LET THE
PEACOCK SING

LET THE PEACOCK SING

LOVE IN A TIME OF RESISTANCE

FRANCE: 1942–44

MICHAEL BARRINGTON

ABOOKS

Alive Book Publishing

Additional copies may be ordered from the publisher for
educational, business, promotional or premium use.
For information, contact ALIVE Book Publishing at:
alivebookpublishing.com, or call (925) 837-7303.

This is a work of fiction. Names, characters, places and incidents are
either products of the author's imagination or are used fictitiously.
Any resemblance to actual events, locales or persons,
living or dead, is entirely coincidental.

ISBN 13
978-1-63132-110-8

Library of Congress Control Number: 2020921576

Library of Congress Cataloging-in-Publication Data
is available upon request.

First Edition

Published in the United States of America by ALIVE Book Publishing
and ALIVE Publishing Group, imprints of Advanced Publishing LLC
3200 A Danville Blvd., Suite 204, Alamo, California 94507
alivebookpublishing.com

PRINTED IN THE UNITED STATES OF AMERICA

10 9 8 7 6 5 4 3 2 1

For Annika, the love of my life.

Acknowledgements

No book typically is the work solely of the author, and this one is no exception. Essentially written during the pandemic lock down I would like to thank most sincerely my three sisters, Kate and Pat in the UK, and Eileen in California, who read and critiqued the manuscript. Each week I sent them a chapter and then we would call each other to discuss. Over time it became more than a book, but a wonderful way in which we were able to deepen our own loving relationships.

Susan Cohen Grossman provided a line item edit and I am deeply grateful for her eagle eye and suggestions. Thanks also to Lois Kaye Pope and Marta Fiehn who gave me constructive feedback.

From start to finish there was one person who not only lived through all of the ups and downs of my writing process while watching the plots and characters develop. She provided me with suggestions and loving support at every step, my wife 'Annika'. I am deeply grateful for everything.

Foreword

On June 22, 1940, France officially surrendered to Germany and under Articles of an Armistice. The country was divided in two: the line ran obliquely from the Spanish border up as far as Tours then sloped eastwards towards to Geneva. By occupying the northern half of the country and the entire Atlantic seaboard, Germany appropriated the richest and most highly populated part of France. The quasi-independent Free Zone was governed by a French puppet administration under an elderly Marshal Pétain installed at Vichy. It became an authoritarian regime and collaborated with the Germans.

More than two million people almost overnight, rushed south to cross the demarcation line. Brive La Gaillarde, in the Correze, a town of less than forty thousand people, mushroomed almost overnight to one hundred and twenty thousand. Papers and passes were required in order to cross the line legally, but few had this privilege. Families were separated, Resistance groups formed on both sides but risked bringing savage reprisals on the civilian population if they attacked the occupying forces. While General de Gaulle formed an army and a government in exile in Britain, he was technically a rebel.

Everything changed dramatically in November 1943 when the Germans in violation of the Armistice agreement, invaded and occupied the Free Zone. The demarcation line was eliminated and all out underground war with the Germans began. The areas of Limousin and Correze in south western France, became a hot bed of large numbers of Resistance groups known as Maquis, and until the end of the war caused a huge amount of trouble and disruption to the German occupying forces. Supplied with arms and explosives by London, intent on sabotage, the Maquis were especially targeted by the German Secret Services (Gestapo) and later by the Milice (newly established by Vichy, French paramilitary organization), determined to exterminate them.

Occupied France 1940

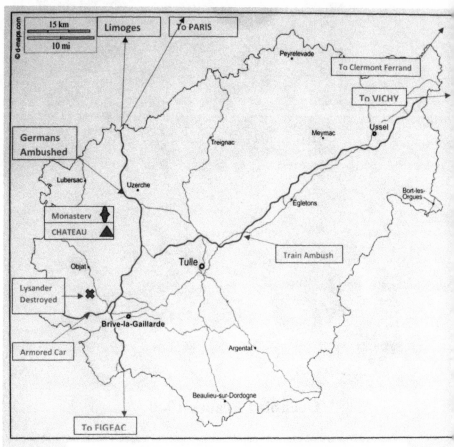

"PEACOCK" Maquis activity around Brive La Gaillarde

Comet Lines 1942

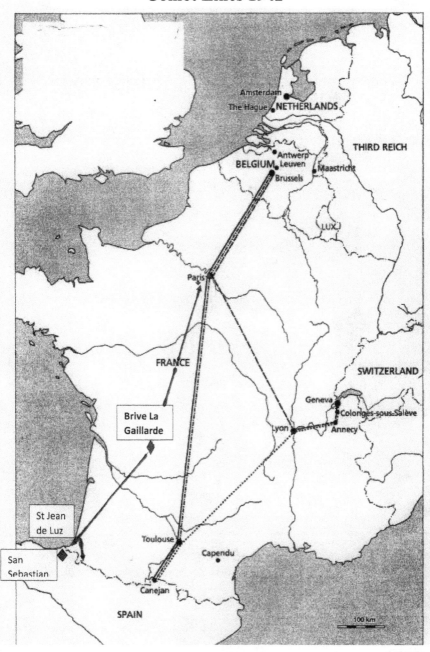

Chapter 1

Henriette

The biting wind driving the heavy falling snow almost horizontally, added to the November chill, forcing her to lean into it as if to get some respite and help her catch her breath. It was rare to have so much snow so early in the season. Was this a sign of things to come? Her heavy winter coat, and warm woolly hat and scarf, provided little protection against the bitter cold that seemed to eat into the bones of her slender body. Her rubber boots left a zig zag trail in the snow as she trudged across the open meadow, heading towards what she knew to be the monastery of Notre Dame de la Paix. Although now hidden by the storm, she knew exactly where it was, since it was she who had given the old farmhouse and three hundred acres of meadow and forest to the monks, twelve years ago.

Henriette Lastiere du Saillant, Countess and sole proprietor of the Chateau de Comborn, was born into a staunchly Catholic family that could trace its ancestry to before the French Revolution. The youngest and most serious of five daughters, her father, Duke Francois Henri du Berry, thought at one time that she would never find a suitor and was afraid she would enter a religious order of nuns, yet at five feet four and finely boned, she was well proportioned. Her dark, shoulder length, auburn hair, and soft green eyes with noticeably long eyelashes, would have made her stand out as a beauty in any female gathering. Regular visits to her two sisters who lived in Paris, ensured that she was aware of the very latest in haute couture. She was always fashionably dressed. After completing finishing school in Switzerland where she acquired a fluency in English, German and

Italian, she seemed to be at ease with her own company, buried in her books. The Duke was relieved when at the age of twenty-six, she met and married a wealthy and committed Catholic Count, who fell madly in love with his reserved and studious daughter.

The Chateau de Comborn had been the ancestral home of the Lastiere du Saillant family since the fourteenth century, and the original foundations and partial walls could still be seen. It commanded an elevated, heavily forested promontory surrounded on three sides by the River Vezière, about two miles from the tiny village of Orgnac sur Vezière. The only approach was by a steep and narrow cart track. Built originally as a small fortress, the entrance was through a gated stone archway leading into a wide, rectangular, cobbled courtyard with stables, a garage, and workshops along one side, and wine making, barrel and bottling rooms on the other.

The wine cellars were underground, cut out of sheer rock, and on their first complete tour of her new home, her husband, explained that the local people knew there was a maze of tunnels under the Chateau. He and his best friend, Gerard, who lived in the village, had sometimes played there as children, though forbidden to do so by their fathers. Gerard, older than Guy, had eventually been conscripted and was killed at Verdun, leaving behind his young wife Agathe and a two-year old baby boy, named Lucien. Bernard, the wine maker, and a widower who had been with the family all of his adult life, and was now sixty-six years old, was the only person who claimed to have explored them all. Even he could not recall what their original purpose was. Rumor had it that the tunnels were used to hide priests and nuns during the Revolution. On just one occasion he had taken the boys along a dark, seemingly never-ending tunnel that exited into a tiny cave in the cliff overlooking the river. It had been a frightening experience and the boys never wanted to return.

A narrow passageway to the right of the main building led

to the rear of the house and a small, ivy covered high walled courtyard, with a row of four neat servant cottages on one side and open wood storage sheds on the other. Bernard the wine maker occupied one with his wife and stepson Lucien, having married Agathe in 1920. In the center was an old well with a hand pump, and immediately beyond the walls, exiting through an old oak gate, the land, covered with almost impenetrable forest, fell steeply down to the river three hundred feet below.

Burned and rebuilt several times over the centuries, the current three-story main house dated from 1748, complete with a private chapel. It was part of a thousand-acre estate of almost virgin land, lying between the Vezière gorges to the east and the valley of the River Rent to the west. The village itself with a population of about eighty, mainly families who worked on the farm, vineyards and in the wine- making caves, was on a small plateau between the two rivers, south-west of the Chateau. Guy's grandfather had planted and developed acres of vines, and the Lastiere wines, especially the delicate, floral whites were much sought after by merchants from Bordeaux. His successful wine business had grown into a major source of revenue, and prior to the First World War he had remodeled the Chateau installing plumbing, and then in the early nineteen twenties, electricity.

Guy, the only son of Pierre-Raymond Lastiere, Count du Saillant, was conscripted at age seventeen. Due to his advanced education he spent two and half years in the French military headquarters as administrative staff supporting General Joffre at Chantilly, near Paris. Although he never saw action, the whole war effort left him disillusioned and distrustful of government and politics. Always a somewhat serious young man, his experiences only served to make him shun society and focus on the work in his vineyards.

Two years after demobilization, his father, who was his idol, model, and best friend, suddenly died of a heart attack. Guy was crushed. The funeral in the beautiful cathedral of St Etienne in Limoges was a grand affair attended by many French nobility, friends of Pierre-Raymond. Among them was his best friend, Duke Francois Henri du Barry, accompanied by two of his daughters, Pauline and Henriette. It was later at the reception for a few selected guests in the Bishop's palace, that Guy met Henriette face to face, and was struck with her sincere condolences, gentleness, quiet reserve, and beauty.

It was two months later while visiting the Duke, this time seeking his help in resolving some of his father's business affairs, that Guy met Henriette again. As the only remaining daughter at home, she entertained him, and it was obvious that there was a mutual attraction. Both were shy and self-conscious at first, but it was the beginning of a deep and intense romance. Eight months later they were married in the cathedral of Limoges where they had first seen each other.

They were well matched, with only two years difference in age; she was twenty-six, and he twenty-eight, and both came from privileged family backgrounds. They adored each other, enjoying the comforts that only wealth can bring, while appreciating the solitude and peacefulness of unspoiled nature. The fact that the Chateau had its own small chapel where a priest came to celebrate mass every day, made it seem that Henriette had everything she could possibly wish for.

But tragedy struck quickly and unexpectedly. While out hunting in the forest, the ground suddenly gave way under Guy's horse and he was thrown violently from the saddle. He never regained consciousness and it was diagnosed that he died from a broken neck. Henriette was devastated; after just three years of marriage she was now a widow. As she tells it, a second tragedy took place shortly after Guy's funeral. The priest/chaplain informed her that due to a shortage of priests in the area he would no longer be able to celebrate mass each day at the Chateau and that the Bishop was transferring him to the village of Beysaac, fourteen miles away. She would have to travel there if she wanted to receive the sacraments and attend mass. This was a situation that she found to be intolerable, something that she was determined to change, but did not know how.

Several months later, still very much grieving the loss of Guy, Henriette visited her favorite sister and confidante Marie-Claude, in the small town of Espeluche in the Drome, and shared that she was thinking of giving her life to the Church and possibly becoming a nun. A fervent Catholic herself, Marie-Claude suggested that her sister reflect seriously about it and spend some time in a spiritual retreat at the Trappist monastery of Aiguebelle, ten miles away.

Call it serendipity or an act of God, but the few days she spent there radically and unexpectedly changed her life forever. On the second day, through the guest master Brother Frederick, she learned that the Order, due to an increase in vocations after the war, wanted to establish another monastery but could not find a suitable site, neither could they afford it. Suddenly, in a flash, she saw how she could serve the Church. After praying over her plan and seeing it as a real message from God, she returned to Espeluche excited and bubbling with her idea. Marie-Claude and her husband sensed immediately that a dramatic change had taken place in her, and since they too were generous patrons to the Church, were not totally shocked with her proposal. Would it be too crazy if she donated a few hundred acres of her land, so that a new monastery could be built near the Chateau de Comborn? She would also support the construction financially and invite other family members to contribute.

This conversation from twelve years prior, was going around and around in Henriette's mind as she struggled through the storm towards the monastery.

Things had happened fairly quickly and where originally an old farmhouse stood, was now a series of solid stone enclosed buildings arranged in the form of a quadrangle, with an inside cloister on three sides and a spired chapel occupying the other. In 1930, five monks were initially selected by the Abbot General to initiate and oversee the construction. Henriette was thrilled to host them herself at the Chateau until the new buildings were completed, since now she could attend mass daily.

Three years later in 1933, a total of thirty monks formed the new community. They were all volunteers from Trappist monasteries across France led by a relatively young Abbot 'ad nutum' (appointed by a superior and not elected by the monks themselves) from Alsace. It was not until four years later in 1937 that an official election took place and Père Louis Albert officially became the first Abbot of the monastery now named by the Trappist Order as Notre Dame de la Paix. He was thirty-nine years old.

Although it was a daily hike of almost half a mile, even with the short cut across the meadow, Henriette, did not mind. Being able to attend daily mass and receive the sacraments whenever she wished, more than compensated for any physical discomfort. Not wishing to intrude into the daily lives of the monks and their silence, she had nonetheless established a deep and meaningful relationship with Père Louis. She also got to know Père André who managed all the accounting and buying and selling of livestock, and her spiritual guide and confessor, Père Yves.

Taking a pair of comfortable shoes from her shoulder bag, she sat in the chapel's vestibule and removed her rubber boots. Her mind was buzzing as she slipped them on, and then standing, removed her soaking wet scarf. Shaking the last of the snow from her saturated hat, she replaced and adjusted it on her head and quietly entered into the warmth and stillness of the chapel. The sweet smell of burning beeswax and the glow from the altar candles gave her a sense of comfort and spiritual wellbeing. She knelt in the first pew directly in front of the altar, and slowly opened her mind and heart to God in silent prayer. For Henriette, this was one place where she could shed her daily worries and concerns and feel spiritually replenished.

Brother Roger the guest master, dressed in a loose-fitting white coweled robe, was quietly finalizing preparations for the public mass as he always did. He acknowledged her presence with an almost imperceptible nod of his head. She was the only person present.

Time seemed to stand still for her, and the mass was over all too quickly.

Signaling to Brother Roger to come over as he extinguished the candles and began putting the materials away, she whispered to him that she would like to meet with her confessor Père Yves.

Without a moment's hesitation the Brother slipped silently away while Henriette removed herself to the side of the chapel that held the box where confessions took place and waited. A buzzer near the door gently sounded signaling that the priest was present. She entered the dark closet, with soft light coming from a solitary bulb above her head which did not bother her, since she was very familiar with the setting, and quickly falling onto the kneeler in front of her she began, "Bless me Father for I have sinned…" There was a long pause.

"Yes, Henriette, do you have something to tell me," the priest said quietly in a tone that invited confidence.

There was another long pause. "Yes, Père," she said slowly, and then taking a folded sheet of note paper from her pocket, slid it under the small window-like, covered screen separating her from the priest.

There was another, even longer, pregnant silence.

A deep, mature but knowing, gentle voice said "Henriette, are you certain about this?"

"Yes Père. I received the information in the night."

"And are all of these details correct?"

"Yes, Père, I'm sure. I completely trust the source. Please give the information to the Abbot Père Louis. He needs to know that the Germans have been amassing troops, trucks, and tanks for days, and tomorrow they will invade the Free Zone. They will drive down from Tours and Limoges on the Route Nationale 20, ten miles from here. It is essential that he attend an assembly tonight, at the Chateau at 5:00 P.M. I have called an emergency meeting of all the area Maquis (the underground Resistance) leaders from Brive La Gaillarde."

*****

It was Monday, November 11, 1942.

Chapter 2
Invasion

Smoke filled the air in the large salon on the ground floor, and the strong pungent smell of Gauloises was unmistakable. It seemed to Jules, the chief of police that everybody was smoking, which of course was not the case. Not everybody, just most of the group. A huge fire crackled and hissed in the wide-open chimney, creating dancing shadows on the walls and ceiling. A group of eight men and women, some standing, others casually sitting on easy chairs set out in a broken semi-circle in front of the fire, were nibbling, drinking, and engaged in animated conversation. A large round table with assorted finger foods, mainly cheeses and cold cuts, and a half dozen bottles of red and white wine, occupied the center of the room.

It looked out onto the main courtyard through four double windows, which were now shuttered to comply with blackout regulations. Not that this was necessary as the high surrounding wall acted as a solid barrier, added to the fact that the nearest habitation was two miles away.

Clotilde, who was responsible for the management and smooth running of the Chateau and had served the family since she was a young woman, answered a knock on the door and ushered Jean Luc into the room. As she took his topcoat and scarf, he said, "It's been a while," greeting her warmly with a kiss on each cheek.

"Yes sir," she replied immediately. "It must have been all of one week," knowing full well that with his quick wit and sense of humor he was joking with her.

It was just a few days ago that she had to make an urgent

visit to his office. As one of the only two dentists in Brive, and the newest, he had arrived from Riom in Auvergne three years ago. At the age of twenty-nine he had started his own practice and was trying to make a living for himself. Having made just one visit to his surgery herself, Henriette liked what she saw and heard, so had asked him to provide services for all the Chateau employees. Clotilde had been a patient almost from the start.

A Breton, he was short, wiry, with a mop of uncontrolled red hair, and was wearing a suit that looked as if he had slept in it. He also detested Marechal Pétain with a passion, and all that he stood for.

Although he lived the closest to the Chateau, Père Louis was the last to arrive.

"Let me take your cape, Père," said Clotilde with a welcoming smile. "And come sit near the fire and get warm."

"Of course," he said, throwing back his cowl and unhooking the front. "It's quite wet out there, and the snow is still falling heavily. I'm soaked," he exclaimed, wiping the top of his shaved head with his sleeve.

He gave her the customary kiss on both cheeks.

As she walked to the clothes closet at the other end of the room, she said to herself that Père Louis was probably the most striking and imposing man she had ever known. Almost six feet tall with a lean body like that of an athlete, when he walked with a very slight stoop and spring in his step, he looked like a lion ready to pounce on its kill. His face tanned from working in the open, had a craggy, kindly, and sensitive look, but it was his bright blue eyes that attracted attention. They seemed to draw a person into his confidence, somehow indicating that this man could be trusted. Clotilde had met many men during her almost fifty years of serving the Lastiere du Saillant family, and she had gotten to know him quite well when he lived at the Chateau, while the building of the new monastery was taking place. She always left his presence with the same impression: he is both a saint and a soldier.

"Good evening Père," chorused the group.

"Good evening to you all," he replied in his deep baritone voice, and moved around the group embracing each one, acknowledging them with a personal word.

"Ah, Raymond," he said approaching a squat, balding man wearing the uniform of a Railway Chief, "how are you managing to keep the tracks open in this storm?"

"Oh, Père, I'm fortunate to have many experienced workers. There's nothing they cannot do on the rails," he softly replied with a meaningful grin. "Perhaps they'll keep most of the trains running. Can I get you a drink?"

"Yes, thank you. I'll have a glass of red."

"So, are we all here?" asked Henriette entering the salon.

All heads turned towards the side of the room where a door had quietly opened, and the Countess was walking towards them. Flaunting the anti-feminine directives from Vichy that women not wear pants, she had on a pair of Paris designed, high waisted navy blue, wide legged slacks, with a long sleeve, hand knitted lavender colored sweater, tied with a narrow decorative leather belt. On her feet were comfortable but elegant wedge heeled shoes; she looked every inch the 'lady' of the Chateau. With her dark hair pulled back into a tight bun, she seemed like a young woman in her thirties, and not the mature forty-two-year-old co-leader of a Resistance group.

"Good evening, everyone," she said, moving quickly around the group, embracing each one warmly. "Does everybody have a drink, food? Please help yourselves."

Moving to a vacant chair close to the fireplace, she signaled with a wave of her hand, "please make yourselves comfortable, we have much work to get through this evening, and thank you for coming out on this awful night. When will this snow stop? But let me begin by telling you why I had to call an urgent meeting. Late last night I received a phone call from Père Louis' brother, Charles, in Paris, asking me to inform all our groups that the Germans are about to invade the Free Zone. He was, as you know, working with the Musée de L'Homme Resistance group that was betrayed, and most of the members executed by the Gestapo earlier this year. He is now using his business as a lawyer to work with Alliance, the largest spy network in France supporting the Allies, and the Comet group which we work with as you know, helping downed airmen reach Spain. Alliance has infiltrated the German headquarters and obtained the very latest and critical information concerning military movement."

A deadly silence took over the room. She paused. The only sound was of the crackling logs in the fireplace and the wind rattling the shutters.

"Using our own code, Charles informed me that the German 7th Army, has been reassembling many troops that had been guarding the Atlantic coast, and about two hundred thousand men, with tanks and equipment are poised to move south and many into our own area. There will be three approaches: one from outside Paris through Lyon and Clermont Ferrand to Vichy in the east, and a second from outside Brest through Tours, Limoges and Brive in the west, starting at 4:00 A.M. tomorrow morning. Another battalion will move from Biarritz eastward along the Pyrenees towards Marseille. The region east of Marseille will be occupied by Italian forces."

There were audible gasps from some of them. Others looked dazed and lost in thought. Henriette could almost read their minds: this was all so sudden. Why were the Germans violating the Armistice agreement with Vichy? Such an invasion would create many more challenges and dangers for themselves together with their groups of Maquis. What should they do next?

"What are you thinking Serge?" she asked, directing her attention to the center of the group, "you and I are in this together, we are the elected leaders of the Brive Maquis groups."

A very tall, well-built relatively young man, (he was thirty-nine but looked older,) with jet black hair, a full beard and legs outstretched, sat upright in his easy chair as she addressed him. A cigarette burned in his left hand, sending little spirals of smoke upwards. He took his time unbuttoning his well-worn leather jacket, as if to create space in which to gather his thoughts. One of the many reasons he had been able to build a successful wood supply and furniture business, was that he carefully thought things through before acting. It was also a reason why he was respected by Maquis groups in the Brive area, and why they had chosen him as their leader.

"This is terrible news," he agreed, "but we must not act too quickly. I believe there are three things we should consider." Then easing himself from the chair, he stood up to his full six feet three inches height, reached over to the table, took a half empty bottle of red wine, and slowly refilled his glass. His steady voice and self-assurance seemed to have a calming effect on everybody.

Standing with his back to the fire he continued and looked around the group, "we need much more information, and then we must, somehow, share all of it with the British."

"Jules, since you're the Chief of Police, we'll rely on you and your team to keep us current of any local operations, and especially changes in administration in Brive." He turned to speak to one of the older people in the room who seemed to have a permanent smile, and behind his spectacles, deep piercing grey eyes, "Henri, as people come into your butcher's shop, you'll need to listen carefully to local gossip, and make a note of everything."

He paused momentarily, to take a long draw of his cigarette with one hand, and with the other, in one quick motion, casually emptied his wine glass. Then taking a step forward, leaned over his chair and set it down on the center table.

"Lucien," he spoke directly to a young man sitting almost outside the group, who seemed shy and slightly overwhelmed by the proceedings, "since you come into Brive almost every day with farm produce from the Chateau and the monastery, you'll continue as our courier."

Addressing the whole group again, Serge continued, "we can all expect that there will soon be additional restrictions on movement of any kind, if the Germans do here what they have done elsewhere. They'll probably issue a new kind of official pass. That could be challenging. We'll need copies or samples of them as soon as possible. But, until we have better information, we'll just have to sit tight."

The group stayed silent. Bernard, Henriette's old wine maker still wearing his stone washed dark blue pants and jacket, his well-worn beret glued to the top of his head and heavy wooden clogs on his feet, shuffled over to a box of logs near the hearth. Taking one out, he threw it onto the fire sending up a shower of sparks and flames. He was a man of very few words but missed nothing that was said.

"The challenge for us," said Serge, "is that we'll somehow have to get word to London of these critical and new developments."

The heat from the fire began to get to him and he slowly removed his jacket, throwing it onto a vacant chair

"We can expect many changes in almost every aspect of our lives. Brive is the largest and most important town in the whole area, and the Germans will surely use it as a central base. It's already a major railway junction serving increased traffic from Paris to Bordeaux, Bordeaux to Vichy, Brive to Toulouse: I'm certain they'll now use our railway system even more, to move men, materials, and military equipment. The marshaling yards will probably start operating around the clock, so Raymond, you and your team must really let us know what's happening." He looked across at the chief of railway operations who simply smiled and nodded.

"In addition, we know that Brive is very important for them, since they are now using the Credit Lyonnais Bank in the town, to hold all of their reserve currency for the army and navy in Bordeaux. They're afraid of the constant air attacks by the British. An armored car comes in every two weeks to make a collection." He went to the table, refilled his glass and then setting his jacket on the back of it, flopped down into his easy chair.

"Any questions so far?" he asked, sweeping a glance around the circle.

The atmosphere had lightened somewhat. Dealing with these kinds of issues was not new for this group; challenging but not insurmountable.

"Yes, I have a question." All heads turned to face Père Louis. He leaned forward in his chair as he spoke. The group knew that when he said anything they should listen carefully. He was not only trusted; he was considered to be a man of great courage and integrity. In any other profession they all knew that he would have been a born leader, a charismatic personality, a serious and clever thinker.

"This is truly disturbing news, and since we don't know what changes will take place administratively, I agree we must wait until we have better information. However, you all know that I have two British airmen staying at the monastery: they arrived three days ago, and one is not fit to travel yet. It will be a few more days before he can take the train to St Lean de Luz. He should never have been sent to us in this state. He has quite a serious leg wound that I am treating, and I need to make sure he will be fit enough to cross the Pyrenees."

"Yes of course, Père," Serge replied. "You must be the judge."

"But perhaps this is a good time to make the crossing into Spain before the Germans really get organized." The comment came from a young woman who throughout the discussion had listened intently to every word being said.

"Very smart thinking Sylvie" said Serge getting up again and walking over to a petite woman standing to the side of the fireplace. He gently put an arm around her shoulder. Dressed in a green woolen top and tweed colored skirt, her straight dark hair cut very short, she looked to be about seventeen years old, but was actually twenty-four. "You've done so much for us not only as a member of our group, but also as a nurse in the Brive General Hospital and as a supplier of medications for Père Louis. Since you're the one to guide the airmen, we need to listen to you. You've made the passage several times now and know just how strenuous and dangerous it is. We are very proud of you."

"Then we must also notify the Comet group in Paris not to send us any more airmen until we know the lie of the land," it was Père Louis speaking again and addressing Serge and Henriette directly. "If we ourselves had been able to make contact directly with London, we might have persuaded them to ask the RAF to fly a Lysander close to here where the meadow is quite flat, then both of these men could have been evacuated. The Maquis in Clermont Ferrand and Ussel get periodic flights I hear, containing all kinds of supplies including explosives and weapons. They also extract important people. The problem as I see it just now, is that the nearest Maquis radio operator, a former Belgian soldier I believe, is in Ussel which is a hundred miles away. And yet it's the only way for us to get out a message quickly. We need a radio operator of our own to serve our six Resistance groups in the Brive area. "Yes," he repeated, "what we need is for London to give us our own radio operator, and we should insist on it."

It was Henriette who replied, fixing her eyes on her priest friend. "Père Louis you make a lot of sense. I support what you are saying. Now is the time for us to reach out to England for a radio operator so we can solidify our position and become much more effective."

"So yes, let's ask for better weapons and explosives too, so we can cause much more disruption to the Boches. They'll be surrounding us now, so we should consider some serious action." It was the railway chief who had spoken.

"I think you might be a little hasty in wanting to retaliate to this invasion, Raymond," said Jules, looking across the room to where the railway chief was pouring another glass of wine, "do you really think taking up arms is the answer? We are so un-prepared militarily. There's no way, even with arms and explosives that we could take on any armed German platoon. It would be amateurs against professionals, and we would most certainly lose. Why don't we just take our time, gather as much information as we can, and then send it to England? I'll do everything I can at the police headquarters to make note of any new administrative changes, and you especially should be able to provide information regarding all of the military movements through the Brive rail system."

Sensing tension arising, it was Henriette who intervened. "So, Serge, can we take some action? Can we agree to send a message to England requesting a radio operator? Secondly can we identify someone who will safely travel with our message, and who will be able to persuade the Maquis in Ussel to radio it to London?"

"Yes of course, Henriette," he said, turning first to acknowledge her, and getting up from his easy chair stood with his back to the fire eyeing each member of the group. "Is there anyone here who doesn't want us to make that request to London?" Nobody said anything.

"Good" he exclaimed, "then whom shall we send to Ussel? Before you respond, know that given this news, there will be huge movement of troops and equipment, all roads will be jammed. Germans will be everywhere demanding priority. The journey could not only be difficult but very dangerous. The roads might be blocked with military vehicles for days."

"Then it has to be me."

All eyes turned towards Henriette as she slowly made her

way to stand next to him.

"I understand that this involves all of us, but I have good business reasons for going to Ussel since we sell wine there. I am very familiar with the town and I have friends there with whom I can stay. I also have a travel pass, but I intend to go by train. If I leave early, I should be able to take care of business and return the next day. Will you please arrange it for me, Raymond? I will need a round trip, first class train ticket for tomorrow morning, from Brive to Ussel." Then turning to Sylvie," I will come back to Brive tonight and stay with you, if that is alright."

"Of course," she replied, "I would love that."

"Since there will only be the French local police at the station barriers," she continued, "if I go quickly before the Germans get established, and travel as Madam Henriette, the Countess Lastiere du Saillant, from the Chateau de Comborn, those unpatriotic buffoons will be too impressed to cause me any delay!"

Chapter 3
Père Louis Albert

Henriette could only think back to the first time she had met this man, this monk, Père Louis, and how he had impressed her. After allowing the monks to live in the Chateau for three years, while the new monastery was being built, she alone had gotten to know about his personal life and what had driven him to enter religious life. For the first time since the death of her husband, she was afraid to admit to herself, that he was the only man to arouse in her strong and deep feelings.

His family was from Saverne in Alsace; his father was a lawyer and his mother made and sold beautiful lace tableware; they were married in the local catholic church. He was born in 1900, the youngest of two boys, attended elementary school there and went to a private high school in Metz run by the Holy Ghost Fathers, a missionary congregation of priests. Some of the staff had ministered in Africa, and he was thrilled and in awe when they shared stories of their lifestyle and experiences.

His father wanted him to be a lawyer, but Gabriel as he was called then, was always one to make up his own mind and follow his own instincts. Instead he opted to be a doctor, completing his studies at the famous school of medicine in the University of Strasburg. Already a German speaker, he now became fluent in French and developed good conversational English.

After graduation in 1925 his parents were hoping that he would practice in Alsace, but that was not to be. While at university he had visited Metz several times to see his alma mater, and got to know the new principal there, Père Henri Gonnet, who had spent nearly twenty years in Gabon. It was he, who first suggested that Gabriel think about spending some time there as a physician.

Living with two priests in the remote village of Ndjole and working long hours each day in a tiny clinic with very limited resources, he fell in love with the people, and saw a level of poverty and sickness first-hand, that made him feel very inadequate. Relaxing in the evening with the priests as they openly shared their personal lives, their struggles, and the importance of prayer and God in their lives, he felt embarrassed and uncomfortable. Religion had not meant much to him since he left high school. At the same time, he admired these men, and their deep spiritual strength, who were dedicating their lives to the service of others. On one short break, he travelled sixty miles to Lambarene to meet the world-famous Dr. Albert Schweitzer. The two of them spent a whole morning together as they toured his hospital, discussing medicine, philosophy, and religion, each one questioning the other as to why they were not only motivated, but driven to provide this kind of service. The meeting left a lasting, and in some ways, disturbing impression on Gabriel.

Back in Saverne, he had no problem finding employment in the emergency room at the local hospital. But even that fast paced and challenging environment could not block his constant memories recalling his two years spent in Gabon. They kept taking him back to the time with the priests, and the fact that they were committed for life to living in a foreign country, away from family and friends; living with minimal amenities and ministering to the poor with seemingly no reward. He admired them but struggled to fully understand from where they drew their spiritual strength. It not only intrigued him, he sensed that it touched and resonated with something deep within himself.

His parents were fully involved in local parish affairs, and although he attended the Sunday mass with them, he felt he was an outsider looking on rather than a participant. He was bored with the mass which was in Latin and which he considered irrelevant to uneducated people, especially remembering the people of Gabon. It just did not make sense to him. He began to slip into the church in the evening on his way home from the hospital. Sitting there quietly on his own, he searched for answers to the many questions he had about life, religion, and about God.

But life took a new direction for him when by chance he met Ernestine, a young doctor like himself, while working on the pediatric ward. He was attracted to her immediately, and they began what turned into a serious relationship. She was from Marseille, and in addition to loving her and making fun of her southern accent, he enjoyed the fact that she was as outgoing as he was shy, as irreverent regarding religion as he was serious. She seemed to be able to laugh in the face of any adversity. Petite, vivacious with dark bobbed hair, wearing short skirts and long drop earrings that exposed her bare neck, she epitomized the post war changing fashion and culture. Gabriel had never felt this way with anyone before, let alone a woman, and was able to share with her his innermost thoughts and struggles. She was a good listener, and sensitive to him and his need to resolve his inner conflicts.

Gabriel's parents were delighted that their son was finally settling down and were hoping that the couple would soon talk about marriage. But people were rejecting pre-World War One values, and society had begun to change rapidly. The nineteen twenties ushered in a new era of emancipation. Even as a single woman, Ernestine was renting a room for herself in a cottage owned by a doctor from Strasbourg, who kept it as a second home and rarely used it The couple were madly in love with each other, and breaking all social and religious taboos, Gabriel began spending nights with her. They talked of building a future together, of starting a family, of opening their own clinic.

The fact that now he was with somebody he really loved yet

feeling the push-pull of needing to spend more time in quiet re-flection, only added to the frustration with his inner struggles. Gabriel finally shared with Ernestine that he wanted to take some time out, not for a long period, just for a weekend. He had seen a poster on the church noticeboard announcing that there was a spiritual three-day retreat for young men, to be held at the Trappist Monastery of Sept-Fons near Colmar. He asked her if he could attend. Without fully understanding it, she simply agreed to his request.

Gabriel had never before heard of what to him was this strange order of monks, dressed in antiquated robes, who lived according to a strict, very old rule of life, and were called to a lifetime of simplicity, hiddenness, silence, and prayer. They typ-ically lived in remote communities set apart from ordinary life. Their days were organized around prayer, study, and work. Speaking only when necessary, the monks used their own form of sign language and they were also vegetarian.

The need to have time for reflection overcame his nervous-ness and anxiousness at the unknown, and the fact that he had never been part of a small group of people who were 'searching.' It was, however, made somewhat easier since the priest respon-sible for facilitating the weekend was a Holy Ghost Father, a saintly older man with snow white hair and a long beard, Père David from Metz. Gabriel had graduated high school there and had lived with members of that Order in Gabon.

The small group participated in the liturgical life of the monastery, attending mass and the chanting of the divine read-ings and prayers several times throughout the day. They even arose in the middle of the night, at 3:00 A.M. to join in the singing of morning prayers.

The priest gave two inspirational talks each day and invited the group to share their own spiritual thoughts and experiences. He also offered himself as a counselor if anyone wanted to talk privately. This level of sharing was just too stressful for Gabriel, and he felt frozen on the inside. On the evening of the second day, he considered leaving and going back to Ernestine. But he still felt attracted to the silence and quiet. When everybody had retired for the night, he went back to the chapel and just sat there, losing track of time, absorbed by the sense of peace and well-being that came over him.

Later the next morning he decided to confide in Père David.

"I'm torn between my need for time alone that is so strong and simply will not leave me, and my life as an emergency room doctor which I thoroughly enjoy. I'm also in a serious relationship," he explained, "with a woman that I love dearly."

"The Holy Ghost Fathers," Père David explained, "are contemplatives in action, they're called both to an active life of ministry and an interior life of prayer. It's a special calling from God; it is very difficult and is not for everyone. These monks have a different calling where they physically leave the world around them to spend their lives in prayer, work, and contemplation. I wonder Gabriel if this is the life-style to which God might be calling you?"

"But that's impossible," he replied, totally taken aback by the priest's words, and beginning to panic. I should never have come here he thought to himself. "I do not have that kind of faith," he blurted out anxiously, "I'm not even a good catholic. I'm not even sure what I believe."

There was long pause before the priest gently said, "the ways of the good Lord, Gabriel are many and diverse, and it's important for our peace of soul that we try to discern what is the path He has chosen for us. I will pray that you find it."

Life quickly returned to normal, and the busyness of his daily life in the hospital and enjoyment of his romance with Ernestine, including a wonderful trip to meet her large family in Marseille, kept him fully occupied. But in the quieter moments especially, on what were becoming less and less frequent evening visits to the church, the call to a different lifestyle seemed to be getting stronger.

Things came to a head five months later, in mid-October. Both had been able to finish their shifts early simultaneously, and decided on their way back to the house, to stroll along the bank of the Canal de la Marne. It was a beautiful evening, with the soft setting sun adding to the gold on the leaves already changing and beginning to cover the ground.

Walking hand in hand, suddenly Ernestine turned and grabbed Gabriel pulling him against herself in a tight embrace.

"I love you so very much," she whispered, "and I just want this moment to last forever."

"And I love you too," he sighed gently responding to her touch, "so very, very much."

"Let's plan a winter wedding," she said coyly, resting her head on his chest. "And let's do it as soon as we get home."

They stood holding each other for what seemed like an eternity to Gabriel as he struggled to find the right words.

"Ernestine, my darling, yes of course I would love to spend the rest of my life with you, I love you more than anything." As he bent his head down and gently kissed her forehead, he could feel her breasts and heart pulsating against his chest. "But there's a part of me that's not free. If I said a whole-hearted yes, it would be a lie. There's something that I cannot control, that keeps pulling me in a different direction. It's nothing that you have said or done, no, it's all about me. It's something that is happening to me."

Tears started to run down his cheeks as he squeezed her ever more tightly. "I don't know what it is," he said choking out the words, "but I'll do my very best to find out." There was a long pause. "This cannot go on," he stammered, "I need to get some resolution."

"Then do it quickly, my love", she urged, "I'll be waiting for you."

They slowly broke their embrace and continued, hand in

hand, along the bridle path leading to the house.

"Do you have any idea what you'll do and when?" Ernestine gently enquired breaking the silence, not daring to look him in the face, trying to be brave but barely able to hold back her own tears.

"Yes, I think I know what to do. I'll call Père David tonight and if he's willing, I'll travel to Metz in the morning to meet with him."

Even after almost an hour with the saintly old priest, Gabriel was still struggling with the decision he needed to make. He repeated several times and in different ways, that the only time he had felt real interior peace was in the chapel at the Trappist monastery. The priest suggested, "then perhaps you might want to go back there for a longer period. God will let you know if He wants you to stay there or not."

"It's breaking me apart, Père, and it's hurting the one person I love the most in all this world. So yes, please help me."

"Let me contact the Abbot for you, he is my friend, and I will explain that you're searching spiritually to find your true vocation in life. Nothing more than that."

All of that was many years ago now. In 1928 after much heartache, tears, more tears and sleepless nights, Gabriel gently broke the news to Ernestine. Sobbing uncontrollably in each other's arms, as she sat on his knee in the sitting room of her cottage, he told her that he would be entering the Trappist monastery of Sept-Fons. She was devastated.

Joining a community of almost sixty monks was unusual in itself, and the lifestyle so unfamiliar that Gabriel struggled for several months to adapt. The regimen was hard and so strange, with the community using such an unusual daily time frame that his body struggled physically to adjust. Retiring at 8:00 P.M. and getting up at 3:00 A.M. each day eventually took on its own rhythm. After six months as a postulant he was given the white robes of a novice, and went into the strict, formal training required before he could be fully accepted into the community. It would take a full year. He also relinquished his old name as a symbol of leaving the old world behind and was given that of Brother Louis.

Three years later, the Abbot General of the Trappists requested volunteers from all the French monasteries to help start a new foundation in the Limousin department, north of Brive La Gaillarde. It was a remote and large area of land, generously donated by the Countess Henriette Lastiere du Saillant.

Five monks were initially selected to establish and help construct the new monastery, that would eventually accommodate up to fifty monks. In 1931 the first monks arrived, including Brother Louis, and were housed by the Countess in the Chateau de Comborn during the construction period. By 1933 the buildings were ready and a new community of thirty volunteer monks was established. In that same year, Brother Louis Albert completed his training and was ordained a priest becoming Père Louis. Identified from the beginning as the natural leader, he had already been nominated as a temporary Abbot, until finally in 1937 he was officially elected as such by all the monks.

From the very moment Brother Louis, as he was then, and Henriette met, there was an immediate and special connection between them. They worked closely with the planning and material affairs of the new foundation, he managing the land and needing assistance in establishing a farm that would sustain the new community, she providing all of the local knowledge and financial support. In return she was able to attend mass daily again. Their living in the same house and having to interact daily, built up a level of trust, confidence, and affection in each other, that would only deepen as the political situation in France worsened.

In late 1940 Henriette's oldest and most trusted employee, Bernard, her wine maker, suffered a serious bout of pneumonia and in fit of panic, she ran to Père Louis asking for his help. Since there was no doctor within thirty miles, he had actually been helping several of the local villagers and workers at the Chateau for some time, so the request was not so surprising. The main challenge for Père Louis was obtaining the necessary medications, but it was Henriette with her many and powerful connections who solved that problem. As he came each day to the Chateau cottage to attend to Bernard, she decided to share with him how troubled she was with the fall of France, the armistice, and how she felt about Marshal Pétain and the Vichy government. She confided in him that two of her sisters in Paris were involved in working with the Maquis and supporting the "Comet Line," by helping British soldiers and airmen get back to England. She herself was playing a role as a safe house and guide. She had established her own very small group and so far, had helped smuggle eight people across the Pyrenees. Arriving by train at Uzerche, twenty-three miles away, they were driven to the Chateau by Bernard's son Lucien. They normally spent two or three nights there in preparation for the rest of the journey. But now she had received an airman who was seriously injured so she asked if Père Louis would help him. It shocked her when he didn't hesitate and answered "yes, but first I will need to share this information with the monastery community. Then I will keep the man in the infirmary where I can care for him properly."

That was almost two years ago and since then he had become even more involved with the Maquis. Two monks who were usually devoted to hand copying old liturgical texts and operating the small monastery printing press, were now able to produce excellent fake German and French travel and work documents. Brother Martin, the tailor, fitted out the visitors with appropriate looking old work clothes and warm coats for the mountain crossing, and Brother Gilbert who made boots and clogs always had a selection of strong footwear available.

Caught up in the ambiguity of two opposites, a world of

silence and a world at war, Père Louis realized that he needed to draw on all of his spiritual and human resources to not only survive, but to give his community a new purpose. In a world now turned upside down, his mission would be to show that a contemplative monastery, albeit hidden and remote, could play a crucial role in helping end the war.

Once the new monastery was opened in 1933, Henriette had seen very little of Père Louis, but now nine years later, the once unimaginable situation of France at war and occupied by Germans, was drawing them together. For her part, while thrilled at being able to work closely with him again, Henriette would always be torn by guilt and fear at having invited him to be a member of the Maquis.

Chapter 4

Sparrow

Shortly after midnight Lucien, his father, and Jean Luc, together with four of his team, took their places spaced out in the snow-covered meadow, standing thirty yards apart, in the form of an inverted letter L pointing to windward. It was a bitterly cold January night and the wind was so strong, they began to wonder if this would be yet another aborted mission. They had already waited for two nights, but the poor weather over the English Channel had made flying impossible. Still they were full of anticipation, since this would be their first real connection with the Special Operations Executive (SOE) in London, and more importantly, their very own radio operator was on board.

It was Père Louis who suggested this potential landing strip just thirteen miles north west of Brive, near the tiny village of Mansac. He and Brother Alphonse had visited several farms in the area some years ago when looking to buy pigs for breeding. They had both wondered why it was not cultivated. It was quite flat, open, and easily accessible from the rough cart-path running along one side. Tonight, it was covered in twelve inches of snow.

At exactly 12:30 A.M., each man switched on his flashlight and waited. A few minutes later the spluttering sound of an aircraft engine could be heard, that slowly grew louder. The three men aimed their flashlights in its direction, and Jean Luc began flashing the letter B for Brive in Morse Code. Moments later, he could make out an approaching dark shape in the sky coming in from the northeast. The Halifax blinked back its own code letter – M. With the signal completed, the plane flew directly overhead, made a tight complete circuit to the right, and came in on a final approach at very low altitude.

Two oblong parachuted canisters could be seen dropping near the entrance to the meadow, but then a third parachute began to fall almost beyond the drop zone; it seemed to hang in the wind momentarily and was suddenly blown sideways outside of the range of the flashlights.

"Quickly, run and take care of the radio operator, he might need help," said Jean Luc, "there is a small, wooded area over there, and take him directly to the Chateau. My men and I will handle the supplies."

Without saying a word, Bernard and Lucien headed across the meadow, their flashlights reflecting on the almost knee-deep snow, created the appearance of a huge white shroud. The drop was not going as expected.

It was Lucien who arrived first and began waving his flashlight through the trees. He saw a flash of white high up in the branches and realized it was a parachute. Suspended and hanging in an awkward position, was a person in a camouflage jump suit wearing a leather helmet that completely covered his head and ears together with large goggles on his face.

"Papa, I have found him," he shouted into the wind, and flashed his light in Bernard's direction.

He arrived, bending over almost double and stopping just a moment to catch his breath.

"We must get him down quickly," Lucien said, "hopefully, this foul weather and wind will keep the Boches away from here."

Without waiting for Bernard to respond, he started carefully climbing the tree, his father shining the light on him. As he reached the parachutist, he saw that he had a blackened face. "Mister, mister" he called in English, "you are with friends, are you OK?"

"Papa" he shouted down, "this man is saying nothing, I think he is unconscious. I'll need to cut the harness and then lower him."

Every Frenchman owns a pocket-knife and as he climbed above the man, took his out and began cutting through the strong webbing of the parachute.

"Papa are you ready?" he shouted, "I'll now lower the man." Inch by inch with just Bernard's light for guidance, he slowly let the harness slide through his freezing hands. It took all of his strength to hold the weight of the man. Bernard left his flashlight on, standing upright in the snow shining at the tree, and finally grasped the body. But not being able to hold the man, they both hit the ground together and the man began to groan.

"Look!" said Lucien, having quickly descended and shining his light on the man, "there is blood all over the side of his jump-suit and there is blood on his forehead."

"Then we must move fast," Bernard insisted "we must get him to the Chateau. Let's see if he can walk between us."

As soon as Lucien tried to lift him up the man let out a scream of pain. "We've no idea where he is injured," he realized, "we will not be able to carry him, we might do even more harm."

"Then what shall we do?" whispered Bernard, as if the man might hear.

Thinking for just a moment, "I have a suggestion," said Lucien, "just train your light on me." Without waiting for his father to respond he turned and climbed the tree again. This time he descended with the remains of the parachute. "Let's put the man in the parachute and we'll drag him across the meadow."

After wrapping him like a mummy, the two men, fighting the wind, slowly pulled the man across the snow until they reached their vehicle. The man continued to groan and moan even though Lucien tried to be as gentle as possible, while laying him on a pile of old sacks in the back of the van.

Bernard drove as fast as he could taking the shortest way he knew towards the Chateau, but he was following tracks made by carts, that were full of potholes and rocks, now hidden by the snow. The old van slithered and shook violently, and both men were worried and disturbed by the continued moans coming from the man.

"Madame, please come quickly," Lucien shouted as he leaped from the van and ran into the Chateau hallway. "There's been an accident and our radio operator is seriously injured."

Henriette and Clotilde were anxiously waiting in the downstairs salon for news of the air drop. A large fire was warming the room and some cold cuts, wine and glasses were set out on an antique dresser. Hearing the urgency in Lucien's voice, both of them immediately rushed outside.

With the rear doors of the truck open and light from Bernard's fading flashlight, they could just make out the mummy-like form trussed in the parachute, curled up in a fetal position.

"Then let's carefully bring the man into the salon where the fire is and lay him on the table." It was Clotilde taking charge. "We will then decide what to do. Bernard and Lucien, can you do this, or do I send for more help?"

"Yes, Clotilde," it was Bernard who responded, "we can do it. The man is not too heavy."

Seeing the man wrapped in a dirty parachute, Clotilde spoke first. "Don't do anything, just let me get my scissors from my sewing box." And moving swiftly, left the room only to return almost immediately with a pair of large shears in her hand. It took only seconds for her to cut away the silk and harness of the parachute, but then she saw the blood oozing from a wound on the thigh, and another high up on the right side. There was also a long diagonal gash across the forehead just below the helmet line, that was bleeding profusely.

"Before I cut away this jump suit, why don't you remove the man's goggles and helmet, Madame. It will make him feel more comfortable."

Without answering, Henriette slid the goggles over the man's head, undid the chin strap firmly holding the helmet in place and as she removed it, gave out a gasp. "Oh my God," she cried, "our radio operator is a woman." Spilling onto the table was a mass of blond curly hair, in sharp contrast to the woman's blackened face.

"Please leave immediately and wait outside," she said with a wave of her hand at Bernard and Lucien, "I'll call you if we need you."

As Clotilde started to cut away the suit with its many bulging pockets the woman opened her dazed eyes, "where am I?" she said in perfect French. At that very moment Clotilde held the woman's right arm to cut away her sleeve, and she screamed in pain and blacked out.

"Madame, it is very late for us, but the monastery will be awake in less than one hour, should we not send for Père Louis? This woman has serious injuries and we don't know what they are. We might make her situation worse if we try to move her."

"Yes, of course, Clotilde, of course. I will send an urgent note to the Abbot immediately with Lucien, but first let's see what injuries are obvious so I can advise him what to bring."

After cutting open the jump suit, they both saw that this was a young woman, probably in her early thirties, dressed in grey slacks with a heavy woolen navy-blue sweater. There was a huge blood stain high on the leg, and as Clotilde cut away the cloth, it revealed a large ugly wound across the top of her thigh that was oozing blood. Then cutting through the sweater and the girl's under shirt, they saw another bleeding laceration to the side of her right breast.

While Lucien went to fetch Père Louis the two women kept a silent vigil. The young woman seemed to lapse in and out of consciousness between bouts of groaning. She was obviously in great pain, and Henrietta saw at one point that her cheeks were wet with tears.

As Père Louis arrived, Clotilde went to open the door. A quick greeting then he entered the salon and gave Henriette an embrace. "I received your message," he said, and taking one look at the young woman on the salon table asked, "is there a room where we can keep this woman safe, a place where I can examine her thoroughly?"

"Of course, Père, we can put her in the visitor's room that we have already prepared. But is it safe to move her?"

"There's no other way," he murmured, "I need to examine her, and I'll need the help of both of you." And with that, he gently lifted up the young woman in his arms who looked tiny against his huge frame. She groaned in pain, but he didn't hesitate and followed Henriette up the stairs and into a large bedroom. Then gently laying her on the bed he said, "please remove all of her clothes except her underpants."

"But Père, is that....?"

"Don't worry, Henriette, I have seen many naked bodies in my life, both male and female. We are all created by God."

It took just a minute for Clotilde to fetch her shears and complete the removal of the jump suit and day clothes.

"I will lift her up," said Père Louis, "and both of you please remove all of the clothing from underneath her and roll back the bed sheet and blanket. Cover her as best you can, we must try to keep her warm while I examine her. Also, I will need warm water and towels so I can clean the wounds and determine their exact nature."

Clotilde left the room and quickly returned carrying a large bowl and several towels over her arm.

As she lay there almost naked, it was clear that this was indeed a young woman who was physically very fit. She was very attractive.

While he was checking her head and eyes, the woman suddenly woke up and shouted in fear, "where am I, where am I?"

It was Henriette who moved quickly to the bedside and gently placed a hand on the woman's shoulder. "You are safe with friends. You injured yourself when your parachute was blown into the trees. We are your friends; we were waiting for you. This is Père Louis, he's a monk, but he is also a doctor."

Still staring anxiously at this strangely dressed man in front of her, her face changed and softened a little and she asked if she could have a cup of water. Père Louis nodded, and Clotilde left to bring it.

After washing away the blood, Père Louis quietly explained, "I need to do several things and it will be a little painful. It seems like you landed in a tree and two branches pierced your thigh and your side. The good news is that although they are deep and long, neither of those injuries are life threatening. You also have a large and deep gash on your forehead; all of these will require stitching but will eventually heal. You will also be badly bruised and swollen for some time."

Clotilde arrived with the water and setting down a jug on the small bedside table poured out a small glass and gently lifting her head, held it to the woman's lips. After just a sip, she slumped back onto the pillow and appeared to lapse into sleep.

Père Louis then reached for her right arm so he could better see the laceration on the side, and immediately the woman screamed and sat bolt upright, her face contorted in pain.

"Henriette," Père Louis called turning and looking over his shoulder, "I'm sure you have a large square scarf you could let me use?"

"Of course, Père, let me bring one immediately."

"I am so sorry, but you have a broken arm" he explained gently and softly. "I'll do my best to stabilize it tonight. I will put it in a sling and tape it to your body until I can set it in a cast for you. I also need to put sutures in the wounds and will start first with your head, but before I begin, I will ask Clotilde to get some more warm water and clean your face. Then I'll give you a sedative and something for the pain."

An hour later, aided by Clotilde, he had done as much as he could. Henriette sat close by the whole time in the one easy chair in the room, with her eyes closed, as if in prayer.

"All of this should help you," he told the woman "and you should be able to rest comfortably for a few hours. But before I go, I would like to ask you a few questions if that is alright."

The woman gave a very slight nod of the head.

"What is your name?"

"Sparrow," she said in a whisper, "just call me Sparrow."

"And what is your birthdate?"

"I was born on April 26, 1910."

"And where were you born?"

"In Manchester." She gave the information in a mechanical manner and tone, almost as if she were not really listening.

"Do you know what day it is?"

There was long silence.

"It maybe January 12?"

"And you know what year it is?"

"I have such a headache; I cannot remember exactly."

"Thank you," he said, rising from the side of the bed while gathering his first-aid materials and placing them in an oblong leather bag. I will see you again in a few hours."

"Henriette, you will have to care for this young woman carefully. I have given her medication, so she should sleep for a while. I am concerned however, that she may have a concussion but only time will tell. When she wakes try to see if she will take warm liquids, perhaps a soup, and in about six hours give her two of these tablets." He placed a small bottle in her outstretched hand as they walked towards the door. "My brother sent me these from Paris some months ago and it is supposed to be almost a miracle drug. It's called penicillin."

"Thank you for everything, Père, we all owe you so much."

"Don't mention it," he responded, "we must all support and

take care of each other in these troubled times. I will return in the evening, but if you think you need me sooner, just have Lucien come and call me. And Henriette, could you please call Sylvie to see if she can get me some more sedatives and plaster of Paris bandages. I really need to set the arm as soon as possible. No need to see me out, you should stay here." A quick embrace and he was gone.

"Madame, I will sit with her during the rest of the night, you should get some rest," it was Clotilde who broke the silence.

"Thank you so much," said Henriette," both of them were standing looking at this young, heavily bandaged woman now sleeping, a stranger, about whom they knew nothing. And a radio operator, could this be possible? Could this really be the person they had been waiting for all of these months? And she mused to herself, the rest of the groups would certainly have an opinion as to her ability, just because of her sex.

"I will relieve you after I have been to early mass at the monastery," said Henriette moving closer to Clotilde and taking hold of her hand. "You have done so much for our family and now this. You are a God given gift and I treasure you." With that she embraced the old lady with a kiss on both cheeks, turned and left the room, quietly closing the door.

It was just after 7:00 A.M. when Henriette returned from the monastery and immediately went up to the bedroom. Clotilde was fast asleep in the armchair covered by a blanket, and the young woman was still lying on her back with the sheet now pulled up to her chin, fast asleep, but the bandage around her head showed that blood was seeping through. "I will let them rest just a little while longer," she spoke to herself, "I need to hear what really happened last night".

The phone line to Brive was full of static, as she made a call to Sylvie at the hospital requesting her not to ask any questions, but to find plaster of Paris bandages and to take them over to Jean Luc as soon as possible. A second call to Jean Luc, let

Henriette know that everybody else was safe; he knew nothing about the parachutist. She informed him about the package he would receive but he told her he couldn't help. Using their own Maquis code, he told her that due to the huge amount of German traffic on the road, he would ask Jules, the police chief if he would deliver it.

Summoning the house maid, she sent her to find Bernard, who was expecting the call and came quickly to the salon. It took only a few minutes for him to explain what had taken place and how he and Lucien had struggled to get the body from the tree and into the van. Thanking the old man profusely for his service and giving him a warm embrace, she suggested that he go home and get some well-earned sleep.

Gently shaking Clotilde by the shoulder, Henriette awakened her and suggested that she go to her own room and rest, that she would look in on her later on in the day. But for now, she would sit with the young woman.

It was not until midmorning that the woman awoke with a vacant stare and fear in her eyes. Henriette was reading in the armchair at the side of the bed, and seeing her, the young woman asked in a whispered voice, "Where am I? Where am I?" Before she could answer, the woman said, "who are you?" She grimaced in pain as she tried to turn her head slightly in Henriette's direction.

It was clear that the young woman did not remember anything from earlier in the night. "I am Henriette, a friend, and you are safe in my house. You came from England last night and parachuted down but had an accident. We've been waiting for you. Can I get you anything to eat or drink? Some water?"

The woman closed her eyes briefly then said, "Yes, please." After Henriette had poured water from the pitcher, she leaned over and very gently lifting her head, held the glass so that the woman could drink. Then taking the bottle from a concealed pocket in her skirt, shook out two tablets as directed by Père

Louis and asked the woman to take them with another sip of water.

"And would you like something else, something warm to eat?"

A feeble "Yes please" came from her lips.

"Then let me take care of it, I shall only be a moment." With that, she left the room, gave the cook instructions, and quickly returned to the bedside. A few minutes later, the maid appeared with a tray containing two bowls of steaming soup.

"Perhaps if I put an extra pillow behind you it might help a little," said Henriette, and very gently raised up the woman's head and began to slowly feed the patient. Almost before she had finished, her eyes began to close, and she drifted back to sleep; clearly the sedative was having an effect. The bedsheet had slipped, and her breasts were fully exposed, so Henriette discretely drew it up to her chin.

She had just finished her own breakfast and settled down with her book when she heard footsteps approaching the room. Clotilde entered looking none the worse for her late-night vigil. "Madame, she said, "You may go now, I'll watch over our guest. If I need you, I'll call you."

"Thank you so much, Clotilde," she responded, I will be working in my study."

It was early afternoon when she heard the sounds of a vehicle entering the courtyard, a sound that she did not recognize. A knock on the door and the maid allowed in Jules followed by Lucien who was carrying two suitcases.

"Please put them near the table," said Jules pointing to a place next to where Henriette who had just entered the room, was standing. "Thank you for your help, Lucien, I hear that you did great work last night. We are very proud of you and your father."

"It's my pleasure sir," he replied, giving him a big smile and left the room.

Henriette gave Jules, a warm embrace.

"You are so welcome. I do hope that there were no problems on the road up here" she began, "we must be extra careful now."

"No none at all. The Germans are everywhere, but I was driving a police car, so nobody bothered me. Before you tell me about last night," he began, "here is the package from Sylvie that she said was urgent," and handed her a carefully wrapped package the size of a shoe box. I hope that this is what you need, and these two valises are also very important. Jean Luc and I checked them out. This one," he lifted it onto the table and opened it, "contains a radio transmitter and spare parts. It was in one of the containers that were dropped; it was well packed, and it looks to be just fine. This other one," he reached down and set it on the table, "is filled with books, ladies clothing and shoes, plus some make up and cosmetics. Based on this, would I be correct in thinking that our radio operator is a female?"

"Forever the policeman," laughed Henriette moving towards a beautiful antique dresser set against the wall that held two decanters of wine and several glasses. "You are correct, so why don't you sit down, and I will fill you in. A glass of wine?" she said, turning to face him.

"Of course," he replied, "perhaps a little red."

Over the next half-hour she proceeded to give Jules the details of what had happened in the night, but also expressed her concerns for the other Maquis groups.

"We have all been waiting so long to get a direct link with London and especially to get our own operator, and now this. So please tell Jean Luc to make sure that nobody knows anything about this situation. We must all act as if she had never arrived, since it may be some time before she will be able to help us, if at all."

"That's so disappointing," said Jules rising from his easy chair and reaching for his cap, "but I do understand. In the meantime, we must continue to keep gathering intelligence and monitor German activity. I'm so sorry I cannot stay longer, but I need to get back to headquarters. We're trying to develop a working relationship with the German military and arrange how the new check points will be manned. I have to attend an important joint meeting this evening."

Once he had left, Henriette went up to the bedroom to see how the young woman was progressing.

"How is our guest, Clotilde?" she asked softly, walking into the room, and taking up a position at the foot of the bed, "has she eaten?" The old lady turned in her chair and smiled, and then stood up out of respect, "yes madame, she has taken some soup."

"Excellent," she said, "I am happy to hear that. Père Louis will soon be here, and we have now received the medications that he asked for."

Then addressing the young woman directly, who was now fully awake, "if you need a bathroom…."

"Madame," interjected Clotilde quickly, I've already explained the options. She knows now where the bathroom is, and I've also placed a chamber pot under the bed."

"Well that's wonderful, replied Henriette," and then smilingly and kindly said, "and what else should I know?"

"Madame, thank you for taking care of me." It was the young woman suddenly addressing her in a very soft voice and in perfect French without the slightest trace of a British accent, "I know where I am, and I know who you are. You are the Countess Henriette de Lastiere du Saillant, also known as Peacock, the Maquis leader of Brive, and I am Simone Carron, known as Sparrow, your radio operator and special agent."

Chapter 5

Simone

"This should make things a little easier for you." It was Père Louis speaking, his deep voice sounding calming and reassuring. He'd just finished placing Simone's right arm in the sling again after setting it in a cast. "Your wounds are clean and are beginning to heal, they're no longer bleeding." He was sitting on the edge of the bed and kept checking her eyes.

"I'm still not certain about a concussion," he explained, "Do you still have a headache?"

"No, Père," she replied, "It only hurts a little where the cut is on my forehead."

"Then for now, I will leave you in the safe hands of Clotilde," he said gathering his things, "and I will check up on you each day."

On his way out, he took Henriette aside, "See if you can get some history out of her. We really need to know if her memory is intact. It seems to be, but one never knows, and in any case, we should learn as much as we can about her, her training and capabilities if she is eventually to help our group."

And so it began, but it was mainly Clotilde who established a trusting relationship with Simone, who nursed her and who learned about her background. Each evening after dinner she would sit with Henriette and relay what she had learned.

Simone was born in Manchester in December 1910, where her father, a professor of physics at the University of Lyon in Central France, was on a sabbatical, studying at the Institute of Science and Technology with Joseph Johnson the Nobel Laureate. Her mother was English, from Droylsden, and was working there as a research assistant.

The family returned to France in 1911 and Simone completed all of her schooling in Lyon. She was completely bi-lingual from a very early age and her parents wanted her to earn a degree in England. Accepted into the University of Reading, she graduated with honors in Mathematics and Statistics. She was not only gifted academically; she was a very good athlete and was considered for the British swim team for the 1928 Olympics in Amsterdam but did not make the final selection.

Returning to France immediately after graduation in 1932, she obtained a position at the University of Grenoble teaching mathematics and also coached the swim team. Surrounded by mountains, ski resorts, forested parks and a cultural center of museums and art galleries hugging the banks of the Isere River, it was just the position and the kind of place she wanted. With short curly, blond hair, hazel colored eyes, and a slim figure, slightly taller than most women, she was constantly sought after by men. Life was exciting, and she enjoyed all the male attention and rounds of parties and night life, that only a major university city could provide.

A close male relationship came in the person of a skiing instructor she happened to meet while enjoying a fun-filled break with friends at the famous Chamrousse Resort. After a short romantic weekend, they quickly fell in love and were soon married, but almost as quickly fell out of love. What she did not know, was that her husband had a drinking problem and became physically abusive when drunk. Fifteen months into the relationship they separated. It was an ugly and somewhat traumatic experience for her. Three years after finding what she thought was her dream job, Simone decided to move as far away as possible. She applied for and got accepted as a teacher at Wallington High School for Girls, a prestigious academy in Surrey, England. She taught Math and French and also provided support as an assistant coach to the athletics teams. It was 1935.

Life took on a new meaning for her and she adapted well to her new surroundings and the novelty of working in a girls-only setting. Sharing an apartment with a teacher from Wales, she found that they had lots in common and they became close friends. It was Iris and her love of singing and dancing that first got Simone into attending a weekly dance at RAF Kenley, an air force base four miles from the school. She quickly learned that with its flights of Spitfires and Hurricanes it was being developed in the event of war as a fighter base to defend London. In 1940, after war had been declared, when the Women's Auxiliary Airforce started to recruit, she decided to enlist and was stationed in the Operations Room at Kenley.

It was at a dance in the officers' club that she first met Squadron Leader Billy Banks who was three years younger than herself, a dapper young man with all of the swagger and confidence that only comes from a wealthy background and the best of education, in his case Cambridge University. He was extremely popular and the life and soul of the party group on the base, as well as being a superb airman. It took four months of a crazy, whirlwind, exciting, wartime romance, before he admitted that he was already married. Crushed by this revelation, she just wanted to run away again, but instead took on extra shifts and cried into the arms of her friend Iris.

But one interesting development did come out of the relationship. Billy would often tell her that with her background and language skills, she could better serve the war effort in another capacity, but never said precisely how or where. Then one day unexpectedly, she received a letter from a Baker Street address in London on His Majesty's Stationery and marked Ministry of War.

The letter was brief and succinct. It simply read: *Should you wish to be interviewed for a government position, please report to this address on Monday April 7, 1941 at 2:30 P.M.*, and underneath was an indecipherable signature with no name.

"Iris," she exclaimed to her house mate, "I'm going to check this out. Maybe if I am accepted, it will really help me participate more in the war effort. I'm bored at Kenley, it's pretty much the same old thing every day, important though it is."

"Yes, you certainly should Simone," she said, "I've known for a while that you had itchy feet, especially after your affair with Billy. A change of scenery and new challenges will be good for you."

Her curiosity aroused, Simone decided to explore the opportunity. What she did not know, was that the brother of Squadron Leader Billy Banks worked for a newly formed war department, expressly ordered by Winston Churchill himself, to 'set Europe ablaze'. It was officially called the Strategic Operations Executive (SOE) and he was responsible for recruitment. Initially it was all done by word of mouth. She did not know it at that time, but it was Billy who had mentioned Simone's name to his brother and provided her address. It was such a top-secret department, that the organization could not be found listed in any military directory. It simply did not exist.

A four-stage training plan had been devised for all potential agents. At preliminary school, the agent's character and potential were assessed through a battery of psychological tests, without revealing to them what SOE actually did. Those candidates not deemed suitable, were soon sent to the 'cooler' where they were encouraged to forget the little they had learned about SOE. Those who passed the preliminary were sent to paramilitary centers known as 'A' Schools.

The schools were based mainly in Scotland and the courses were especially grueling. They lasted ten weeks. Classes included physical training in which Simone excelled, even though it meant running for miles in miserable, Scottish wet weather, crawling on her belly through obstacle courses, and trekking up mountains with forty pounds of equipment on her back.

Weapons handling, unarmed combat, silent killing, demolition and explosive training, map reading, compass work, and radio communication were all part of the curriculum. Whether it was her mathematical mind or simply a fascination with the technology, she became the most proficient in her group in using Morse Code.

Her screened phone calls every week to Iris only indicated that she was happily working now for a war department in the midlands, dealing with statistics, and that she would make a visit home later in the year.

Having passed with flying colors each early step, she was then sent to Manchester's Ringway Airport for parachute training, where she did several jumps, first from a static balloon and then from an aircraft. She had to practice low level jumps at three or four hundred feet and would hit the ground within ten to fifteen seconds. Simone was afraid of heights, and this part of her training terrified her, and she barely passed.

The final course of her training took place in a secluded manor house in the New Forrest in Hampshire. Here agents learned survival skills: clandestine life, personal security, how to maintain a cover story, and how to act under police surveillance. It was also the stage where her false identity was provided to her. A great deal was based on personal background information she had provided, and the more immediate from weekly intelligence reports received from agents in the field. She also learned that her new code name was "Sparrow." By this stage in her training, Simone was fully aware that she was being trained as an agent and that she was agreeing to work for SOE. Four months earlier she could never have imagined being in this role, let alone actually volunteering for it, and yet here she was almost ready to take on her first assignment.

In 1942, SOE was operating in almost every European country and each agent was matched to a country, as much as possible, based on language skills, but also on the specific demands and needs of the location. Each country was also given a code letter and Simone was assigned to Section F. She would be going to France.

A final detailed briefing took place with the Air Liaison Section that had procured a country home close to the airfield used for clandestine operations. It was there while waiting for suitable flying weather and sufficient moonlight, that Simone was introduced to her assigned group for the first time. She was being sent to support the well-established Maquis groups of Brive La Gaillarde in the former Free Zone in South West France, an area only recently occupied by Germans. Due to the huge increase in the volume of intelligence being gathered and sabotage plans being developed, the group especially needed a radio operator and a person able to handle explosives. It was led by a woman, a Countess called Henriette de Lastiere du Saillant, code named "Peacock."

It had taken the best part of three days for Clotilde and Henriette to gently tease this information from Simone, as she slowly began her recovery. Père Louis came each evening to change and dress her wounds, and each time he had Clotilde help the young woman sit on the edge of the bed so that he could better examine and treat them. To cover the more serious one on her side, he had Clotilde hold up Simone's arm a little so that he could pass the bandage all the way around her body. He was concerned that her broken arm would rub up against the injury and possibly affect the sutures. A pressure dressing would help somewhat, but every time as he gently lifted her breast to wrap the bandage, he could sense even without turning his head, that both Henriette and Clotilde were uncomfortable with the situation. It was not that they were judgmental of him, it just seemed to conflict with their concept of Catholic modesty. That a monk was involved even as a doctor, simply added to the shock and uneasiness. He checked each time for a concussion which now was beginning to look highly unlikely.

Henriette could contain herself no longer but was having difficulty finding the appropriate words without seeming to be too prudish or appearing to be ungrateful. As she was escorting Père Louis out, she suddenly stopped half way down the stairs and as he turned to face her she hesitantly said, "Père when do you think I could give Simone a brassiere?" As the words came out of her mouth she almost felt faint and could not look him in the eyes. Just saying that very word to a priest, a monk, did not seem right. Then she hurriedly added, "This house is full of draughts and even with a fire in the hearth I would hate her to catch a cold."

"I understand Henriette," he said gently, "I know that this is hard for you, but there is no sin in what we are doing. This is God's work. Why don't you take a moment when you have time and discuss it with your confessor, Père Yves, he's one of us and you know you can trust him implicitly. We must wait until I remove the sutures before you can dress her, just another week or so."

"You are right Père," she said, as they continued down the stairs towards the front door, "Your advice is always so helpful, I will do that."

The two women took turns watching over her and as the hours passed it was clear that Simone was beginning to feel a little better and also needed to talk. Propped up on pillows, and with a colorful shawl from Henriette over her shoulders, she did not hesitate to answer questions about her background and training, clearly wanting to impress, and not taking for granted that she would be accepted into the Maquis group.

"Initially I thought that I would be flying in a Lysander which would actually land near Brive, and I almost felt giddy with excitement and expectation. I felt truly ready for my first assignment. Then as the poor weather continued, they told me about the snowy conditions and that they would be using a converted Halifax bomber, that I would have to parachute into the landing area. You can imagine how I felt. My excitement quickly burst, and I was filled with a terrible dread of everything going wrong. In all of my training the one thing I hated most was using a parachute."

"As the airplane approached the target area, I was offered a double whiskey, which I downed very quickly. I was terribly nervous about the fall. As soon as the crew member got the call from the pilot on the intercom, he opened a hole in the floor of the fuselage, hitched a static line to each of two long canisters, then tied one from my parachute and the other lines to a hook above my head. He checked and re-checked to make sure that my line was well attached. I was standing near the hole with the wind blowing right at me and I thought "I can't do this." I could feel the plane banking steeply while making a righthand sharp turn, then straightening itself up. The red light changed to green, the crew quickly slid the two cannisters through the hole, then pressing me down shouted "sit on the edge." I was too terrified to think and just let my legs dangle over the edge. I felt a push on my back, the rushing of wind and then a huge jerk as my chute opened. For just a few seconds I had a feeling of euphoria, but it was completely black below and I could see nothing. Suddenly a huge gust of wind blew me sideways, and I remember fighting with my harness to gain some control, then just blackness. I recall hearing French voices but also excruciating pain all over my body, especially my right arm. And then I was here in this bed with Père Louis talking to me."

"Well you are with us now," said Clotilde, fluffing up a pillow and gently placing it behind Simone's head, "and Madame will make sure that you are safe. You'll come to no harm here. Just rest and get well. When the time comes, you will meet the others. Your radio transmitter and your valise with your clothes have also arrived. I'll bring them here and help you change your underwear."

"You are so very kind," Clotilde, "may I ask how long you

have worked here?"

"I came here when I was fourteen as a junior maid, but that was almost fifty years ago. This is my home, my life," she said in a quiet voice as she moved towards the door. And then in a slightly more severe tone, "Madame is a very special person and I will never let anyone, or anything harm her. You are her guest and as such you are in my care. Do not worry about anything." And with that she quietly left the room.

*****

"But what is our next move?" it was Henri speaking as he poured himself a glass of red wine. "We have so much to do and with Simone still not sufficiently recovered to help, we need to reorganize ourselves."

The Maquis leaders gathered at the Chateau had already been meeting for almost an hour and confronted with some serious issues, seemed to be creating even more problems than answers. If the atmosphere in the room were to be described as subdued it would be an understatement. Morale was flagging.

"Henri, please," it was Serge speaking. "Let's not exaggerate. We'll do what we need to do." They were all in their usual place, in the large salon, and several of them had stood up and were walking about the room. "We can discuss Simone at another time. She is not physically able to help us at all just now, and with a broken right arm she cannot even use her transmitter, so we cannot send intelligence reports to London."

"Not so, Serge." All heads in the group turned to look at Père Louis, "I think that in a week or so her wounds will be healed sufficiently for her to move around. And yes, she will be able to use her radio and transmit even with her right arm in a cast, you see, Simone is left-handed!"

"While that is excellent news, we also have some bad news," Henriette walked slowly to the center of the group and sat in an easy chair. Sylvie, as some of you know, is being watched by the Germans, they are just suspicious of her work at the hospital. Due to some mix up with the guides she was delayed returning from St Jean de Luz where she left the airmen. She had waited in the Basque safe house and ended up missing three days of work at the hospital. We have told her to lie low for the moment until things cool down. We now need to find a new guide to take some British airmen to the Spanish border. There are two of them currently at the monastery. Does anybody have a suggestion?"

She moved around in her chair so that she could actually see everyone's face. "But let me add first that the Gestapo are making it their business to track down Maquis all over France. An Alliance cell near Toulouse was denounced by a traitor last week, and seven men and two women are now being deported to Germany. However, the Comet Line near Pau is still operating well, and perhaps that might be the one we should use. Any questions?" This was typical Henriette and at her best; informed, able to make decisions and completely cool headed.

It seemed like an eternity before anyone spoke. Jules looked around the group of Maquis leaders, "It cannot be just anybody. The guide must know what he is doing, be very self-assured, able to handle going through multiple check points which are increasing almost daily. The Germans are very paranoid about an underground army being formed. There's nobody on my team I could trust just now."

"We need to use extreme caution with our groups," explained Serge getting up and facing Henriette. "We have got to avoid recruiting an informer, this is what I fear most. Since the Vichy French police and now the Germans are searching for young men to work for the Germans, they're forcing men between the ages of 20 and 30 to register for paid work in Germany. Many are literally running to the hills to avoid conscription, and we ourselves seem to be getting a sudden increase in the number of people wanting to join the Maquis."

He turned from her to look around the group. Then taking his time and reaching inside his jacket he took out a packet of cigarettes, flipped out a Gauloises. "Anybody?" he said offering them around, but there were no takers. The light from the match in his cupped hands briefly illuminated his face, which looked tired and haggard. He took a long, slow draw and tried to blow a smoke ring as he exhaled.

"While this is wonderful on one hand, on the other we have not yet established a screening system for these men, and I am a little paranoid. We have just got to do a better job; our very lives depend upon it. We need to reorganize into much smaller units so that fewer people know fewer people, so if anybody is caught, they will have less information to give to the Germans. I'm also hearing from my sources in Marseille and Paris that the Gestapo are getting smarter. They are using radio detector equipment and are beginning to terrorize anybody suspected of being in the Resistance."

Serge had the full attention of everybody, so he continued.

"I suggest that we keep as little paperwork as possible. Burn everything after reading. Next week, I suggest that we each bring a diagram showing how we have organized our cells and the names of the people involved. Once we have reviewed and discussed them, we will destroy them right here."

Again, there was a nodding of heads. Nobody said anything.

"Then I'll take on the responsibilities of the guide." Standing up from his chair, Père Louis looked directly at Henriette knowing that she would disapprove. "Since there's a greatly increased German presence everywhere, let me use my German language skills to good advantage. For this next trip, I could simply be a wealthy farmer taking my farm hands to help me buy cattle from farms in the south for the German military. But afterwards, what I am about to suggest might come even more as a shock, I need to either obtain a German officer uniform or the material to make one. Brother Martin is a wonderful tailor and should be able to create one, but better still if we could find one that will fit me, together with boots and weapon. I must look like the real thing. I'll become a German Major General, but also a Senior Field Veterinarian. My sole mission will be to find cattle for the army, and I'll always have a couple of workers with me. There cannot be many officers in this area, if any, with this specialty."

A stunned silence took over the room.

It was broken by Henriette, who had taken a chair at the end of the semi-circle, "Père, this is madness!" she cried, and jumping to her feet stood directly and defiantly in front of him, "There must be another way."

"Yes, I know that you worry for me," he replied in a caring voice, "but if I do this, then I can virtually travel all over southern France gathering intelligence, as well as taking people to the Spanish border."

"No, I'm against it," she stammered, and in a completely uncharacteristic way, with her voice breaking slightly as she held back her tears, turned away from him and said softly, "You are too valuable to us, and God forbid that anything happens to you. I cannot support this crazy idea."

"We are all taking risks," he replied, moving towards her even with her back turned, and gently reached out to put an assuring hand on her shoulder. She quickly brushed it away. They both just stood there frozen in the moment.

"We are all in danger," he softly whispered to her, "but we all know that we can't sit back and just let the Germans not only take our country from us but rape our land as well. You of all people know that, which is why we are even here tonight. Just remember what they have done to your father's chateau, his farm, his cattle, his vineyards and his poor workers."

His words seemed to kill any further discussion. Nobody spoke for a while. Henriette seemed immobile and lost in thought.

Then surprisingly it was she who spoke up, but in a very odd, and for her, unusual way. Turning to face him, she reached out and took hold of both of his hands and in a soft and slightly shaky voice, said, "I am fairly certain I can get the boots you need Père. My sister in Paris has many contacts," It shocked her to suddenly realize what she was doing, that in all of their thirteen years of knowing each other, she had never held his hand.

Chapter 6
The Package

"Let me try to work on the uniform," it was Jules following up quickly in response to Père Louis's need to dress like a German Officer. "The Germans have established a commissary in the large building behind the town hall in Brive that used to be a store for all community event equipment. They've also changed how they are staffing the different areas, check points and special operations. Most of the troops coming into this part of France are coming from active duty on the fronts. This is really just a place for them to do some soft assignments, get some rest, recreation and allow units to re-tool. They'll eventually be rotated back mainly to the Eastern Front. But what's important for us to know, is that the whole of the Town Hall is now managed by only one officer and five *Band of German Maidens* (BDM),young girls from the Nazi party who are starting to control everything; telephones, typing, filing, producing new passes and ration books and so much more. They issue requests and payment for any produce or cattle sold to the German army. They also control the commissary."

"Then I don't need to remind you to be extra careful," said Serge moving to the table to refill his glass, "but this might well be a very useful resource we could exploit. I've an idea but must discuss it privately with Henriette first." And then in a much more sarcastic voice, "Let's meet again in one week, perhaps by that time our radio operator might be of some use."

"There is one other piece of bad news," it was Jules again taking the floor, "a small detachment of Secret Police (Schultzstaffer), the SS, that was based in Clermont Ferrand arrived in town five days ago and the officer in charge, the Polizeifurher, called Otto Kreips, is now responsible for our region right down to the southern border. He's taken over the house near the square, next to Henri's butcher's shop, belonging to old monsieur Gardin, as his headquarters. His reputation precedes him, and from what I hear he's a nasty piece of work. Some might say that being next to the butcher's shop is 'appropriate' for him, as he has committed many atrocities. There's some talk in the police station, that the SS were brought in to focus on eradicating the Brive Maquis groups. The Germans are paranoid about an underground army being formed here and equipped from England, and that is exacerbated by the number of Maquis cells that have already been infiltrated and uncovered." He paused as if to gather his thoughts again while walking over to the buffet and pouring himself a glass of water. He returned pensively to the center of the group.

"By far the most troubling information we've received to date," he continued, "is that Marshal Pétain, with the help of the Germans, has recently established a paramilitary group called Milice, headed by Pierre Laval the Prime Minister. The real director of operations is the General Secretary, Joseph Darnand. Their purpose is three-fold, to root out any Maquis cells, round up Jews for deportation, and disseminate propaganda for the administration. They are openly fascist, anti-communist, anti-Semitic and anti-republican."

"But why is Vichy doing this?" asked Henri in a concerned voice. "Why another organization in addition to the SS and the Gestapo?"

"I think the real reason is that these are native Frenchmen who understand local dialects fluently, have extensive knowledge of the towns and countryside, and they know the people and informants. I've personally read reports of torture to extract information, even resulting in murder and random executions. What makes them especially dangerous, is that the Gestapo is allowing the Milice to keep a large part of the money and other valuables confiscated from their Jewish victims."

The group was strangely silent as Jules shared this intelligence, and it was clear that the shock factor of this bad news was being felt by everybody. Père Louis, Bernard, and Lucien moved their chairs closer to each other and huddling together shared a whispered but brief conversation. He continued, "I know that they are already very active in Lyon and Grenoble, and several Alliance cells have already been uncovered and the members executed. What's more important for us, is that they have now established their headquarters in Limoges at the old army barracks and have started recruiting almost any young man whom they can find. I am certain it will not take long before they come recruiting in Brive."

"Thanks' so much, Jules," said Henriette, looking ashen faced under her make-up, "we are lucky to have you! You have a huge responsibility and you walk a very fine line for us every day. I do not take you for granted and I pray for you and your family that your work for the Maquis will always remain hidden." With that said, she walked up to him and gave him a kiss on both cheeks.

She had known Jules for many years as he had been a close friend of her husband, and together with his wife Sofie, had dined several times at the Chateau. He was a local boy, educated in Brive but attended police academy in Limoges. Married and with two sons, both gendarmes, one in Dax and the other in Ussel, he'd worked his way through twenty-five years of postings and promotions all over the area, and just five years ago was made police chief of Brive. He was very competent, extremely intelligent, universally well-liked by his own men and those of many surrounding towns, and had a vast knowledge of peoples and villages of the Correze and the Auvergne. The Germans quickly identified him as a person they needed to help impose their new controls. But like most of the people in the region, that had always been staunch traditionalists, resistance to oppression almost came as second nature to him. He didn't know it at the time when asked by Henriette to join the Maquis and to form his own cell, that he was also becoming part of the largest and most active grouping of Resistance cells in France. Within a year they would number about ten thousand men and women.

Many French people saw the creation of the Free Zone and the Marshal Pétain regime, as bringing stability back to the country, and creating the opportunity for French people to return to their daily work with some degree of normalcy. Jules, always a serious thinker, had a different point of view. For him, it stood for collaboration with Germany and abandonment of French values. He quickly saw that the government had embarked on a mission to kill parliamentary democracy, and install an authoritarian regime modeled on that of Nazi Germany. He was viscerally opposed to the Vichy government.

"And before we close then," Henriette signaled to everyone to wait a moment, "in the light of Jules' information, I would like to bring up one other item. We have got to be even more careful than ever with our own movements, and while we are isolated out here in the countryside, you just never know whom you can completely trust. There have just been too many Maquis cells destroyed recently. So as a precaution, I suggest that we use our old barn just outside of the village for concealing your vehicles."

"Henriette, what are you really saying?" asked Raymond who had been quiet for the whole of the meeting.

"I am suggesting that should the Chateau ever be targeted by the Gestapo, there is only one narrow path up here and escape would be difficult. If they found your vehicles it would be easy to trace you. Let's use the old barn since there are several escape options from there. When we have a meeting, leave your vehicles there, and I will have Bernard or Lucien pick all of you up in the van and bring you here."

"Well that sounds good to me," replied Jean Luc, nodding his head.

"And I would also add," she continued, "that you vary your routes whenever you come and leave. Thank God there are still many small lanes and tracks that are passable. While we know almost everyone in the villages, if they hear or see frequent traffic, or a vehicle they do not recognize, it could cause gossip, and who knows what it could make them do? The Germans pay well for informers and money is scarce."

"Henriette," it was Serge signaling to her as the group was preparing to leave the Chateau, that he wanted her attention, "can we talk for a moment?"

"Of course," she replied, leading the way back into the salon. "What is it?"

"We need to get copies of the new ration books and especially the new travel pass as soon as possible so that the monastery can start preparing to reproduce them." They both took chairs next to each other at the round table, Henriette looking quizzically at Serge. Lighting another cigarette, he continued, "the commissary is also a major development as it's now the center of the German administration. Short of infiltrating their system, we need to know as much as we can, as soon as we can, about how it functions. My suggestion is that since Lucien is the person who takes the monastery milk and produce every two days to the collection centers, in all probability he will now have to deal directly with the BDM women. Perhaps you could discuss with him how he might ingratiate himself with them. He is young, good looking and is able to obtain country food products which every German wants. We have heard that food is so bad and so scarce, that even some officers are not averse to trading on the black market."

"You have a Machiavellian mind, Serge, she replied, her face registering concern, "but perhaps that is what is needed in these troubling times. Let me discuss it with both Bernard and Lucien, it is best that both father and son know how important, yet how dangerous this assignment could be, even though I am quite sure what they will say."

"I have one other piece of information that I did not share," he said looking almost absent mindedly at the smoke spiraling up from his cigarette. "I learned this morning that the Gestapo are in Tulle and have rounded up twelve hostages. Some uncontrolled Maquis group spent the night cutting all of the telephone lines in the area and ended up shooting two sentries. There's a regular disagreement between some elements of the Secret Army group supporting General de Gaulle, and despite his urging nonviolence, are bent on active confrontation with the Germans. They are also not in agreement with the local group of Francs Tireurs who support what we are doing. A random selection of men regardless of age or health, took place immediately. Twelve of them will be executed in the marketplace tomorrow. That's only fourteen miles from here."

*****

It was a phone call and in code, a very strange call, and it came late at night, and had Henriette not totally trusted the caller, she would have quickly hung up. But it was from her sister Therese. She was asking her to pick up a very important package containing a special hedgehog that was sick, and asking if she could take care of it for a few days. It would benefit from being next to the Bull and should then be sent to Sparrow's land. She knew immediately that it was a person who was sick and needed attention from Père Louis. Only a few people knew about his Maquis name of Bull and even fewer that he was a doctor. And still fewer people knew of Simone's alias. The package would arrive by car which she should pick up at the Catholic church in Uzerche after the 10:00 A.M. Mass.

While attending the early morning Mass at the monastery,

Henriette called for and confided in Père Louis regarding the message from Therese. "Père, the decoded message states that a very important person is being sent to us and needs medical care. After some days of recuperation, the person should be sent to England. I must trust Therese that this is indeed an important task, she sounded very anxious that we take care of this person, but of course was afraid that the line might be tapped, and so gave no further information. Will you be able to help us?"

"Of course," he replied, "you know I will. Once the person is at the Chateau, send Lucien for me and I will come and see what's needed."

With Bernard driving, they arrived at the parish church of St. Peter near the square with plenty of time to spare. Passing through the checkpoints was just the usual tedious process and without incident. Sitting directly opposite the main entrance, Henriette waited until the first person exited the church. Then stepping out of the car, she walked up the steps and stood at the side of the large double doors. All women entering a Catholic church were required to have their hair covered, and Henriette was dressed appropriately and discretely, but very fashionably for the occasion, wearing a long calf length, navy blue woolen coat, and on her head a beautiful damask silk scarf.

Three old ladies walked past her, each of them wearing a black dress and head scarf, offering a simple "good morning." They were followed by a middle-aged woman carrying a wicker basket filled with vegetables, and an old man who even with the help of his cane was having trouble walking. A quick greeting and they were gone.

Henriette entered the church, and it took a little while for her eyes to adjust as she moved from the bright morning sunlight into the more subdued lighting of the ancient building. It smelt of hot beeswax and incense and had the feel of an old shawl, well used, comfortable and warm. But it was empty, save for one person sitting in the last pew, and as she approached she knew from the head covering that it was a woman, and when she turned to look at Henriette it was obvious that she was also quite young.

"You must be 'hedgehog'?" enquired Henriette. "Yes, I am," she replied in a tired voice, "and you must be 'Peacock'?"

"My car is waiting outside, let's go quickly." The woman reached down to pick up a small suitcase, and as the two of them walked side by side out of the church, Henriette could not help but notice, that the woman walked with a severe limp.

"Please hand me your travel pass," requested Henriette, I will manage the formalities at the checkpoints." Driving a new model Citroen made her car stand out among all the vehicles in line, and it was the French police who recognized it.

"Didn't you pass through here a couple of hours ago?" asked the sergeant.

"Yes, we did," Henriette replied, "and I told you then that I was coming to pick up my sister who is sick. I am taking her to my home so she can rest."

He walked slowly around the car, clearly wanting to examine the model itself rather than find any fault with it, then checked the passes, peered through the window, and satisfied with his scrutiny, signaled to Bernard to drive on.

After a short distance, it was Henriette who spoke first, "Just for now, I suggest that you try to relax and enjoy our wonderful countryside, we will soon be at the Chateau where there will be lots of time to get to know each other." She laughed lightly, "and you can call me Henriette. You will be safe with us and we will take good care of you," she said in a warm and comforting voice.

"My name is Madeleine, and all I know is that you have a wonderful sister, and that your reputation as a leader in the Maquis, is known from Paris to the Pyrenees. I'm looking forward to a long rest."

Père Louis arrived within the hour and was escorted by Clotilde into the dining room, just as the maid was serving them lunch.

"Welcome," Père, said Henriette, with a big smile and rising to meet him, gave him an embrace. "This is Madeleine." After he had greeted the guest and Simone, she pulled out a chair next to herself, "do join us, but of course I know you will not eat." He could see immediately that this was a young petite woman in her early thirties with dirty looking shoulder length brown colored hair, dressed in badly fitting clothes and who at one time must have looked very pretty. But he also noticed the dark blue patches under her sunken eyes, and that she looked gaunt and pale.

"Is there something wrong with the food or would you prefer something else?" asked Henriette, noticing that Madeleine was simply toying with her food.

"Not at all Henriette," she replied, "I'm just not used to such rich and substantial food and am constantly nauseous. I've also got scratches and scrapes all over my body and am very uncomfortable."

"Then why don't we take you to your room and let Père Louis examine you, he's a doctor and will be able to take care of you. I apologize, I should have been more sensitive to your needs."

In spite of her superficial injuries, severe scratches to both ears and the side of the head, lacerations to the shoulders and knees, and general poor health, Madeleine was in excellent spirits. It was obvious she was a very intelligent and articulate woman. She suddenly surprised them by pulling at her hair and they saw it was a wig. Her own hair was very short and quite blond. The most severe damage was to the soles of her feet that were badly skinned and bruised. Père Louis was surprised that she could actually walk. She jumped and cried out when he tried to manipulate her right leg, explaining that she had had a displaced hip for a long time. Realizing that there was nothing he could do to fix it, after treating her wounds, he ordered complete bed rest. "When I return to the monastery, Henriette, if you will allow Lucien to accompany me, I will send back some medicine that will help as a tonic and reduce the nausea. I myself will come back in the morning."

"But Père, do you and Henriette not even want to know who I am, how I got here and where I'm going?" asked Madeleine feeling a little left out of the conversation.

He paused for a moment, then replied gently, "Madeleine, as a monk we learn in our training not to ask unnecessary questions, and as a member of the Maquis, I try to say as little as possible. You were sent to us by Henriette's sister and that's all I needed to know. I can only assume that you are part of the Alliance network, and that if you have to go to England, you must be an important person. If you wish to share with us more information, and especially if it will help both you and us, then I will happily listen to you. More importantly, we do understand that you will need our help to get to London."

Before she could reply, it was Henriette who continued the conversation. "Madeleine share with us whatever you wish, and most certainly you can stay with us just as long as you think it is necessary. We would very much need to know how we and Simone can help, I will call her to come and join us. But first, why don't you get ready for your bed rest, I can help you if you need any clothing."

"If you would excuse us for a moment Père, I'll help Madeleine, so could I ask you to go down into the salon and wait there for ten minutes. Also, would you please ask Simone to come here, she's probably reading there."

"Thank you both, yes, I would like to share some information since I need the help of your radio operator to help arrange a flight for me to London. When I was in Paris, I was able to send a message to SOE telling them I would be staying with the Peacock, and that you would contact them for further instructions."

Henriette invited Clotilde who had arrived to make sure Madeleine had everything she needed, to stay and be part of the conversation. The two of them, together with Père Louis and Simone, were sitting around the bedside as Madeleine, now propped up with pillows and looking bright eyed, but quite fragile, recounted her story.

"A few days ago, the Gestapo came to my apartment in Aix La Chapelle looking for a man suspected of being the head of the Alliance, Charles des Isnards, and were so focused on finding him that they did not recognize who they were talking to. I was taken to the soldiers' barracks and put in a cell, arrested for being a simple spy. The Gestapo only had my forged identity papers. I knew that very soon they would figure out who I was. I feared being tortured and even worse, of giving away critical information, and so decided to try to escape. I needed to warn the rest of my group and let them know what had happened and to stay away from the apartment. During the night I stripped naked and was able to squeeze through the bars of a window, injuring myself in the process as you can see, but was able to reach our safe house in the countryside. I immediately used another disguise, travelled to Paris and then to here."

Madeleine paused to take a sip of water. "Would you prefer something else?" asked Henriette.

"No thanks," she replied, my stomach is still very upset," and continued with her story.

"The head of London SOE operations has been requesting for weeks that I go there to give a full report on the operations of Alliance, and they also knew that I've been sick. Your sister Therese and her husband were extremely helpful, and I stayed with them last night. I know that you have a radio operator here and am hoping that you can send a message to London, telling them where exactly I am, and asking what they want me to do next."

It was Simone who four days later announced that SOE was sending a Lysander with supplies, but primarily to pick up 'hedgehog', and would be arriving at the usual place the following night. They were all extremely surprised that London had responded so quickly.

At that time, Henriette, Simone, and Père Louis never did fully understand who it was they were taking care of, only that she was an important leader in the French resistance movement and in the Alliance network. It was not until after the Liberation that they discovered the truth. In 1941, at the age of 31, Madeleine Fourcade became the head of what would emerge as the largest and most important Allied intelligence and spy network in occupied France. All of the leaders took the name of an animal for security purposes, and the organization became known among the Gestapo as "Noah's Ark". Numbering 3,000 people at its height, it also lost more than four hundred and fifty operatives who were captured, shot or sent to camps in Germany, but was never short of recruits. It had agents in England, Belgium, France, North Africa, and Morocco. Throughout the war it supplied the British and American high commands with vital German military secrets regarding troop movements, submarine activity, and number, type, and location of aircraft. It provided details of train movements, fuel dumps, storage of armaments, tank depots, and information about the V1 and V2 rockets. Alliance's successes included giving the Allies a 55-foot-long detailed map of the Normandy beaches that proved vital on D-Day,

After resting for those few days at the Chateau, Madeleine Fourcade was flown to England where she spent the next six months debriefing, planning, and recuperating. She then parachuted back into France and continued her espionage work with Alliance until the end of the war.

Chapter 7
Monastery

Early in the project, in 1931, while on the way back from Uzerche with Brothers Alphonse and Louis after helping purchase farming equipment from a friend of hers, Henriette mentioned the subject of Black Bottomed pigs. For the monks, being driven in a new luxury, Renault Monastella, which had been the star attraction at the Paris auto show in 1929, was of no concern or embarrassment. Their life of poverty and simplicity taught them to just accept what is given and could not see the incongruity of themselves riding in the very latest model car while dressed in their monk's robes.

"You mean that you have not seen or heard of them," she laughed mockingly. "No," they chorused, laughing back at her.

"But please do explain," said Brother Alphonse, as he turned around to speak to Henriette and Brother Louis on the rear seat, "We are all ears."

And they all laughed loudly again.

"Well," she began, "the Black Bottomed Pig of the Limousin region was once known as the pig of "Saint Yrieix" and has lived for centuries in the west of the Massif Central Mountains. The animals roam freely and are fattened on chestnuts. They are a great delicacy," she continued, "and are much sought after by buyers everywhere since they are scarce. Typically, they are slaughtered at Christmas which is what I do each year, for my staff and the villagers who live near the Chateau. Isn't that right, Bernard?" she asked, directing her question to the driver. "Yes, Madame," he replied, "it's a wonderful feast and everybody has a happy time."

Ever the one to query and ask probing questions, it was Brother Alphonse who spoke up.

"Well, Madame Henriette, I'd like to know more about this breed, but also why you have brought up this subject?"

Without a hesitation, she continued. "This medium sized pig, with black feet, a white trunk, head and rump covered with two black patches, holds its head and ears straight up. The breed grows slowly, is not very choosy in what it eats, is rustic, and well adapted to walking among the chestnut and oak trees.

"Are you suggesting that the monastery invest in some of these?" Brother Alphonse replied quickly.

"Alphonse," it was Brother Louis who interjected, "if I may, I think Madame Henriette is asking us to look at our options. You know even better than me that we have a large number of acres of chestnut trees on the property, and based on what she's saying, it might be a good idea to explore commercial opportunities. These pigs would have access to almost free food!

For the monks, after being secluded for several years in their monasteries, and now having to speak freely, travel on trains, buy and sell items, and meet an unknown group of new monks, was a major upheaval to what had been their daily routine. Being housed in a Chateau belonging to a Lady was nothing that life in the monastery had prepared them for. It was Brother Louis after the formal greetings were completed and they were together in the large salon, who took it upon himself to introduce the group. Seated at a large round table, "Madame the Countess," he began, but before he could continue, Henriette interrupted. "Please, each of you, while you are in my home, just call me Madame Henriette."

"Thank you Madame Henriette" he replied hesitantly pronouncing her name, "what I would like to say, is that we are all privileged to be part of this new mission, and we know that it is due mainly to your generosity and that of your family. You have been informed by the Abbot General that even though I did not want it, I have been asked to act as a temporary Abbot until such time as the community will elect its own. Out of obedience I have accepted. If it is convenient, I would like to suggest that you show us where we'll be sleeping, where the chapel is, where we will be eating, and then perhaps we can reconvene here to discuss how we might proceed each day."

"An excellent idea, Brother Louis. But first can I offer anyone a cold drink."

No one answered.

"Pardon me, Madame Henriette," it was Brother Louis addressing her, "It's now almost 5:00 P.M. and usually we gather for our evening prayers at 8:00 P.M. and then turn in for the night. At what time is the evening meal?"

"Once we have finished showing you around your new home, Brother, we will serve your meal at 5:30 P.M."

It took just a short while to first see the dining room on the ground floor and the kitchen, then down a long well lighted corridor, a solid wooden door opened into a beautiful but small chapel that could hold at most fifteen people. It had several kneelers, a few chairs, an altar, and all that was needed to celebrate Mass. All of the monks immediately fell to their knees, and with bowed heads, remained in silent prayer for almost five minutes. Henriette and Clotilde just stood, awed by the sight, silence and wonder of the scene before them. She could never have envisaged such a moving moment taking place in this chapel that had hardly been used for some time. Overcome with such deep feelings of gratitude, Henriette quietly shed tears of joy and happiness.

Dinner was a simple rustic meal and immediately afterwards they all took a seat in the salon. "Brothers, I know that each of you internally is struggling to understand how we will adapt our rule of life to our new surroundings," said Brother Louis. "It will be strange for all of us. But it's no stranger than the fact that each of you for the first time in many years is now wearing a wristwatch. There are no monastery bells here yet. My suggestions are that we arise as we are accustomed to at 3:00 A.M., and have morning prayers in the chapel at 3:15. Holy Mass will be celebrated by Père Clement at 6:00 and he has brought all the necessary materials, but we will need to arrange to get more. Breakfast will be at 7:00. It will be simple and taken in silence. At 7:15 we should be ready for work. Any questions so far?"

"Yes, I have one," it was Brother Alban addressing the group in a somewhat nervous tone. "Not having a monastery bell to awaken us, how will we manage to arise for morning prayer? I would not trust myself to wake up in time."

"Thank you, Brother," said Brother Louis, "and that issue was brought to me before I left Sept-Fons. The Abbot gave me an alarm clock as a practical gift. So, Brother if I give it to you, would you accept responsibility for making sure all of us will be in the chapel at the same time? A simple knock on each person's door would suffice?"

"Of course," Brother Alban replied, with relief written all over his face.

Then addressing Henriette directly across the table, Brother Louis continued, "it goes without saying that you and your household are more than welcome to join us in any of our liturgical services." And turning to the brothers, "we are all guests in somebody else's home so I know that you will respect their privacy and sleep, especially when you rise for morning prayer."

"Oh no, Brother," it was Henriette addressing him with a look of concern, "do not worry about waking me. I am the only person sleeping near the chapel, and I will certainly be joining you for morning prayer and Mass. It is such an honor to have all of you staying in my house. And do not worry about materials for Mass, I will visit the local priest in Beysaac later on in the week and get as much as you will need."

And so, the work began, and with two professional construction companies working on different sections of the buildings, the speed of construction was impressive. But what struck Brother Louis most forcibly was the dedication and attention to detail that Madame Henriette was bringing to the project. He had not worked closely with a female for several years and in some ways, it was both refreshing for him and challenging at the same time. The pure pleasure and enjoyment she took from having the monks live under her roof, was evident in everything she said and did. Being able to pray with them and attend the mass daily was something she could never have dreamed of. Her staff noticed, that for the very first time since the death of her husband, she was clearly very much alive. Brother Louis early on had to explain that while they were working together, she did not have to keep apologizing for having to speak to him. "Madame Henriette, this is a very special project and we must adapt the Trappist rules to suit our current situation, especially our rule of silence. You and I need to be able to dialogue freely and openly, so please, do not be anxious. We both, each in our own way, should practice silence of the spirit."

"I understand Brother, but I still feel guilty," she replied, "and I am just so afraid that I will spoil this marvelous gift that God has given to me and my family. I do not want to offend any of the Brothers and least of all you."

Several months later an incident occurred, and Brother Thomas was at the center of it. While they were having their usual evening round up of the day's events sitting in the salon, he surprised everybody with an announcement in his typical Ardeche blunt and no-frills manner, "Brothers, I believe somebody is stealing our wood." All heads turned towards him and it was Henriette, who spoke first.

"Brother, this is a serious allegation, are you sure?"

"This afternoon there was a delivery of lumber for me," he continued, "from the same supplier and yard in Brive where all previous materials were purchased. The foreman for our con- tractor, Mr. Boblin was there when it was unloaded. I was somewhat suspicious with a delivery last week, but only after I'd started to use the wood. I was not certain any was missing, I just seemed to be short of material. Anyway, this time I checked the amount of wood delivered against the invoice, and we are missing about twenty-five twelve-foot lengths of board."

Everyone at the table looked mystified and shocked. But Brother Thomas continued. "I confronted the driver and the foreman, and an argument broke out. The foreman was upset and angry and could not explain the discrepancy. He's afraid that he will lose his job. The driver, however, said that this has happened several times before on other contracts, and that it's the lumber yard that's cheating. I rechecked the pieces and my count was correct. I left them to resolve their problem. I have the invoice with my count here," and reaching into his robe, pulled out two pieces of paper.

"Thank you, Brother," it was Henriette taking charge, and addressing him directly, "this is totally unacceptable and of course I will personally deal with this immediately. In the morning, after breakfast, Brother Louis and I will travel to Brive to meet with the manager and owner of the lumber yard. He and his father have been good friends to us for a long time, and helped my husband, several years ago. I will get to the bottom of this problem. Do you not agree Brother Louis?"

"Yes of course, Madame Henriette," he replied, "we can go together, and thank you for offering to do this."

The trip to Brive was without incident and Henriette spoke very little, her mind clearly on the business in front of her. She had telephoned before they left, just to make sure that the owner of the lumber yard would himself be present.

"Madame the Countess, how nice to see you again, I trust that you are well?" An older gentleman with a shock of long white hair and a white well-trimmed goatee stepped forward to meet her and embraced Henriette warmly. "It's been too long since we last met," she commented and turning to Brother Louis,

"This is the Abbot of the new monastery that I told you about, Brother Louis."

"You are welcome Brother," he said greeting him with an embrace. "Please come into my office, it's much cooler inside."

Realizing that she had failed to introduce him, Henriette turning to him said, "I do apologize, and please excuse my bad manners Brother, but this is a very old friend of our family, and the proprietor of this establishment, Mr. Jean Pierre Huteau."

Looking around, Brother Louis realized that this was the same lumber yard he had visited with Henriette several months earlier. Wood of every description was piled everywhere in high, neatly ordered stacks, clearly sorted by variety and sizes. The sound of a circular saw at work almost drowned out any conversation and the air seemed to be filled with heavily scented dust. The office was upstairs overlooking a long open sided workshop and he could see at a glance where the noise was coming from. They sat on two wooden chairs that clearly had just been wiped clean from the dust that seemed to permeate everywhere, facing an old desk covered with some tidy files and papers in a two-tier tray. In the far corner a young woman was working at a desk heaped with heavy binders. Brother Louis acknowledged her with a nod. "Jean Pierre and I go back many years," said Henriette, "and he even longer, having worked in the Chateau before the war. It was he who helped renovate several rooms including our little chapel."

At that moment, the door opened, and a tall thin man in his late twenties, dressed in dusty blue coveralls entered, and after greeting the visitors, gently embraced the old man. "I've just turned off the sawmill," he exclaimed. "We can now have a discussion without having to shout," he said laughingly. Then turning to the woman at the desk, "Agnes," he asked, "would you please bring some water for our guests."

"Let me introduce my son," said Jean Pierre, "this is Serge Huteau, my eldest son and the manager of all my businesses.

Henriette you know him well, but Brother Louis, I hope that you'll also get to know him."

"Thank you, but yes I know him, but not well, we met some months ago when I first arrived in the area. Henriette introduced me to him."

"We know unfortunately why you are here," it was Serge who opened up the discussion, as he dragged over another chair and placed it next to his father behind the desk, "but we also want you to know we believe we know what is happening to your orders. It's an internal pilfering issue. And let me assure you that we will make good on any lumber that you believe has gone missing. I'm only sorry that you've had to come all of this way to meet with us."

"As I explained on the phone, Serge," said Henriette picking up the conversation, "I have total confidence in you and your father, our friendship goes back too far to be spoiled by this upset, and I know that you will take care of it. But the real reason I wanted to come, was so that you both could have time to meet Brother Louis. The monastery as you know, once it is completed, will house at least thirty monks and they will need all the help they can get to make it sustainable. As an eminent and highly respected businessmen in both the Catholic and the local merchant community, it would be most helpful if you could introduce and help connect Brother Louis to important businesspeople in the Brive area. They need opportunities to sell their farm produce and especially their pigs."

*****

The car stopped with a sudden jerk as Bernard parked it in front of the main door of the Chateau, but Brother Louis continued sleeping. "Brother Louis, Brother Louis," it was Henriette gently shaking his shoulder, "we have arrived home."

"My goodness," he replied somewhat sleepily and rubbing

his eyes, I had no idea I was so tired, I do apologize."

"No, not at all, not at all," she replied in a motherly tone, "your body was just telling you what it needed. We have all arrived safely and have time to freshen up before our evening meal."

*****

Tending to a wounded airman in the monastery infirmary, Père Louis, pondered as to what his next move should be. He needed to decide quickly. Getting the man prepared and ready to hike across the Pyrenees was difficult enough. Even more challenging in some ways, was how to get the man with a serious leg wound on a train, even as far as St Jean de Luz, without drawing too much attention from the Germans, and possibly the Gestapo. In recent months physical check points on roads and at train stations had increased considerably. The monastery had fitted the three men out with suitable clothing and boots, and Brother Anselme the printer, now turned into a forger *extraordinaire*, had created authentic looking ID cards and passes that would stand the most intense scrutiny. But would all of that be enough?

As he looked out of the window, he could see heavy, grey clouds coming from the south west, and the line of chestnut trees near the river tossing about and shaking their heads furiously, as if in disagreement with the coming storm. He needed time to think and clear his head.

Leaving the infirmary, he went to his own room which was close by and taking his heavy white robe to help stave off the cold, pulled up his cowl, went downstairs and pensively walked round and round the cloister. But for the noise of the wind, the monastery was silent and at rest. He loved these precious moments when in spite of nature making its own voice felt, the world seemed to stand still. "How did I get here?" he asked himself. Why had he said a quick and such an easy "yes" to Henriette when she had asked him to help a wounded airman? Why had he gotten even deeper involved and without further invitation, expressed a desire to be part of the Maquis? Was all of this not just against the Trappist way of life and a commitment to a life of prayer? Even worse, what would the Church say if the authorities knew what he was doing?

He had cried the night he heard that his brother Charles in Paris was almost caught by the Gestapo and that all the others in his group had been betrayed and shot. Just four months earlier, Charles had brought two of them to the monastery for a weekend, as a respite from their intense and stressful work. And now, they had been executed at Fort Mount-Valerian, and for what? For wanting France to be free again. It was Henriette herself who had come to the monastery to give him both the good and bad news. It was she who had witnessed his tears and heard him cry out that "true Christians should not stand idly by and watch poor people suffer injustice after injustice."

Sitting side by side in the chapel, it was she who listened sensitively to his pain but also to his commitment. "Yes, we can pray for the poor and oppressed, we can pray for the suffering and sick, but we can do even more. Praying is simply not good enough. People are sick, cold, hungry, have lost all of their possessions, are homeless, are starving, are being treated like animals." His voice trailed off into silence. "These are extraordinary times, Henriette," he finally continued in a subdued voice, "and we must use extraordinary means to help our people. We have to be Christians in action."

"So, Père," she quietly asked, "what do you intend to do?"

"I will follow your lead," he replied, "I am not a man of the world, I have been sheltered from it. So now I must rely on you to help me, to show me the way. I know that you care about me and these monks, so I know you will never put us in danger."

With those words still ringing in his ears, Père Louis, paused in his cloister walk and then decided to sit for a moment on a bench near the chapel door. He shivered slightly with the cold and drew his robe tighter around himself.

Just seven years after starting the new foundation, he had been ordained a priest and was no longer 'Brother' but 'Père' Louis, the officially elected Abbot of this new monastery. Under his leadership it was now totally self-sufficient. It had also grown and there were almost forty monks in the community. While he was grateful to God for all that had happened, he was also now beginning to question his own judgement. Three years ago, he had never heard of the Maquis, and what little news there was of the Resistance came through Henriette. But he decided as Abbot, once he learned of the fall of France and the partition of the country, that for the safety of everybody, there would be two material changes in the monastery.

The Germans had divided France into an Occupied and Free Zone, which caused a massive exodus from the North. Brive itself with a normal population of forty thousand people, almost overnight swelled to one hundred and fifty thousand. Terrible things were happening everywhere, and Père Louis knew that the monastery needed to stay informed. With Henriette's help, a small radio was purchased, and twice a day, two monks were assigned to listen to the news, take down notes and share them with the everybody by reading them out loud at the evening meal. He himself listened to broadcasts in German and English and shared pertinent information with the community.

A second item had been discussed many times in the past, and the community was split on its value. The monks involved primarily in buying and selling produce were very much in favor, but the majority were opposed. After speaking with his brother Charles by phone from the Chateau, and hearing more about the Comet Line, Père Louis uncharacteristically made a unilateral decision and asked Henriette if she could use her influence and have a telephone installed in the monastery.

"I wonder what other changes we will have to make before this war is over," he mused, "we have come so far, and have achieved so much since those first days."

The sound of a door slamming in the wind brought him suddenly out of his reverie. He realized that he must have been dozing for some time and was now ready to retire. The booming bell high up in the chapel steeple seemed to come in waves as the wind gusted across the roofs, announcing that it was almost time for the final prayers of the day and an examination of conscience. As the monks silently filed passed him into the chapel, he followed and took his place in the choir stall. But he was struggling with some of his most recent decisions; they would not leave him in peace, and he could not fully focus on the prayers being chanted. "Here I am the spiritual leader and role model for this community," he said to himself, "at least that is what I had committed to be when I was elected as Abbot. Yet tonight I am sheltering British airmen in the guest rooms and infirmary and preparing to take them to the Spanish border. But even more than that, I have given medical care and nursed back to health a foreign agent and saboteur, and more damning still, I've taken a leading role in helping plan a major resistance operation; to derail a German train and release more than seven hundred conscripts."

Chapter 8
Comet Line

It was while Henriette was in Paris meeting with Père Louis' brother Charles and the leaders of the Comet Line, that significant events took place that severely impacted the Maquis groups in Brive.

The Comet line itself was the initiative of Andree de Johngh, a twenty-four-year-old Belgian woman and nurse, who had come into contact with wounded Allied servicemen, mainly aviators, hiding in safe houses throughout Belgium. Together with family and friends they established a network which protected these men, and then escorted them through France into what was technically, but very superficially, a neutral Spain. Stopping at numerous safe houses on the way, the pilots and crewmen, were moved slowly through France towards Saint Jean de Luz in the Southwest. From there, they were escorted by Basque guides across the Pyrenees.

Charles who had survived the assassination of the Musée de L'Homme group in Paris, was now heavily involved in Comet Line operations and had recruited Henriette. On a visit to see her elderly and ailing father in the Occupied Zone, who was being cared for by a trusted family companion, she saw firsthand the negative effects of the Occupation, and in particular what it was doing to her family. The demarcation line had cut in two the Department of Cher and the Berry where her ancestors had lived for centuries, leaving the family chateau just inside the Occupied Zone. It was now forcibly commandeered by German Officers and their staff, and her father was restricted to just two rooms and use of the kitchen. He was too proud to leave and live with Henriette or any of her sisters. The once beautiful grounds were now unkept and overgrown, all the staff had fled south for safety to the Free Zone, after the armistice. The acres of vines, once the pride of the area, stood bleached and shriveled, and the very productive farm reduced to providing a few eggs daily.

Her feelings of helplessness, resentment and anger clashed with her Catholic values and belief in a loving God but were somewhat assuaged when she arrived in Paris and stayed with her sister Therese. Over the course of several days Therese confided in Henriette that she and her husband Victor were involved in helping distribute a clandestine anti-Nazi newspaper *Combat*, and through a Catholic action group had been introduced to the Comet Line. They were now acting as local couriers and also provided a temporary safe house. It all came as a shock to Henriette as she struggled with the idea of her family taking up an active role in the Resistance. All of that changed, however, the evening that Charles was invited to dinner.

"So, Henriette," he chided, "what are you afraid of? Afraid for us or afraid for France?"

She was stuck for words, and although she had met Charles several times in the past, that night as he leaned over the table looking directly into her face, all she could see were the eyes of Père Louis. They had almost finished a very satisfying meal complete with stimulating conversation regarding various controversial topics, not the least being why they needed to be part of a Resistance group. They were relaxing with a treasured glass of brandy, reserved for such a special occasion.

"We are following our own consciences and that means staying true to our Catholic principles. This is the way we are trying to live out the Gospel message. And when Boris Vilde and the other members of my group were shot, I just wanted to run as far away as I could go." Charles's voice softened and he began to choke on his words. "But I needed to recognize that my mission was not completed. It was not just survivor's guilt." His voice broke completely, and he began to quietly sob, turning away from the table in embarrassment. Therese moved quickly and standing in front of him, gently leaned over and held his head against her breasts. "It's OK Charles, it's OK," she murmured comfortingly.

"I needed to do more than just distribute anti-Nazi propaganda," he said earnestly, pulling a handkerchief from his top pocket and drying his eyes, "even though that itself is an action that could result in imprisonment or deportation if I am caught."

"I can understand that, Charles, and it takes great courage, so what more are you planning to do?" Henriette gently asked. Therese and Victor said nothing, but waited for Charles to continue, knowing what was surely coming next.

"Well, Henriette, it's actually what I'm doing now. So, I have a confession to make. I'm one of the leaders of the Comet Line, helping downed Allied airmen get back to England through Spain. We do it through a series of safe houses and use of couriers. You also know now that your sister and her husband are deeply committed to this work."

There was a brief lull in the conversation and Henriette toyed with a dessert fork, before replying, "I think I understand Charles what you are all doing, but if all of this is so secret and hush hush, why are you sharing the information with me?"

"Because, Henriette," he said, reaching over the table to touch her hand, "we need your help. My job is to recruit strong and reliable people and help set up safe houses along the line. And in these days when there is a great fear of our groups being infiltrated by spies and collaborators, I know that you are neither. I also know that you are already working with Maquis groups."

For a while, the two of them sat there in silence. She was conflicted. It was not a question of using the Chateau as a safe house, for she certainly had the space and the means, and it was so remote as to not raise any immediate fear of being noticed by the Gestapo. But this new activity would involve a Maquis travelling 500 miles in a round trip to the Spanish border, escorting men who did not speak French. The risks were huge and given the recent increases in military and police check points and travel document controls, very dangerous. She wished she could run to the monastery and consult with Père Yves, but instead had to try and imagine what he would say. She first looked at Therese and Victor whose eyes were expectantly focused on her, then at Charles and said, "Tell me specifically what I need to do, and how I can help you."

*****

That conversation with Charles had occurred almost two years previously and so much had taken place since. It took just a few weeks for her to get organized with some trusted friends and set up the Chateau as a safe house and recruit Sylvie, a nurse in Brive general hospital, as an escort. Some years earlier they had been partnered at a special Catholic workshop for single women, and their friendship had developed. Under Henriette's direction several Maquis cells were already formed and operative, with control of Resistance activity around Brive La Gaillarde. Now they were ready to support the Comet Line to the Spanish border. With Père Louis also now a member, it enabled Comet to send wounded people to the Chateau, knowing that they would get essential medical attention before continuing their journey.

With increased police patrols everywhere and German military check points springing up almost overnight at cross-roads, train stations, bridges and outside most important buildings that had been commandeered by German military, travel was becoming extremely difficult. There were now additional and frequent document checks on all trains. What changed everything was the arrival almost overnight of a detachment of Gestapo troops that immediately took forced occupation of buildings in the center of Brive. The three-story house next to Henri's butchers shop became their headquarters and lodging for their commander, colonel Otto Kreis.

In spite of the increased controls, Père Louis made two successful trips to Saint Jean de Luz. Dressed as a wealthy businessman and with perfectly forged credentials, courtesy of Père Anselme, he travelled with four supposedly, Polish workers. who had been conscripted to work with him in selecting cattle as provisions for German troops. The most hazardous part of the journey was actually entering the town of Brive itself with its multiple and various controls operated both by French police, German military and occasionally by the Gestapo.

It was Brother Thomas the carpenter who offered a solution for transporting the Allied airmen to the railway station. He created a false wall behind the cab in the Citroen van used for transporting produce to market. The space was just large enough to conceal three people for a short period of time. Two more people could sit up front on a bench seat with the driver. Since the military routinely used German shepherd dogs to check out vehicles, Brother Thomas had concocted a mixture of pig manure with crushed peppers, and liberally coated both the outside and insides of the van. Both the dogs and the military recoiled at the smell. Once on the train, each of the airmen looked their part, complete with dirty work clothes smelling strongly of pigs and hens.

On his second trip however, when they arrived at the station in Saint Jean de Luz, the contact informed Père Louis that the safe house where the Basque guides usually came to lead them into Spain, had been compromised. The group would have to move to another location. Taken to a small farmhouse they were given old bicycles, and led by the guide, pedaled spread out in two's, eleven miles to an alternative safe house in the village of

Sare. It was almost too physically challenging for one injured airman, and it was clear that from now on, the Comet line would have to move more inland and develop alternative escape routes. The guide who was also a member of the Alliance group, insisted that there would be no special consideration given to any airman who was sick or injured, as the routes now being planned were extremely physically taxing. If a person could not keep pace with the group, he would be left behind. It would also mean taking on extra risks for Père Louis since now they would have to travel to villages further inland for the actual crossing. Units from the German 7th army and the French police seemed to be everywhere, and he realized that he would have to change his identity if the Comet line were to stay open.

He had reduced his visits to Simone considerably and after removing her sutures, did not see any immediate need to continue. He learned from Henriette, that she was now, apart from her arm, fully recovered and was able to transmit information to London daily. Lucien brought in messages several times a week from Brive, passed on to him by Jules. Most of the secret information came from three members of Jules' group, a French policeman, stationed near the Bordeaux seaport and the other a construction worker in the port itself. Essential information regarding the movement in and out, of German supply ships and submarines, was passed on to London every few days by Simone. The Allies discovered for the first time, that the base being built by the Italian military next to the Bordeaux harbor, could house up to thirty submarines; it had dry docks and two basins connected by locks. Shore barracks accommodated a security guard of sixteen hundred men of the San Marco Regiment. They also learned that in December 1942, the Italians would hand over the submarine base to the Germans. They would take responsibility for the northern Atlantic, the Italians would manage a sector south of Lisbon. That same month fifty-five hundred men from the German 7th army would be stationed in and around the city.

A constant stream of information was obtained from a third Maquis who had infiltrated the German Luftwaffe airfield as a permanent laborer at Cazeau, twenty-five miles south west of Bordeaux, where four-night fighter squadrons were based. All flight movements were being monitored and the markings of all aircraft noted. A daily log was being kept and was passed up the line to Simone.

In spite of her typical evening work of transmitting coded information, she was becoming bored and was eager to utilize her training by working more closely with the Maquis. Six weeks had passed since her arrival, and she had expressed this to Henriette who did not respond to her, other than to have Clotilde give her a guided tour of the Chateau, its farm, vineyards, and wine making cellars. It was while they were visiting the chapel in the Chateau that the topic of religion was raised by Simone. "I know that Henriette is a Catholic since she goes to the monastery everyday for Mass. But what about you Clotilde, are you Catholic also?"

"Everybody who works here is a Catholic, and this family's faith can be traced back five hundred years. Yes, we have fought hard for our religion. And what about you?" Clotilde asked, somewhat coldly, sensing that there was a question behind the question.

"Oh, no," Simone responded with a smile, as they walked back down the hallway. "I have no religion; I don't believe in religion. If God does exist and He is good, then why does He allow people to go to war?" she asked provokingly.

"Well, you can ask Père Louis that question, he's coming shortly to remove your cast."

"Yes, I certainly will," she replied, "and I'll ask him to give me a tour of the monastery."

They were just outside of the main salon when Clotilde hurriedly opened the door and almost pushed Simone into the nearest chair. Still standing and with arms folded and in an icy but intensely calm voice said very slowly teasing out each word, "Simone, we are grateful for your being here and the great risks you are taking to help us all, but just a word of caution. As far as you are concerned, the monastery, the monks who live there and all the work they do are strictly off limits for you. Do not ask about them, do not mention them unless you are spoken to, and do not even ask to visit the monastery or think that you will ever visit it, that will not happen. If you deviate from my directives in the slightest, I know that Madame will not hesitate to have you moved far away from here immediately. Do I make myself clear? And now I suggest that you go to your room and get ready, Père Louis will be here very soon."

"Good evening Père," said the maid opening the front door, "how are you?" "I am well, thank you," and gave her the customary kiss on both cheeks. "Miss Simone is waiting for you in her room." "And Clotilde?" he asked. "She's speaking on the telephone with Madame who is in Paris. She'll join you as soon as she is finished."

"And how is my patient today?" said Père Louis after knocking on the door and being invited to enter. He directed his question to Simone who was sitting in an easy chair with a book on her lap.

"I'm well, Père," she replied getting up to greet him.

"Fine, then shall we take what is hopefully a last look at your arm; I think that it's time for the cast to be removed. Please sit on this chair here," indicating one that had a straight back, "it will be easier for me to work on it." It took just a few seconds of asking her to perform some simple finger and hand exercises, to show him that it was indeed time to remove the cast. Working quickly and meticulously, he soon removed it and then very gently pressed several areas of her arm, checking for any residual pain. "It seems to me that you are fine," he told her. "If you have any kind of cream, I suggest that you use it for a while to help rejuvenate your skin, it's typical after wearing a cast that the skin dries out."

"Thank you so much Père," she replied, "it will be such a relief not to be carrying this around with me anymore," pointing
to the opened cast. "It made sleeping so uncomfortable."

"Yes, I am sure it did," he replied and proceeded to gather
up his instruments. "But before I go, why don't I take a final look
at that cut under your arm, it was very deep; I just want to be
sure it is fully healed. Does it still bother you?"

"Only a little," she replied, "it's in an awkward place."

"Alright, then let me see it," he asked, "would you please remove your top and undershirt?" Simone quickly did as he requested.

"It looks like the strap of your brassiere goes right over the
wound. Why don't you remove it and let me take a look?" She
quickly did as he asked and sat there bare breasted while he gently and professionally examined the wound.

"It looks to be just fine," he announced, it is healing nicely
and there really is nothing else to be done. Please put your
clothes back on." She hesitated for just a moment, almost imper-
ceptibly, but he noticed it, and quickly turned away. *That was
provocative, he thought to himself, why is she doing this to me?*

At that moment Clotilde burst into the room. "I'm so sorry
Père," she exclaimed breathlessly, "but Madame was very busy
taking care of an urgent business matter."

"That's just fine, Clotilde," he responded kindly, "I have just
finished here anyway. You can now put Simone to work full
time," he said jokingly, "she has a clean bill of health." And with
that he picked up his bag from the side table and headed for the
door.

"Père," it was Clotilde following him down the stairs, "Yes,
what is it?" he asked.

"Madame just wanted me to let you know that your brother
is well and is enquiring about you. She said to tell you that she's
found a tailor for you in Paris, and that you would know what

that means."

"Thank you, Clotilde, "I am sure I will get a full report when she returns. While I am here, would it be possible to have a word with Lucien; I have not seen him for several weeks?"

"Of course, Père, I'll get him at once, he's working with Bernard in the winery. Why don't you wait in the salon?"

Five minutes later, a dirty and disheveled Lucien arrived, smiling and happy to see him. "Please don't try to greet me Père," he said apologetically, "I'm really dirty. Let me sit over here on a hard chair otherwise Clotilde will be very upset with me."

"How are you Lucien?" greeted Père Louis, "we have not spoken in a while and I am curious as to whether you have been able to make any progress with developing a relationship with any of the BDM ladies in Brive. I think about you so often and I worry for you. Can you bring me up to date or is there nothing to share?"

"Of course," he replied. "You know Père that I drive the van or truck every other day and take the milk into the distribution center. I also take cheese, eggs, and butter, but now I have to register all of the produce at the town hall where everything is recorded. It's the same when I go with Brother Alphonse or Brother Gaspard to sell pigs or cattle. We always end up in the town hall either completing or receiving paperwork. The systems are managed by BDM Nazi women, but as Madame and my father instructed me, I'm beginning to get to know one of them quite well and her name is Marta Feldmann. She's younger than the others, about my age, and also is the best French speaker."

"That is wonderful, Lucien," but you must be extremely cautious. You need to watch out for the Germans and the French police, most of whom cannot be trusted, but especially around civilians, you must be doubly careful. It is sad to say but some people will report you to the authorities if they suspect anything at all, as it will mean more money in their pockets. You must be above suspicion."

"Yes, Père," he replied soberly, but I do think that I can help us get what we need. I've learned that soon there'll be new ration books issued, and a new travel pass is being prepared. We'll all need these special passes for travelling anywhere. I'll see what additional information I can get from Miss Feldman."

"Then, do what you have to do," he replied, rising to his feet, "but you cannot afford to make a single mistake. I will pray for you."

And with that, the two men walked side by side out of the door and into the night.

Chapter 9
Marta

It took only a week before Lucien made further progress with Marta. She was inquisitive about his work and asked how he was connected with the monastery that produced so much dairy produce and meat.

"You are fortunate to work there," she said one day as she was filling out his paperwork. "You look as if you are well fed, and unlike the rest of us, don't have to rely on what is rationed, if and when food is available."

"Well doesn't the military feed you?" he asked.

"No," she replied, "at least not adequately." Then realizing that perhaps she had said too much, lowered her voice and leaned over her desk to whisper, "everyone has to use the black market, even the officers." But then she quickly pulled back and said, "I'm sorry, I shouldn't be talking like that, least of all to a Frenchman." Lucien made a joke of it and replied, "but your French is impeccable, and you have such an interesting accent. Where did you learn to speak so well?"

"I went to school for two years in Switzerland, in Geneva," she explained, and Lucien saw that she was somewhat embarrassed.

It was shortly after that while going through the typical registration process, and while there was nobody close to her desk, that Lucien carefully slipped her a small package of fresh cheese. She didn't quite know what to make of it, but also did not refuse it. At the next visit, she was clearly eager to show her thanks without being too demonstrative.

"You are very kind and I'm very grateful" she said, and shyly turned her head away. "Then you must also take this." Lucien slipped another package to her, a block of freshly made butter. Looking widely around to make sure nobody was watching, Marta quickly placed it under her desk. "Why are you doing this for me?" she asked softly and urgently, "because your face lights up when you blush," he quickly replied.

Several visits later, each time bringing her a small gift of food, Lucien sensed that she was really waiting for him, not just to come and check in his produce, nor to receive his gifts, but just so she could talk. It was obvious to him that she was becoming attracted to him, and him to her. She was after all a very pretty woman, with short blond hair even under her dark green forage side cap, that made her look much younger. He later discovered that they were almost the same age. The tight-fitting uniform showed off her petite shapely figure, which he thought was quite sexy. Summoning up courage, and knowing that he was taking a huge risk, he decided that he would ask Marta to meet him after hours.

It took another week, and when on a Monday he passed her a package of cheese, he also included a note asking if she would meet him at his friend's dental office. He suggested Thursday evening of that week at 5:00 P.M. and provided the address. It would be closed, but all she would have to do would be to knock, and he would open the door. On Wednesday when he came in for his paper work, her face lit up as she saw him, but signaled quickly that one of the other BDM women was watching, that he should leave and come back a little later when there were more people around. Once he saw several people enter, he followed them and went directly to Marta's desk. Carefully slipping her a package of eggs and cheese, he waited for her to say something, but she focused on her work and then passed him his receipts in silence with a simple "thank you sir."

Disappointed, Lucien wondered if he had done something to upset her, and tossed and turned things over in his mind, trying to see what he had done wrong. Was it something he had said, or done? It wasn't until he arrived home that night and was checking his paperwork, that he saw it. Carefully written on the back of a receipt, in a clear and educated hand were the words "I will be there." He was so excited he could not sleep but kept trying to remind himself of the words of warning given to him by Père Louis.

Arranging things with Jean Luc was easy as he usually did not see any patients after 4:30 P.M. and he gave Lucien a spare key with instructions to just make sure the door was locked as he was leaving. He understood that finding a place to take a lady could be difficult for any young man, especially in these troublesome times. The office space had three sections, a tiny receptionist office, and next to it a small but comfortable waiting room with a love seat and two fireside chairs. Behind that was the surgery room itself. A rear door from the surgery led into an alley way that ran behind the building for about thirty yards, before joining a street that during the day was quite busy. In the evening it was quiet save for a few people strolling in the park opposite.

It was 5.05 P.M. when the knock on the door came, and Lucien was literally standing there in the shadows, waiting for it. In a flash he had it open, and Marta entered with a quick look over her shoulder, checking to make sure that she was not being followed. "Thank you for coming," he said rather breathlessly, giving her a chaste brotherly embrace. "I was so looking forward to seeing you."

"And me too," she exclaimed, "but I'm so very nervous and scared that somebody might see me."

"Well we are here now, so please come in and let's enjoy some time together. I have a bottle of white wine from our own vineyards, and some madeleines baked by my mother."

Sitting side by side on the love seat, but looking straight ahead, both of them seemed too shy to speak, and were afraid to look the other in the eye, until Lucien opened and poured the wine. "I hope that you like French wine, Marta," he said offering her a glass. "Yes of course," she replied, I'm starting to enjoy it. The couple in whose home I am staying always have wine with dinner."

"So, you are living alone?" he asked. "Yes," she answered, "there are five of us working in the office as you have seen, and we were each assigned to a household in the town. It is difficult to socialize together, added to the fact that sometimes we work different shifts. I share my ration coupons with the couple I live with, but food is so difficult to find it does not help very much. What you bring to me is really appreciated, and I'm asked all the time where I get it. I just tell them that I have a very good friend."

Beginning to relax, Marta took off her side cap, placed it on the coffee table, then shook her hair as if to set it free, quickly running her fingers through it. Lucien was struck by just how pretty her face looked. "But please tell me about yourself," she asked, "and why you bring me so many gifts."

Still nervous, he rested his arm on the seat behind her head and took a sip of his wine. "It's a long story," he explained, but then shared with her his life at the Chateau and that of his family, and how he was also the driver for the monastery.

"Well that makes a lot of sense," she exclaimed, turning to face him, "now I understand where you get the food."

"And what about your family," he asked. Without any hesitation she replied, "I'm from a village just outside Munich and have two sisters and a brother. My father works in a munitions factory and my mother died four years ago: she had a weak heart. My parents sent me to Switzerland to finish my high school studies, they wanted me to be a doctor but when I came home, I joined the Hitler Youth movement and got caught up in the whole organization. Two years ago, I had the opportunity to serve the Fatherland as a military assistant because I spoke fluent French and was first assigned to a dreary office in Paris. Then with the recent removal of the Free Zone, I came here last

November. You've seen me at work each time you come into the town hall."

"And have you made any friends?" he asked. There was a short pause before she gave a cautious reply as if somebody were listening. "No, we are not supposed to fraternize with French men, and French women hate us. At times it's very lonely. There are of course our soldiers, but most only stay for a very short time and are then sent back to Germany, and it's absolutely forbidden to establish any relationships with them."

Lucien sensed a need in her to be touched and reaching out gently held her hand. She didn't resist but allowed him to take it, then turned her head slightly and looking at him directly said, "I really like you, and hope that we can continue to be friends." "Yes of course," he replied, "and I like you too, and very much want to see you again. We can meet here at the same time next week if that will work for you? But if you ever have time off during the day, I'll arrange something special."

"Yes, to both of those she said smilingly. Every two weeks I get one day off, and it's always a Saturday. In fact, I'll be off a week from this Saturday."

"Then, consider it done," replied Lucien. If times were different, I would take you to a beautiful place on the Correze River where I used to go as boy, it's very secluded and only known to a few local people. However, as you know, moving around is so difficult now."

"If it's a travel pass you need," Marta suggested, "then I can certainly take care of that. The next time you come into the office, just give me the details of your driving license and I'll issue a new one. In fact, new passes are being prepared and, in several weeks, everybody will need one as well, so I'll make sure you have one too."

"Wonderful, then let's consider it a date," he replied, then quickly corrected himself, "no, it will be two dates since we'll meet here again next week."

Chapter 10
The Train

"The main reason we're here tonight is that a major disruption to the German administration has been suggested by the Francs-Tireurs (FT) group and they have asked us to be responsible for the planning." Serge had taken off his well-worn leather jacket and was rolling up the sleeves on a shirt that had not been laundered for some time. "The only other person who knows about this is Henriette. We have first to decide if we can in fact design and execute a plan of action. Henriette," he asked, turning towards her, "why don't you explain?"

Standing up from her usual chair at the end of the semi-circle, she moved forward and with her back to the fireplace, looked around the group whose eyes were now rivetted on her, waiting eagerly to hear what she had to say.

"We have learned that the Germans will round up hundreds of young Frenchmen for forced labor in Germany, and that they will be held for about two days in Brive, at the soccer stadium before being loaded onto a train. Both Jules and Raymond have confirmed this information, as well as a member of FT who has infiltrated the German administration. We do not know the exact day and time of departure, but it will probably take place in about ten days. After leaving Brive it will pass through Tulle, Ussel and stop in Clermont Ferrand for coal and water before proceeding to the border at Noveant sur Moselle. There, German engineers will take over the train and the French crew will return to Brive. We also know that the Germans are treating this as a low-level operation. There will only be a minimal number of troops guarding the train. The main danger will come from bombing by the Allies, but that will probably take place four hundred miles from here." She paused to look around the group and could see from their facial expressions that they had many questions.

"So, what is the plan?" she asked rhetorically. "Our principal goal is to derail the train, quickly neutralize the guards without shooting them, and let the conscripts know they are free to run and hide in the hills. In fact, they can go home. If we can do this quickly with a strong show of force, there should be no bloodshed."

"But how will that be possible?" interrupted Henri. "The Boches will shoot us once they see us."

"That is not necessarily so," she replied. "First, we will need to find an isolated spot between Tulle and Ussel, which would provide lots of cover for us. Then we set explosives on the rails and wait. Once the train is derailed, we will wait a short while, and when the Germans see no further action, they will certainly get down to see the extent of the damage. Raymond will guarantee I am sure, that the engineers will be members of his Maquis cell. They will tell the Germans that they are outnumbered and that if they lay down their arms they will not be harmed." Then looking directly at the railway chief asked, "are you OK with that Raymond?"

"I am a little surprised with the plan," he replied, "but yes, I'll make sure the crew will be Maquis, and let them know that this will be their last trip. I have more than a thousand workers, and will be able to move them later to safer work where they'll be hidden. Closer to the departure, I'll also have the details of the train, the numbers of conscripts and exact number of military personnel. A similar train a few weeks ago only had four armed guards, two in the last carriage and another two in the front, plus one officer."

"Thanks so much Raymond, I know that we can rely on

you," she said. "It is thirty-eight miles from Tulle to Ussel and we need to find a suitable location outside of Tulle for the derailment. If we cut the telephone lines, it will take quite some time for the station in Ussel to realize that the train is not running on schedule. Raymond will be able to tell us just how long we should have to take care of business and make our escape. I would imagine that we might have about thirty minutes maximum."

"If I can interrupt again," it was Serge moving toward Henriette and unfolding a sheet of paper. "I want to share a few details that we've worked out with the FT Group. We'll take a total of twelve men, six from our cells and six from theirs. Everybody will wear a face covering so that there'll be no recognition. The two section leaders will be identified by wearing a red bandana around their necks and a red arm band, and that means me and the FT leader. Once we find the location, we'll split ourselves on either side of the track, and at my signal, a single gunshot, we'll rush to the train and open the doors yelling at the young men to get out and run for their lives. Is everybody clear so far?"

There were nods all around. "Then the next two issues are of critical importance. We need to explore areas east of Tulle station and find the optimum place for the derailment. For this assignment I'm proposing that we ask Simone to do it. She is the only one among us professionally trained in sabotage and the use of explosives. She could accompany me posing as my wife"

Again, it was Henriette taking control, "I am not sure about that Serge", she replied, "we should give it more thought. In addition, there is the question of cutting the telephone lines between Tulle and Ussel. Jean Luc has a member in his group who works for the PTT (Post, Telegraph & Telephones). We need him to survey the area and ensure that the two stations will not be able to communicate with each other."

"And what will we do with the Boches?" Again, it was Henri interrupting, this time in a slightly agitated voice. Getting up from his chair he began to pace nervously up and down behind the group.

"I hear your anxiety Henri," Henriette, continued, "but please listen carefully. We will do no harm to anyone. This operation is to strike a blow at the German occupiers, to let them know that we are watching them, that they cannot be safe anywhere they go. It will also liberate many of our countrymen who are forcibly being taken to work in Germany. They are all young in their twenties, so they should be able to look after themselves, and I am sure will be happy to do so."

"But to your question, Henri, our intention is to get the Germans to lay down their arms, knowing that they are outnumbered. If they do that, we will blindfold and gag them, remove their uniforms, and leave them tied up at the side of the tracks. They will be found soon enough." Then turning to Père Louis, "you are very quiet Père, what do you think?"

There was almost a hesitancy in his voice as he replied, "perhaps there is one very important element that has not been discussed," and all heads turned to look at him. "What's that Père?" demanded Serge quickly, leaning over so that he could see his face. "What am I not taking into consideration?" It was said with a sharp tone that shocked everyone in the room. But it was Jules who intervened and broke the tension. Getting to his feet and eying each person as he looked around the chairs said, "Serge let's be clear, this is not your operation, it's ours, we're all in this together and we'll all do our very best. Nobody has a monopoly on ideas or suggestions. This is a dangerous, complex, and challenging plan, and people could get shot. We all need to hear what Père Louis has to say." And with that, sat down again, and looking over said, "Père, please continue."

"Thank you, Jules and thank you Serge for all that you are doing for us, for our land, for France. If I understand you correctly, it will be the locomotive drivers who will let the Germans know that they are surrounded, outnumbered, and will ask them to surrender, is that correct?" "Yes indeed, Père," said Serge, "that's the plan." "Well," Père Louis continued, "that assumes several things: first that the Germans will speak and understand French, which I for one think is highly improbable since these troops are headed back to Germany, and will only have been here for a short while. This is not a return trip; they are going home. Secondly, if they do not speak French, who will speak to them in German? Again, I think we can safely assume that the locomotive drivers will not be able to do that. We will need a German speaker?"

The silence in the room was palpable. "You are correct, I think, Père," said Raymond. "None of my crew can or would want to speak German." And then addressing the group, "so what should we do? What other options do we have?"

"I'm not sure," Serge began, "the FT group are relying on us to plan the derailment, and I'd be surprised if they have a German speaker in any of their cells." He paused to light a Gauloises. "Perhaps we should call the whole thing off? None of us speak German." The group remained silent. "I've put many hours into planning this action with the FT," he reflected, "but maybe this is just too risky after all. Shall we take a vote?"

"I suggest that we all take a deep breath and listen again, very carefully to what Père Louis has shared with us," answered Raymond as he got to his feet and started walking back and forth behind the semi-circle of chairs. "If what Serge says is correct, then we're also ignoring the two people who do speak German, Père Louis and Henriette. And I'll speak for all of us, by saying that we will not involve her in any way with the actual physical operation."

"But what are you saying, Raymond?" interjected Henriette quickly, "are you suggesting that we involve Père Louis in this? That's just a crazy idea," and she moved towards him defiantly. "It is not even a question of 'how', I do not want any further discussion on this topic," she snapped. She walked over to the bureau and poured herself a glass of water.

"Well Henriette, I respect your position as a leader, but can we hear from Père Louis, himself," he responded, "he has raised the questions, and may have a solution." Returning to the group she signaled with a slight nod towards Père Louis that he should speak.

"Raymond," he began, "I first must ask you a question. How many engineers normally operate the locomotive?"

"Typically, two Père."

"And do you ever use three?"

"Yes, sometimes on a very long haul or if there's a night schedule. But why are you asking?"

"And what about this train?" he asked. "Could you put three engineers on it without raising any suspicion?"

There was a lull in the conversation and everyone in the room was wondering what was coming next.

"That wouldn't be an issue, Père. It's almost four hundred and fifty miles to the border, and there are two problems that could take the train longer than the usual eight hours. There's a steep gradient and slow section just outside Tulle, all the way to Clermont Ferrand and that section alone could take hours. Then within one hundred and fifty miles of the border, there'll be very slow sections due to Allied air attacks. The last train took seventeen hours to reach Noveant sur Moselle, the border change over station. With a third engineer, they would each rotate and take a spell at the controls and firing the boiler."

"Then my question becomes, Raymond, do you think I could ride on the locomotive dressed as a third engineer? If the answer is yes, then we can figure out the details. I could be that German speaking member of the crew."

"This is ridiculous," cried Henriette, losing her normally calm and controlled voice. "Why are you talking like this, Père?" and unable to look him in the eye as her emotions momentarily took over, she walked to the bureau and with her back to the group pretended to refill her glass of water. Then turning round, she asked, "do we want to risk losing our guide for the Comet line? Is it not enough that he gambles with his life every time he takes Allies to the Pyrenees? No, no, I will not, cannot support the idea, it is just too dangerous."

"But you yourself said that in this action there would be no bloodshed," interjected Simone, "that you did not want any shooting. Did you not say that the intent was to have the Germans lay down their arms?"

If looks could kill, Simone would have died instantly. Walking slowly back to the group, Henriette shot her a withering look as she sat next to Père Louis, too close in Henriette's opinion, but now back in control, said, "you are new to this work Simone. Blood is being shed all around us and I do not want to add to it. The group will decide what the best course of action will be, and I have stated my opinion clearly," and with that took an empty chair in the semi-circle.

"I think it could work," said Serge gravely, taking a draw on his habitual cigarette, "but we would need to really get down to details and specifics. We'll need to address many 'what if' scenarios and ensure that in the event of things not going according to plan, that Père Louis will be able to defend himself; that will mean carrying a side arm." He paused for a moment as he exhaled a cloud of blue smoke. "All of the engineers in addition to their goggles, will have their faces covered at all times as will all of the Maquis. At all costs, we must not allow the Germans to be able to identify anybody after the event. In addition, for the rest of us and the FT group, we cannot all try to pass through the check points at the same time or even close together. It's very complicated and dangerous since we'll all have to get out of Brive, and then get through Tulle which is crawling with military, Gestapo, and police. Then we must all figure out how we'll get home."

"So, let me suggest something," it was Henriette, speaking

softly in a leadership tone, and in such a way that the whole group focused on her. Standing up and taking a position next to Serge, she continued. "we have lots of friends and safe houses in and around Tulle, so once we know the exact date of the departure, all of our cells that are involved, should be in the Tulle area at least twenty-four hours beforehand. Secondly, we should use as few vehicles as possible to avoid suspicion, but sufficient so that we can leave the area quickly. My suggestions are that we do not return to Brive but cut across country westwards towards Uzerche. You all know the backroads and villages, and you can head back to the Chateau. I have lots of room where people can stay for a few days until the noise and repercussions have died down. Thirdly, I suggest that we have a small group comprised of Raymond, Jules, Simone, and Serge plan the details of the derailment. Finally, once that is done, we must have a joint meeting with the FT leadership in Brive as soon as possible."

*****

Three days later, Simone and Père Louis, drove to a safe house in Tulle to meet the person responsible for the FT group. Bernard should have been the driver for Simone but was sick, and Lucien had already left for Brive with the pick-up truck. Père Louis was simply the backup driver; there was nobody else close by who could be trusted. Serge was to lead this exploratory trip but was also unable to participate. The increasing numbers of executions by the Gestapo had put a huge demand on his business for coffins, and he was unexpectedly called to a business meeting with an SS officer who controlled the sale of polished wood.

Dressed appropriately for the occasion, and driving the smelly monastery van, at the roadblock to Tulle lined up with many other vehicles, the French police barely looked at Père

Louis' papers and accepted the reason for travelling to Ussel. The German SS were less polite, much more demanding and scrutinized both the IDs and travel permits of himself and Simone.

"So, who is this person with you?" demanded the soldier speaking in broken French

"It's my wife," responded Père Louis handing over Simone's pass.

"Then why don't you have the same name?" The soldier discussed in German this issue with a second soldier while turning the passes over and over in his hand, as if somehow that action might reveal some additional information. They were unaware that Père Louis understood every word and knew that they were just showing off their authority. "Because we refused to marry in the Catholic church, and just signed papers in front of the mayor of Barassac."

"And where again are you going?"

"We are travelling to Ussel for a funeral."

"Then remember that there's an early curfew in that town, and you will be shot if you are found on the street." After a "Heil Hitler" salute, he signaled with his arm for another soldier controlling the barrier, to raise it and allow the van to pass. Neither of them spoke for the rest of the journey. After parking the van outside a house behind the church, and passwords had been exchanged, an old lady dressed completely in black opened the door leading them into a small sitting room where two men were waiting.

"Hi, I'm Remy, from Jean Luc's cell." A young man in his late twenties wearing heavily stained work clothes rose to meet them. "I work for PTT and so can travel pretty much anywhere. I'm here to assess where best I can cut the telephone lines once we have a location for the ambush."

"And you can just call me Hatchet". A short thickset man who spoke French with a heavy Spanish accent, and was clearly

Basque, offered his hand to Père Louis. "I'm from the Francs Tireurs group. And who are you?" he asked brusquely. "Just call me Bull," said Père Louis, "I'm with the Peacock group, and we're responsible for planning the attack, that's all you need to know."

"And why did you bring along a woman?" he snorted in a dismissive tone.

Sensing his resentment of Simone, Père Louis uncharacteristically retorted back, "You may have experience fighting against General Franco, Hatchet, but what do you know about planning an ambush, setting up a derailment, and using plastic explosives? This woman's name is Sparrow, and we will all follow her instructions down to the smallest details. Our lives may depend on her. She is a professionally trained saboteur and demolition expert. And since we do not have much time, let's get back on the road and start work. We have consulted with the railway chief in Brive, and he suggested that we start looking at an area about eight miles out from Tulle, where there's a narrow gorge. The nearest village is Touza, about four miles away. We will all travel together in my van. Since you have a German pass Remy, you should ride in the front with Sparrow and myself. At the checkpoint we can say that you also are coming to the funeral with us." Then turning to Hatchet, he said, "you will need to hide in the secret compartment in the van. It will be uncomfortable and smelly, but we should have no problem passing the barrier and, in any case, it won't be for long."

Getting through the various checkpoints proved to be a tedious but uneventful experience, and once leaving Tulle, Père Louis kept the River Correze and the railway line which ran alongside of it, on his right hand-side. Turning off the main road they followed for about half a mile, what appeared to be from its appearance, a rarely used narrow cart track and found an ideal spot to conceal the van. Remy explained that he needed to check the telephone lines which he noticed some miles back, that also ran along the edge of the railway tracks. After synchronizing their watches and agreeing to meet back at the van in about four hours, he set off down the slope, and was quickly hidden by the thick forest.

The way down to the river and the railway line was so steep, that with the exception of Hatchet, who moved down the slope like an agile mountain goat, Père Louis and Simone had difficulty with their footing and were constantly grasping at branches and bushes to prevent their falling. At one point with Père Louis leading the way, she slipped and screamed, and as he turned, she crashed into him, clinging tightly to his arms. As they rested momentarily, he felt her deliberately press her body up against his. Once at the bottom, Simone could see that the place was not suitable for the movement of so many Maquis.

Walking side by side with Père Louis along the railway line eastwards and Hatchet following close behind, she noted that they were walking up a very steep grade that would slow down any train. About a half mile further on, with the tracks still climbing, they followed a sweeping curve to the left following the course of the river. The gorge suddenly opened up to a narrow plain flanked by dense forests on either side. Five hundred yards further, the tracks curved again, but sharply to the right.

"This might be the perfect place," said Simone. "There's good coverage for all of the men. In addition, the two curves will force the train to slow down even more after the climb up the gradient. Let's pace out the attack."

"What do you mean?" asked Hatchet.

"We need to estimate the length of the train," she explained to him, "and assuming that each passenger coach is 60 feet long and there'll be twelve or fifteen of them, then we need to calculate where we want to have the actual derailment, and where we want our men positioned. In other words, we need about 900 feet at least in which to operate"

And with that, pointing to a small boulder, asked Hatchet to bring it over to the side of the track, "This will be our starting point." Then turning to Père Louis, "you have the longest legs Père, will you please measure this out, it should be about three hundred paces." And with that all three moved up the line, with Père Louis counting out aloud. "This is just about fine," she said, looking around. At that moment, a train whistle sounded in the distance, and the three of them immediately ran towards the forest scrambling for cover. Five minutes later, a train belching black smoke pulling a line of freight cars came into view and inched its way past the group as they watched its every movement.

"It was just like I anticipated, "whispered Simone while the three of them crouched low, as if the trees could hear what she was saying. "Did you notice how slowly it was travelling?"

"Yes," replied Hatchet, "you are correct. Then what's the next move?"

"Let's go back to the tracks first," she explained, "I need to put a marker where I'll place the explosives." It took just a few minutes for her to roll a small boulder close to where she wanted the actual derailment, and then said, "we don't want any confusion among ourselves, so let's agree that the FT will take responsibility for the six rear carriages and the German guards. We'll take the rest. All three looked along the line and then at each other, realizing without saying a word, that this would be a major event for the Maquis, and an even bigger blow to the German occupation.

"Getting out of here carefully and quickly will be critical for all of us," Simone, reflected. "We also need to find a better place to hide the van, rather than the one where we first entered this gorge." With Hatchet in the lead, the three worked their way up a gradual slope and through the trees so close together they shut out the bright sunlight. It was ten minutes later, that Hatchet signaled with his hand for the others to stop. Working his way back, he said, "there's a small clearing ahead, and I'm not sure if anybody's working there or not."

"Then why don't you take a closer look?" suggested Père Louis. Without saying a word, Hatchet took off and was soon out of sight; it was obvious that he was comfortable working in this kind of terrain. Père Louis and Simone sat on the pine needle covered ground with their backs against a tree. She wanted desperately to talk, and get approval for her work, but she intuited that this was not the time. Père Louis with his eyes closed, was using it to pray.

Twenty minutes later Hatchet was back. "Excellent news," he reported, "it looks like this is an old logging site since nothing has been freshly worked. There are two overgrown cart tracks that must lead back to the main road. I only followed them for a short distance as the weeds and grass were knee high, but they would both be passable in a vehicle."

"Great said Père Louis, "then maybe that is the site where we should have everybody gather. Why don't we split up now, we have about half an hour left before meeting up with Remy? Hatchet, first show us the paths then take Simone and follow one, and I'll follow the other. Hopefully, they'll both join the main road."

Getting back to Tulle, dropping off Hatchet and Remy, and then cutting across country towards the Chateau, was uneventful, save for the usual, time-consuming process at several checkpoints. They travelled for the most part in complete silence. Simone wanted desperately to reach out and just touch him; he caught up in his own thoughts about his role as a priest, monk and abbot, and the ambush he was helping to plan. But he was also remembering those seconds when she pressed her body up against his – and all he could think of was Ernestine.

*****

"Bless me Father for I have sinned."

"Yes, what is it Henriette?" replied Père Yves softly.

"Père, I continue to have deep emotional feelings about Père Louis, feelings that are only appropriate between a married man and woman…"

Chapter 11

The Ambush

The room was thick with smoke and with only two small windows high up in the wall, there was almost nowhere for it to escape. Simone's eyes were constantly watering. There had been a catholic church in Brive since the 12th century and after many modifications and partial rebuilds, the current collegiate church of St Martin held pride of place in the old town. What had not changed was the crypt, made up of several rooms one of which was used regularly for various meetings. The parish priest, a member of Henri's cell, had no issues with it being used by the Maquis.

About thirty men and women were crowded together around an oblong table, on which there was a large sheet of white paper about three feet long and eighteen inches wide. Many were seated, the rest standing and peering inquisitively over their shoulders. While all eyes were on the hand drawn diagram on the paper, all ears were on the young blond woman standing up against the center of the table, explaining how the operation would be executed.

"It's important that we all work as one team," explained Simone, "and it's essential that each one of us knows exactly how to get to the site undetected. We need to conceal the vehicles, take up our positions early, execute the derailment, capture the German guards quickly, and successfully exit the site as fast as we can. I have one major change to our plans. We'll need more than twelve of us to complete this operation. We need to strike swiftly and as silently as possible and then vanish from the scene. However, I received an additional piece of information that this train will have approximately fifteen carriages, so we'll need twenty-four Maquis, twelve from FT and twelve from our own Peacock group. I suggest that you break into your two groups and decide who will take part in the operation and how."

The murmuring and shaking of several heads indicated that that there was some disagreement with that decision. The three leaders next to Simone, Hatchet, Serge, and the leader of FT named Sabot, looked at each other and discussed the change in plans, and after about fifteen minutes agreed on a new arrangement. It was Sabot who explained, "Tulle is crawling with Gestapo and German SS, since they publicly executed a group of twelve men two days ago. They're searching for Maquis everywhere. First, we have to avoid the town and its check points, which means getting to the site the day before and sleeping out in the woods. And we must plan in detail how we will exit, remember there will be hundreds of conscripts with the same intention. Secondly, we need to decide how we will take care of the German guards in the last carriage, I need to hear from you how exactly that will take place."

"And the Peacock group," needs to decide," said Serge, "how we plan to get on site, take care of the guards at the front of the train, and who will actually work on the Germans themselves. Let's group ourselves over here," he indicated a corner of the crypt, "and have Simone help us."

The train was set to depart from Brive on the following day at 10:30 A.M. It would arrive at the gorge at approximately 11:00 A.M., and by that time everything including the charges would need to be in place. It was agreed that everybody would be on site by tomorrow evening, except for Père Louis. He said nothing but listened intently to what was being presented, trying not to miss any detail. The discussions in each group seemed to him to drag on interminably, and he was conscious of the time and the upcoming curfew. But it was Serge who realized that time was running out and closed the meeting.

It was just after curfew, and almost dark, when Père Louis and Simone left the church and headed across the Pont Cardinal bridge, past the Denoix distillery and the market square, hurrying towards Raymond's house, close to the railway yards. They were to spend the night at his home, where he had a small extra bedroom. Turning left at the small park, they suddenly saw three SS Officers about thirty yards away, laughing and joking, walking directly towards them. In a flash, Père Louis grabbed Simone by the hand and pulled her into a shop doorway. Then he squeezed her into a tight embrace and held her in a long kiss, cupping her face in his hands while the officers walked by. They were still laughing as they watched the couple, and Père Louis heard them say in German, "lovers are the same everywhere."

Still holding her close, Père Louis waited until the sounds of their boots on the sidewalk died away. Then without saying a word he walked on quickly with Simone trailing behind, past the rail yards where several locomotives were belching smoke and steam, and the clanking and squealing sounds of carriages being shunted, filled the night air.

"You're welcome my friends," greeted Raymond, and turning to a grey haired, buxom, smiling woman, "this is my wife Claudine. She's prepared supper for us." As they dined, Raymond explained what the arrangements would be for the next day. "Simone," he began, "you'll be picked up by Serge at 9:00 A.M. and taken to his yard. He has all of the explosive materials and guns we received from London, and you'll be able to select whatever you need. You'll ride with him to the site."

"That's fine with me Raymond, but first let me thank you and your wife for your generous hospitality."

"You are both very welcome," he responded, "but Père, your schedule tomorrow is a full one. We'll leave here at 8:00 A.M. I have a special railway yard pass for you, we'll go directly to the locomotives. There are two in the sheds, and one of my Maquis will train you on the basics. One of these will be used to pull the train. In the afternoon you'll ride in the cab, while the carriages are shunted back and forth into position and the train assembled. There will be fourteen in total not fifteen as initially thought. It will be hot, smoky, and hard work, but it's not dangerous. There will be a German officer poking his nose into everything, and if he asks why he hasn't seen you before, you can say that you're a former driver that I've asked you to come and help out. He knows I'm short staffed. I've also seen the German arrangements. There will be three armed soldiers in the last compartment that's been reserved for them, two others plus an officer in the first, right behind the tender. My sources tell me that I was correct in my assumptions, they're all going back to Germany then probably onto the Eastern front. Do either of you have any questions?"

"Yes, I do," responded Père Louis, "what about clothing for me, and also Serge said that I must carry a side arm?"

"Oh, yes, I nearly forgot some other items. There are two sleeping places in the bedroom, a typical single bed, and a folding bed on the floor. You'll find a toilet and a wash bowl outside your room with soap and towels. I've also put two sets of old work clothes on a small table, Père, I'm sure one of them will fit you, in addition to a bandana, cap, and goggles. The boots you are wearing will be just fine. And regarding the side arm, let me show you." With that, he left the room, appearing quickly with a shoe box which he placed on the table. Sliding it over to Père Louis, he said, "please take a look, just so you know what you'll be using."

"Oh, it's a Walther P38, nine-millimeter," cried Simone, an excellent weapon."

Père Louis looked at her in astonishment, and surprise. "Is this what they taught you in training camp?" he asked. "Yes," she replied, "I've used one of these many times."

Then taking it out of the box, he held it in his hand as if not knowing what to do with it. So many conflicting thoughts were crowding his mind. This was the first time he'd ever been close to a gun, let alone holding one, a weapon that could kill a person, and he shuddered at the thought.

"Shall I show you how it works?" asked Simone. And without waiting for an answer, took the gun from his hand and in seconds broke it apart in five pieces, and just as fast had it reassembled.

"Wow, that was amazing," said Raymond, "do you think that we should put a loaded magazine in it? There is one in the box."

"Well," it was Simone taking charge again, "Père Louis will have to have this in his hand and will point it at the officer. If the officer is well trained, and you can be sure that he will be, he'll see at a glance if the gun has a magazine or not. Since the gun is not intended to be fired, I would suggest that we put an empty magazine in the gun, and nobody will know the difference."

"That's a great idea," said Raymond.

"Yes, I agree," said Père Louis, "so go ahead, Simone put one in now?" And almost before he could finish, she reached over, released the magazine, emptied it into the box and replaced it in the gun. "But how will I take the gun onto the locomotive?" he asked.

"That is already arranged, Père, it will be in your lunch box which my wife will prepare. Now I suggest that we retire for the night, as the morning will come around all too quickly." he joked. "It must have been a particularly long day for you Père, "at what time do you usually arise?"

"Yes, I agree, Raymond, I am feeling more than a little tired this evening. My day started at 2:30 A.M. and I like to enjoy a full six hours of sleep."

The bedroom was larger than he had imagined and in addition to the two beds, a straight-backed wooden chair stood next to each one. A small table near the door held the clothes, cap, goggles, and bandana for Père Louis. Taking them from the table, he placed them on a chair, then turning to Simone asked, "would you like the regular bed, the lower one will be just fine for me?"

"Certainly, if that works for you," she replied.

"And would you like to use the toilet first?" he asked.

"Yes, thank you," she answered.

"Good, then while you're in there, I'll try on these work clothes."

When she returned, Père Louis had already made his choice, put the work clothes over the chair holding his other items, and had removed his boots. Simone sat on the edge of her bed trying hard not to look as he removed his shirt, revealing a hairy chest and torso, toned from daily hard physical work.

He saw that she was under her blanket when he came back into the room, and it seemed like she was sleeping. After switching off the light near the door, he sat on a pillow with his back to the wall and tried to meditate. He missed the quietness and solitude of the monastery, and time for silent prayer. He didn't know how long he sat there, but sensed he was falling asleep and so slid under his blanket.

'Louis, Louis," she whispered.

"Ernestine," he murmured and felt her breast and nipples on his chest as he pulled her close to him. His hand reached down, and he heard her gasp and shiver a little as he felt between her legs and fingered the wetness in her pubic hair. He tried to visualize where they were, and he remembered it was the cottage in Saverne, and they were making passionate love. The scent and softness of her skin easily aroused him, and as she slid her hand into his pants and fondled his genitals, he sighed and moaned with each touch. He desperately wanted her. "Ernestine, I love you so very much," he whispered, his hips thrusting in urgency and desire. But as she started to undo his belt, he suddenly woke up. "What is happening?" he stammered. And trying to pull himself upright, realized that Simone was on top of him, and he could feel that she was naked. "What are you doing?" he demanded, "what are you trying to do?"

"I love you Louis, I love you," she whispered, "and we should make love. I know that you want it too."

"Go back to your bed, Simone," he hissed while pushing her away, afraid that they would wake up Raymond and his wife in the adjacent room. "It's something that will never happen no matter how much you might feel attracted to me. It's not even a topic we will ever discuss, so block this moment from your mind. My response was purely animal, physiological. I have no interest in you sexually. Go back to sleep, please and forget about this."

He spent most of the rest of the night in prayer, examining his conscience and slept very little. The incident with Simone troubled him greatly not because of what actually took place, but because of the thoughts and desires he still had for Ernestine. Those feelings were still so strong and powerful, that even tonight he was struggling to clear them from his memory. He thought he had dealt with them many years ago and eliminated them forever, but now realized that he had buried them alive.

In the morning, dressed in his blue fatigues and cap with goggles on top, he looked the part as a driver. The day was spent as Raymond had indicated, working on the locomotive with the two experienced engineers who would be driving the train the following day, learning the intricacies of operating a huge steam engine. By evening time, it was ready and finally chugged its way to the number five platform in the main station, to await the arrival of the conscripts the following morning. The German officer did show up accompanied by Raymond, but together they were simply inspecting each carriage for the long journey to Berlin, not paying any attention to the locomotive itself or the engineers.

The following day, a knock on his door and Raymond's voice

saying that coffee was on the table, awoke his aching body from a deep sleep. It was 5:00 A.M. and he needed to get to the station and help fire up the locomotive. Unusual for a man with a normally balanced and calm temperament, Père Louis was anxious as he walked to the railway yard with Raymond. Perhaps it was the fact that he was now carrying a concealed weapon and had to pass through both military and police check points. But at this early hour there were only a few workers in line and noticing that he was accompanied by, and chatting with the Railway Chief, there was barely a glance as he offered his pass for scrutiny.

Out in the forest it had been a cold night, and Serge and Simone in spite of being prepared with extra layers of clothing, spent most of the time shivering in their van. As the sun came up, the Maquis groups started to come alive, a few people emerged from their vehicles, rubbing their eyes, stretching, and yawning after what must have been an equally uncomfortable night. Others had simply camped rough on the ground, covered only with a blanket or heavy coat, and had probably slept very little.

Anticipating that they would not be able to light a fire, Serge had come prepared. Proceeding to light two spirit stoves in the back of his van, he began brewing some ersatz coffee for his group. With only a half dozen cups the men had to take turns sharing. But he had also brought enough croissants, two per person, which were devoured with gusto, even though they were not fresh. By 8:00 A.M. it was already beginning to feel warm, and the atmosphere in the group changed noticeably once they were fed. Serge gave the order to start moving into positions. They looked very much a motley group, and although they were under strict instructions not to use them, every man was armed with a British Sten-gun, courtesy of recent Lysander flights.

Simone had already selected her explosive materials the night before, and had everything she needed in a large black canvas satchel which she slung easily onto her back. "Let's go," she ordered, "and let's get these charges set up." At that moment, a man on a bicycle was seen and heard approaching, and a small group closest to him quickly pointed their weapons and started walking towards him. Getting off his bicycle he began pushing it while shouting "don't shoot, don't shoot, It's Remy, it's Remy."

"Put your arms down," commanded Serge, and walked over to greet him. "What brings you here, shouldn't you be at your post?"

"Yes," he replied, "but I have some latest news from Brive. There'll be an unscheduled freight train leaving Brive at 8:10 and passing through here at approximately 8:40. Raymond also asked me to tell you, that there are now three soldiers guarding the rear of the train, not two."

"Thank you, Remy, and good luck with your work!"

As anticipated, the freight train was almost on time, and once it was out of sight, Simone walked towards the boulder marking the spot she had chosen for the explosives. It took her about half an hour, making sure it was all secured and wired correctly, and the line to the detonator carefully covered over all the way back into the trees. It was now a waiting game.

Back at the station, Père Louis, high up on the engine footplate, was leaning over the side watching the lines of young men as they were brought from the sports stadium, and carefully assigned by number into the carriages. There were German military and French police seemingly everywhere. It was a long but meticulous and very orderly process, with troops holding and checking names off clipboards before a person entered the carriage, and another soldier making sure each person took their assigned seat in the compartment. The final count for the train was eight hundred and seventy passengers, and there was only one scheduled stop in Clermont Ferrand, where the train would take on water and coal and the passengers would be fed. It had been announced and emphasized all over the region that these young men were *volunteers* and were valued workers for the German homeland - that the Reich would reward them well for their labor. In fact, they were all conscripts, part of the STO (Service Obligatoire de Travail), a compulsory work program for men aged eighteen to thirty.

With the doors closed, Père Louis saw Raymond walking the length of the platform with a smiling German officer looking up at the carriage windows, and as he reached the locomotive he stayed bent down and out of sight.

"Pierre and Georges," Raymond shouted above the hissing steam, to the two men whose heads could just be seen above the top of the metal gate, "are you ready to go?" An older stocky and muscular man in well-greased coveralls and a bandana around his already sweaty face, leaned out of the cab and shouted back, "of course sir, and I'll bring you back some German sausage." He blew the whistle. They all laughed including the officer. Seconds later the German officer entered the first carriage and compartment, and at precisely 10:30 A.M. after the Railway Chief had waved a green flag, engine number 7997, a Model P106 and weighing one hundred and six tons, with a tender and fourteen carriages, slowly pulled out of Brive La Gaillarde Central Station, heading for the German border. In the engine cab were two engineers and a monk trainee, all three were members of the Maquis.

At the exact same time, Serge walked around all of his men, checking their positions, and then strolled over to where Hatchet and Sabot were arranging their own people. Everything appeared to be in place. Satisfied that he had not forgotten anything, he strolled back and took up his station next to Simone.

The train could be heard long before it appeared, and the unmistakable sound of its laboring up the steep grade filled everybody with anticipation. Spewing black smoke and steam, the locomotive very slowly came into view round the first curve onto the plateau and slowed down even more as it approached the second curve. It never reached it. Suddenly an explosion erupted sending dirt and rocks high into the air, that tore the tracks apart leaving them as a mangled heap of steel. The locomotive momentarily thrown into the air, remained upright but continued forward, ploughing into the soft shoulder alongside the rails, and finally stopped amid the squealing of brakes and hissing of steam.

It all seemed to happen so quickly and yet so efficiently. Nothing else moved. Waiting just a few minutes, the two regular drivers got down from the cab and while wiping their oily hands, walked slowly to the front of the engine to examine the damage. Seconds later a major and two soldiers climbed out of the first carriage and hurried to meet the two drivers. In broken French the officer asked what had happened, and the men played a game of not understanding. The two soldiers were standing back twenty feet away, gazing towards the forest with a look of sheer terror on their faces, waving their rifles back and forth as if they expected an attack of some kind.

"Put your hands up." Père Louis had come quietly around the other side of the locomotive and was standing right behind the officer. He repeated in German, "put your hands up," and continuing said "don't reach for your weapon, if you move, I'll shoot you." Then speaking to the train driver said, "Horse (Pierre) remove the officer's weapon," and then to the major, "tell your soldiers to put down their arms and sit on the ground, you are completely surrounded by an army of Maquis." Allowing himself first to be disarmed, in a loud and tremulous voice, the officer then shouted to his men explaining that this was an ambush; the man was clearly afraid for his life. The soldiers quickly complied, and the two drivers walked over, picked up their rifles and stood guard over the frightened men.

"Walk in front of me to the rear of the train, to the last carriage," Père Louis commanded the major. Without hesitating the officer did as he was ordered followed by Père Louis holding his gun. Many heads were leaning out of the windows, but everybody was watching in silence. Fifty feet from the last door, he said, "Now call on your soldiers to come out and throw their weapons on the ground and understand that I speak fluent German." One soldier had already opened the door and was standing on the step with his rifle slung over his shoulder, looking towards the front of the train. There was no hesitation, after the instructions were given, the soldier threw down his weapon and started to descend. Two more rifles were flung out of the door followed by two terrified soldiers.

Serge who had been carefully watching every movement, once he saw the rifles hit the ground, fired a single shot in the air as the agreed upon signal, and all the Maquis rushed from their concealed positions towards the train. Six men ran directly to the soldiers in the rear and took them, their officer, and their rifles back towards the damaged tracks. Serge and four men joined the drivers who were holding the other two soldiers under guard. The rest were opening the carriage doors shouting, "run for it, we are the Maquis and you are free to go home." Bodies began jumping out of the doors and hundreds started running into the forest.

Meanwhile Serge and Hatchet were supervising the next step, and after blindfolding them, were having the Germans strip down to their underwear. All of the uniforms, weapons and boots were collected and taken to the van and hidden behind the secret partition. The soldiers were gagged, their hands and feet securely tied, and were left sitting at the side of the destroyed tracks. Père Louis was nowhere to be seen; he was already inside the van changing into regular work clothes, his railway 'uniform' hidden with those of the Germans. Minutes later Serge arrived and checked that he was not harmed and was preparing to leave. "One minute Serge, he called out, "please return this to Raymond, I won't be needing it anymore," and reaching onto the passenger seat, picked up and handed over the Walther pistol.

Seconds later Simone came rushing through the trees crying "wait, wait Père. I need to hide my equipment." It took just a few moments for her to climb into the back of the van, secure her satchel, then jump into the passenger seat saying in an animated voice, "you did a great job Père, were you afraid at all?" She was clearly energized by the whole experience. He didn't respond but focused on driving the van out of the forest and taking only the smallest roads to avoid check points, headed back to the Chateau and the monastery. The whole action had lasted a mere fourteen minutes and as Madame had requested, 'no blood was spilled.'

Chapter 12
The Picnic

Reprisals came quickly. The SS chief in Brive, Otto Kreips was said to be apoplectic when he heard about the ambush. He worked in conjunction with the Gestapo from Tulle and Ussel, and the newly formed Milice, to help round up possible suspects.

Ussel had recently been the center of much Maquis activity with anti-German graffiti appearing on buildings, and the ubiquitous V for Victory sign painted all over the area. There had been several ambushes of small German convoys carrying food for the troops, and telephone lines were constantly being cut. And in all three towns the underground newspaper *Libre* mysteriously appeared each month in the train stations and in marketplaces, which angered the Gestapo and made the Germans determined to capture the perpetrators. The assumption was made, wrongly in fact, that the Maquis from Brive and Tulle were not directly responsible for the ambush, but that Ussel was the center of operations.

It came as a relief to Serge and Henriette when Jules informed them, that the Maquis in Brive were not being especially targeted. But now knowing how the authorities, and especially the Gestapo were operating, they were still very much concerned that railway workers would be targeted. Henriette in particular was afraid for Père Louis, and shared her concerns with her confessor, Père Yves.

"I feel so guilty, Père," she explained, "I should never have agreed to let him do it. My mind is not at rest, and I'm so afraid that somehow his role will be uncovered. I could never live with myself if anything happened to him."

"Those are noble sentiments, Henriette," he responded gently, "you and I have known each other for many years, so I would suggest that you look a little deeper into yourself, and see if they're not coming from several different places. Sometimes our concerns for another can go beyond the obvious and if so, we should ask ourselves "why?" Not that it is necessarily a bad thing, but just so that you can be honest with yourself and get to know better who you really are. Père Louis is a mature and intelligent man who is more than capable of making his own decisions, and I do know that he respects, admires, and cares about you greatly. I will pray that no harm will come to either of you."

"Père, your words are always full of wisdom and kindness. I'll reflect seriously on this."

Hundreds of troops were needlessly deployed from Ussel in sweeping the countryside for escapees even though the derailment was forty miles away. The planning of the ambush was so effective, that by the time troops did arrive at the site and found the trussed-up Germans, it was almost two hours later by which time the conscripts were scattered across the area, and the Maquis long gone. Remy's work in cutting off telephone communications had exceeded expectations.

That very afternoon, Raymond was arrested and brought into SS headquarters in downtown Brive. After several hours of questioning by two SS and Gestapo officers, he refused to divulge any information. They were mainly concerned about the engineers: who were they, were they members of the Maquis and where did they live? As a precaution and anticipating reprisals, Raymond had selected two single men who lived in rented lodgings, to work that train. They had no families that could later be targeted. The third, Père Louis, had been given a false address in Bordeaux, and all his fake hiring papers matched his identity.

The question as to whether his workers were in the Maquis was an easy answer. With more than a thousand employees, "how could I know who was working against the Reich or not?" Later that night, with a badly beaten face, a broken nose and a dislocated shoulder, Raymond was released. The authorities realized that he was such a key component in keeping all of the trains on schedule, they needed him to report for work the following day. Needless to say, he would remain under suspicion from that time on, and an SS soldier was usually within hearing distance of his conversations whilst he was working.

From in and around Brive, Tulle and Ussel, nineteen men and women suspects from Maquis cells that had already been under observation, were brought in for questioning. All were beaten, some to within an inch of their lives, and multiple, techniques of torture were used. Only three confessed to knowing anything about the ambush, and the information they had was all second hand. None were directly involved.

The Vichy Administration led by Prime Minister Laval, upon hearing about the ambush and the subsequent round up of Resistants, urged that moderation and leniency be used since no soldier had been killed. They argued that yes there was a serious interruption in the schedule for sending volunteer workers to Germany, and that some embarrassment had been caused to the Reich, but that overreacting would possibly result in further action by Maquis groups all over the region. The Vichy Administration was also afraid they would lose their much-needed support of the local people. The voice of reason was partially heard. The Gestapo continued to brutally torture and interrogate each suspect, but also understood that male workers were urgently needed and that they could actually serve the Fatherland. The men were eventually sent to work camps in Germany and the women to a female concentration camp at Ravensbruch.

Without the physical resources to scour the countryside or visit every small town, only sixty-eight conscripts were eventually found or turned in by collaborators and brought into the German authorities for questioning. However, since none of them were involved in planning the ambush, and could not identify any of the Maquis, they were later released as there was no place to hold them. All were advised that they would be given further opportunities to serve the Reich.

The effects of the ambush had a rippling effect on the regions of Limousin and Auvergne. To avoid conscription and being sent to Germany, hundreds of young men left their homes, went into the countryside, and were employed as much needed farm laborers, often working by day, and hiding at night. Others began searching for Maquis groups with the intention of joining them. While this influx of recruits significantly increased the numbers of Resistants, for their part, the leaders of the Maquis struggled to fully screen each new applicant. It exposed the groups to possible infiltration by collaborators. The consequences in 1943 proved to be dramatic and in some cases catastrophic.

Administratively it took another three months before a train for conscript workers could be assembled which severely set back the production of armaments in Germany. Locally it caused the authorities to revise how special trains should be guarded. From now on, each one would have three armed soldiers in the rear with a machine gun, and two attached to each compartment. Three more with a machine gun would occupy the front of the train and a low-ranking officer was assigned to ride on the footplate with the drivers. But more importantly, the ambush caused hundreds of soldiers to be pulled from more important duties, as they were placed at every rail junction and station leading to the border 450 miles away.

Most people were unaware of what had taken place and were busy just trying to keep some degree of normalcy in their lives. In spite of food and clothing shortages, lack of gas and restricted travel, people were still going to work and attempting to earn a living.

Lucien made his regular visits with the farm produce and each time he saw Marta she kept her head down, afraid that people might see her blushing or the excitement in her eyes. Thursday evening came around and as arranged, after her work she arrived at the entrance to Jean Luc's dental surgery. Waiting just inside the door, as soon as she knocked, Lucien quickly opened it and taking her gently by the arm, pulled her close to him giving her a tender kiss on the lips. "I've waited all week to do that," he said, "and watching you at work and not being able to touch you or say anything, has been so difficult for me. I can't stop thinking about you."

"And I too about you," she replied, "ever since the last time we were here, you have constantly been on my mind. It's been difficult to concentrate at work."   As they entered the waiting room, she removed her forage cap which she had been wearing all day and placed it on the table. Lucien loved to watch her as she shook her hair and ran her fingers through it. He couldn't stop looking at her. Taking off her jacket she folded it carefully and draped it over the back of the armchair, loosened her tie and undid the top three buttons of her shirt. "Now I can relax a little," she said, sitting demurely next to him on the love seat but looking straight ahead, "it's been a long day and I have something for you. Reaching into her purse, she took out a small document. "This is the new travel pass," she explained. "When you came into the administration the other day, you probably didn't notice that I kept you waiting, I was copying your old pass. Now you have the newest one and should have no problem moving around. Everybody in the coming months will need one, but since there are only five of us to handle all requests, it could take months, even a year, for people to get one. It will of course put less traffic on the roads which is what I believe the Administration wants."

"That is so sweet of you," said Lucien taking it from her and pouring her a glass of white wine. "Why did you take such a risk for me?"

"Well, you're taking a risk for me every time you come in and bring me food," she replied with a smile.

After he had draped his arm across her shoulders, he could feel the warmth and softness of her skin through her shirt. "I really like being with you," he said, "and even more than that, I think I'm falling in love with you. But I have a confession to make. I've never had a lady friend in my life, and I'm twenty-five years old. I live out in the countryside where there are few suitable women of my age, and since the war started and travel so difficult, there is even less chance I might meet somebody. I know my parents would like me to settle down and start a family. They don't say anything directly, but they also understand how difficult it is just now. You're the first lady I've ever invited out. I hope my saying that won't make you leave. But how about you, have you ever dated anyone?"

Marta took a sip of wine, then putting down her glass gently pushed him into a corner of the love seat, curled up her legs and leaned back with her head on his chest. He responded by pulling her closer to him and holding her in his arms. The feel of his strength and the lavender scent of his shirt created strange and new emotions within her. "I too have never been in a serious relationship," she began, "there was just what you might call a brief infatuation while I was in high school in Switzerland, but it didn't go anywhere. Then I came home, got caught up in the whole Nazi Youth movement, as I have already explained to you, then later enrolled in the military, and here I am. My only knowledge about dating and relationships, comes mainly from my sisters and other women, describing their real or imagined amorous adventures and experiences. I can tell that many of the troops here would like to invite me out, but it's forbidden; we're not allowed to fraternize at all. And "no," she said assuringly, "I won't walk out on you."

Relieved to hear her words, he leaned down, gently kissing the top of her head allowing his fingers to feel the soft texture of her hair. She suddenly looked up at him and pulled his head down with both hands holding him in a long passionate kiss. Her warm, soft mouth pressed against his shaking lips sent wild tremors along his nerves, evoking from him sensations he had never known before, or imagined he was capable of feeling. As his head spun around and around, he knew that he was kissing her back, creating undreamed of emotions.

"Lucien, I love you," she murmured, and with one hand began to unbutton her shirt, then taking his hand gently slid it inside and helped him cup her breast. She trembled slightly as he felt and touched her hardened nipple through her brassiere. Lucien was lost in a sea of new responses but was momentarily embarrassed as he knew she must be feeling his penis becoming hard underneath her, and he was powerless to stop it.

"I love you too Marta," he whispered, "I really love you."

Moving her hand from his, she reached down and pulled up one side of her brassiere, and taking his hand again, pressed it hard against her beast. She moaned and shivered again as he gently kneaded her nipple, allowing his fingers to explore the silkiness of her skin and the texture of her nipple.

Briefly breaking from their kissing, Marta lay back with closed eyes took Lucien's hand again, and began to push it slowly down her body, letting his fingers feel the softness of her skin and explore the contours of her navel. He could scarcely contain himself and was afraid he would ejaculate.

Then just as quickly as it had started, Marta opened her eyes and withdrew his hand. He was spared. "Oh, my darling," she said, kissing him all over his face. "I know that you want to make love and me too, but now is not the time or the place. Please don't be angry with me."

Lucien held her tightly. "No," he said reassuringly, "I'm not angry. I really love you and am happy with whatever you chose to do. I just need a minute to calm down; you've set me on fire."

Marta stood up and began rearranging her clothes, "I think it's time for me to head home," she said, reaching for her jacket.

"Well, before you leave, asked Lucien, "shall we talk about Saturday? Do you still want to come with me? Are you still able to have the day off work?"

"Yes, of course," she replied, "and I'm so looking forward to it."

"Then where should we meet?" he asked, "my father has said I can use the Chateau pickup."

"I must be very careful and discrete," she explained, "I just can't be seen to be going anywhere in the town with you. I need to make sure that none of the other girls know what I am doing. Can you meet me behind the Catholic church?"

"Of course, I can. How about at 9:30?"

*****

Dressed in a light summer frock with a small floral pattern, and buttons all the way down to the hem, white sandals, holding a white floppy hat in her hand and a black leather purse over her shoulder, the only one she had and it was military issue, Lucien almost did not recognize her. He could not stop himself from smiling. He was dumbstruck by her beauty; her almost translucent skin and her blond hair being ruffled by the slight breeze. As he jumped down and moved quickly to open the door for her, she gave him a chaste kiss on both cheeks.

"How did you explain to your landlords what you're doing?" he asked as they worked their way out of the town.

"I've travelled before on my day off by both train and bus to neighboring towns, so they rarely ask questions, and besides, they're old and don't remember things. I told them I was going to Uzerche. Today is market day and I've been there before.

Getting through the checkpoint was a different experience

for Lucien. After handing over both his and Marta's passes, the soldier almost fell over, quickly returned the documents and with a sharp "Heil Hitler" salute shouted to the other soldiers at the barrier to let them through immediately. "What was all that about, what happened?" he asked as they drove off.

"Well my pass is special," she explained, "there are only five of us women working for the Reich and the local troops know about us. We take care of many of their needs through the commissary. They really like working with us. And oh, I have something to give to you, so please stop when you can."

Intrigued by her request, a mile or so down the road, he pulled over to the side of the road and turned off the engine. Marta immediately slid over on the bench seat and holding his face in her hands, gave Lucien a long warm kiss. "I've been waiting all morning to give you that," she said a little breathlessly. "Now we can go on and enjoy the rest of the day."

Seven miles outside of Brive they branched off the main road and followed a narrow lane for about half an hour. The countryside began to change. There were only a few scattered farmhouses and the fields were uncultivated, with just the occasional cattle grazing here and there. He slowed the truck down as he looked for a landmark, and finally seeing it, turned on to a narrow cart path that judging from the height of the grass and weeds had not been used for some time. It climbed up hill and as he engaged a low gear, the truck rumbled through the vegetation and over rutted and uneven tracks, making conversation impossible.

Suddenly they found themselves on a narrow grassy plateau between two areas of tall and dense pine forest. Pulling the truck over into the shade, he switched off the engine. "We're almost there," he said, "are you ready for a short walk?"

"Of course, I am," she replied cheerfully, "it'll be good to stretch our legs."

Reaching into the back of the pickup Lucien hoisted onto his shoulder a large wicker basket the size almost of a travelling trunk. Taking her by the hand he led her downhill through the forest until they suddenly emerged into bright sunlight. Immediately in front of them was the beautiful and unspoiled, shimmering blue Lake de Causse. As far as the eye could see there was not a single house or person in sight. Placing the picnic basket on the ground, Lucien made a proposition. "Why don't we take a walk along the water's edge, then we can come back and have our picnic?"

"Oh, I would love that," she answered happily, and took off laughing and running down towards the edge of the lake. A narrow strip of beach ran the whole length of one side, and as Lucien caught up with her, she had removed her sandals and was drawing patterns in the sand with her toes. After removing his boots, he tied the laces together and threw one over his shoulder. Then he reached out for Marta, put his arm around her waist holding her close as they walked together leaving their footprints on the pristine sand. He could feel the warmth of her body as she slid her arm around him, resting her hand inside his back pocket.

"I often used to come here as a child with my friend on our bicycles," he told her, "and we would swim and fish. In the hot weather we sometimes would camp overnight. I've such clear and lovely memories, and I've never ever shared them with anybody before." They stopped briefly to kiss.

"It's so peaceful here as there are no sounds except for the birds. It's truly beautiful," she said, "thank you for bringing me and sharing it with me."

An hour later, relaxed, and ready to eat, they arrived back at the picnic spot. "Please take these and lay them out on the pine needles under the tree," said Lucien handing Marta two thick blankets. "And lay this on the ground next to them." He gave her a square plastic flowered tablecloth. "This is what it means to be loved," he laughed, as he passed her the items from the basket: freshly baked bread, three kinds of cheeses, butter, ham, pickles, rillettes, and a potato galette. "My parents are real country people who say little and rarely show any emotion, but there are other ways they let you know that you are loved. My mother got up early this morning to prepare this food. She knew that I was taking a lady friend for a picnic, that was all."

Finally, taking out two bottles of wine Lucien opened the white and poured two glasses, handing one to Marta. "Let's make a silent wish as we drink together," he suggested, and they touched glasses and quietly sipped the best of his father's wine.

Even under the shade of the trees, it was hot as the sun reflected off the glimmering lake, and without thinking Lucien removed his shirt revealing his tanned, and well-toned body. Marta loosened the top buttons of her dress and began to fan herself with her hat. "But where on earth did you get all of this food? I've never seen such a variety since I came to France."

"It's all a benefit of living out in the countryside," said Lucien, "and now you know where your little gifts come from. My mother is an excellent cook and almost everything we eat is home grown. You've eaten her madeleines before, and I cannot take them back home," he joked. "Maybe later you can squeeze some into your purse?"

Lucien was stretched out with his hands behind his head, relaxing, staring up into the cloudless sky, when Marta snuggled down beside him and rested her head on his chest. As he toyed with strands of her hair, feeling its soft golden texture, and delicately letting his fingers discover the shape and outline of her ear, her body trembled involuntarily. He kissed her ear lobe. Neither of them spoke, each of them lost in the sensation and thrill of the moment.

Using his powerful arms, he gently lifted her up, surprised at how light her body was, and laid her down next to him. Leaning on one elbow he bent over, and nibbling her ear and tasting the delicate scent of her skin, whispered, "I really love you,

Marta and I don't want either of us to ever forget this time together." She momentarily kept her eyes closed, afraid that if she opened them, she would break this magical spell. Then slowly opening them, she reached up to him, drawing his head towards her and started to kiss him softly and sweetly, tugging at his lip with hers. Then she grabbed his hair and pulled him even closer.

Unsure at first, Lucien responded as she placed her tongue inside his mouth, setting off an outburst of unimagined responses. She felt short of breath and as he lowered his head and slowly kissed her neck, her body shuddered against him.

She began undoing the buttons on her dress as far as she could reach, and as it fell open, the sight of her breasts sent tremors through his whole body. Taking his hand, she held it as he cupped her left breast, pressing it firmly against her. As his thumb began to trace the outline of her nipple through her brassiere, she shivered and softly moaned. Her eyes closed again and as their bodies touched, they covered each other with passionate kisses

Briefly sitting up, she slipped the dress off her shoulders and let it fall to her waist. Then she reached behind herself, and quickly unhooked and removed her brassiere, revealing her beautifully shaped and rounded breasts. Lucien was mesmerized as she then lay back with her eyes closed, looking so beautiful and trusting. This was the first time he had seen a woman's breasts, and they stimulated him as he reached over and hesitantly fondled each one, aroused by their beautiful softness and the paleness of her skin.

Opening her eyes and looking up at him, "I love you so much," she whispered in a sultry voice, "please Lucien, please, I want you," and put his hand on the buttons of her dress. One by one he opened them until she lay there, completely vulnerable, wearing nothing but her ivory-colored panties. Then leaning over he kissed her breasts again as her fingers held on to his hair, slowly running his tongue around her nipples moving from one to the other. He marveled as her body quivered when he touched her. As he took a nipple between his lips she sighed with pleasure and her body arched and twisted under him. He let his hands explore the shape and contours of her hips and the softness of her buttocks as he straddled her legs.

As he gently leaned over her, she rubbed her hand against his groin then started to undo his belt buckle.

His own body took on a life of its own and he could not control what was happening as his penis hardened and he felt the throb of passion. Moving down her body he allowed his tongue to explore the contours of her navel, sending him sensational shock waves never before experienced. Marta cried and began pushing her body against his.

"Please, Lucien" she pleaded, "please, don't stop," and pushed his hand under the top of her panties until he could feel the softness of her pubic hair. As he gently removed her panties, his hand brushed against her pubic mound and she shivered, moaned, and began thrusting her hips. He had never seen a naked woman before, let alone make love to one, and was not sure how to proceed. But letting his instincts and his passions take over, he quickly removed his pants and underwear then gently spread her legs apart. As he looked at her, he became so excited he felt that he would not be able to control himself. He was afraid he would ejaculate prematurely. Kneeling between her thighs she felt him begin to push against her.

Marta gasped and pleaded, "Please, Lucien, please, I want to feel you inside me." As he began to enter her, she cried out and he wondered if was too painful for her, so quickly withdrew. "No, no," she whimpered," please don't stop." Seconds later her pain was a distant memory and nothing, absolutely nothing in this world felt as good as the sensation of him sliding into her. He quickly climaxed as they held on to each other, their voices forming one wild unbearable cry, "I love you."

He held her, like a fragile child, exhausted but content. "I am just so happy, "she whispered, so utterly happy, I could never have imagined that love could make me feel like this. I feel totally lost and yet secure at the same time. I don't ever want to leave you, Lucien. I want to be with you forever."

"Yes, my love, and me too.," he replied, kissing her ear. You are so beautiful, and I am so very lucky."

Lying together locked in each other's arms, they enjoyed the powerful emotions of first love, and the thrill, intimacy, and sensations of experiencing the physical closeness of their bodies. Time seemed to stand still. The war and the German Occupation a million miles away. There was no need for words.

She was the first to move after Lucien finally suggested that it was time to head back to Brive and standing up she reached for her panties. "Don't move, just stay there for a moment," he said, looking up at her. From his low angle he could now see her body in a different light: her beautifully sculptured pointed beasts and blond pubic hair contrasting with her delicate pale skin now looking almost translucent in full sunlight. "I want to carry this image of you with me wherever I go," he said. "Today is the most wonderful in my life," and standing up, he held her again in a tight embrace and smothered her with his kisses.

Chapter 13
The Uniform

Waiting on the platform for the 8:30 A.M. express train from Brive to Paris, wearing a beautiful navy blue ankle length coat by Schiaparelli, with white fox fur collar and cuffs and a fedora styled hat complete with matching feather, Henriette stood out, with both men and women staring at her. It was a rare occurrence, a very rare occurrence to see such an elegantly dressed lady in public, and especially so in these times of material hardship and rationing. Holding a small leather tooled suitcase with her initials emblazoned in gold on the front, Henriette was almost oblivious to the attention she was drawing. She focused on locating the first-class coach at the front of the train, trying to ignore the hundreds of German soldiers with their personal equipment waiting to board.

As it slowly came to a stop, the few people exiting were almost prevented from doing so by the crush of people wanting to board. Waiting until the crowd had thinned, she climbed the steps, helped by a courteous German soldier who handled her suitcase, and with ticket in hand searched for her compartment and reserved seat. The carriage was filled with junior officers all jostling for a place, with many still standing in the corridor, blocking her way forward. Finally reaching the correct section, she saw that it was filled with military personnel and that her seat was occupied. As she looked around feigning complete helplessness, an officer, an older man, stood up and asked her in perfect French if he could help. Noticing the number of his seat, she replied, "You are occupying my seat, sir, and I'd be very much obliged if I you would vacate it."

"My sincere apologies, Madame," he answered, and turning to the other soldiers, ordered them to get their baggage and leave the compartment, and not knowing that she spoke fluent German, added, "I want to be alone with this lady." Then addressing Henriette, "Our men are excited about returning home, and seem to have forgotten their manners, Madame, please excuse them. But allow me to assist you," and as she offered it, almost without looking at him, he took her suitcase and placed it on the rack over her seat.

"Thank you, sir," she murmured, "you are very helpful." Henriette's seat was against the window, and until the train began to move, she ignored the officer, turning her attention to watching the hustle and bustle on the platform, all the while sensing that he was scrutinizing her. As the train pulled out of Brive, she removed her gloves, and opening her purse took out a small book to read. At that very moment, the train suddenly jerked forward, and the book fell to the floor. Sitting opposite in the middle seat, the officer quickly stood up, reached down for it, and with a glance at the title handed it back to her.

"Thank you, officer," she said, "I am grateful."

"Madame, may I present myself, I'm Lieutenant Colonel Karl Bomelburg," he announced with a bow and click of his heels, before retaking his seat. His name began to resonate at the back of her mind, but she could not clearly recall what the association was. Unfamiliar with German uniforms and insignia, Henriette had no idea which branch of the military he represented, but did notice the numerous decorations including an Iron Cross on his grey green uniform, and the SS flashes on his collar. "I see that you're reading "Nuptials" by Albert Camus," he said, "I assume it's an interesting book? I read his other volume of essays last year, "Betwixt and Between" (L'envers et L'endroit) and found them most entertaining."

Something in his demeanor and his earlier comment to the soldiers, made her cautious, and not knowing whether she wanted to engage with this man in conversation or not, she did not immediately reply to his question. And yet there was something intriguing about him. He was in his middle sixties, or so, with snow white hair, immaculately groomed and spoke impeccable French. They were both about to face each other for the next six hours.

"Yes," she finally responded, "I find Camus fascinating. It's a collection of four essays dealing with absurdity and suicide. He examines religious hope and rejects religions and life after death. Instead, he advocates for living now. In these troubled times, where we're surrounded by so much death and destruction, it's a fitting read."

"Indeed Madame, and may I say, it's a rare pleasure to meet such an educated and sophisticated lady." Henriette chose to ignore the flattery, and instead wondered if there could be any advantage to her or her group in knowing more about this man.

"And you sir," can I ask why you as a German read modern French literature, that also must be a rarity?"

Leaning forward, his body language was clear, he wanted to engage with her. "Well I studied French as a student and spent five wonderful years in France, including three at the Sorbonne. I like everything French; music, poetry, art and especially your wonderful food," he added with a slight chuckle. "But of course, I also love my own culture and in fact in Paris I'll be attending the opera tomorrow night to see the 'Magic Flute', music from one of the great German composers for the Fatherland."

Without showing any inviting facial expression, but looking him directly in the eye, "Oh," she replied with a touch of sarcasm. "I am familiar with the fact that Mozart wrote his opera in German but did not know that it was considered to be Nazi music. Wasn't he born in Austria, in Salzburg perhaps? And then quickly continued, "Is that the only reason you will be in Paris?"

"No," he explained, his stony face not showing any reaction to her correcting him. "I've been in the Paris Administration since the Armistice was signed, and now have been transferred to Vichy. I'm taking care of some final items of business. And how about yourself?"

"I'm visiting my family. My father is quite sick and may not have long to live."

Unsure whether she wanted the conversation to go any further, she opened her book and searched for her bookmark.

"I am sorry to hear that," the colonel replied with fake concern. "But I wonder if you're free on Saturday evening. I'd be honored if you could be my guest at a small private soirée with the singer soprano Elizabeth Rethberg at the Hotel Lutetia. It's a very special event and I'm sure you would enjoy it. If not, then perhaps if you're ever in Vichy, you'll allow me to take you for lunch."

"You are too kind," Henriette responded, and now wanted to know a little more of who this colonel was, since it was clear from the way he spoke, he was not directly engaged in military operations. "However, unfortunately I do have a previous engagement this Saturday," she demurred, "but should I come to Vichy, lunch sounds like a nice idea, I'd be happy to call on you."

"Excellent," he replied with an animated voice, clearly enjoying Henriette's company, "then let me give you my calling card. And if you're ever in need of anything at all, you have simply to call me. I'll remember our meeting and our pleasurable conversation." And with that he reached into an inside pocket of his uniform, pulled out his wallet and handed her his card.

Barely able to keep her composure, as Henriette read the name and his title, she suddenly discovered that she was sharing the compartment with one of the most hated and frightening men in the whole of France.

"And may I know who I have the pleasure of speaking with?" he asked politely.

A little startled by his request, but also knowing that he had the resources to discover who she was if he really wanted to, she said, "I am Henriette Lastiere du Saillant, Countess du Chateau Comborn."

"Of course," he replied, "your refinement, elegance, and beauty shine through, and I'm privileged to have met you."

Karl Bomelburg had been, until the previous month, the head of the Gestapo for the entire country, based in Paris, but had reached retirement age as a Lieutenant Colonel. He had been assigned to Vichy to head up and reorganize the Gestapo there, and to control central and southern France. He was ultimately responsible for the deportation of seventy-five thousand French Jews and an estimated twenty-four thousand Maquis.

On September 7, 1944, following the Allied invasion of France, as security-chief, Bomelburg helped Marshal Pétain and members of the Vichy government cabinet travel safely and relocate to Sigmaringen in Germany, together with two thousand supporters. Then on April 29, 1945 he authorized Pétain's departure for Switzerland. He was later condemned to death in absentia for war crimes but escaped using the name and identity of a dead soldier. He died in 1946 by accidentally slipping on ice and breaking his neck.

Staying with her sister Therese was one of the main purposes of her visit as well as to see her ailing father. Henriette needed some rest away from the stress of coordinating six Maquis groups. The 16th District where she lived, was commonly thought to be one of the richest areas of Paris, and featured some of the most expensive real estate in France, including the famous Auteuil villas, heirs to 19th century high society country houses. They were exclusive gated communities with huge houses surrounded by gardens, which was extremely rare in Paris, and created an air of security, quiet and calm.

Over dinner which included two cheeses Henriette had brought, as well as a bottle of the best Chateau white wine, she shared much of what was happening with her cells and gave a detailed account of the train ambush. Her recounting of the experience in the train with the Gestapo Chief was troubling at first, as all Maquis in the Paris region were on edge, due to the large number of recent arrests and executions. Therese was concerned that somehow Henriette may have let slip where she was staying. She was quickly reassured, and Henriette showed them Bomelburg's calling card saying that "you just never know, it might be useful in the future." But it was Victor, Therese's husband who changed topics and surprised her by saying, "I hope you will not mind, but through our contacts, I heard that the leader of all the Maquis of Limousin, Georges Guingouin wants to talk with you. Knowing that you were coming to Paris, I said that I'd help the two of you meet. What do you think?"

"Well, interestingly enough I know a great deal about this man," Henriette replied, "but he operates out of Limoges, further north than us, we mainly operate out of Brive. I also know that he is far more military minded than me, is managing very large numbers of men and women, and has completed many major acts of sabotage all over the region. And incidentally, although we've never met, I worked together with some members of his Francs Tireurs group when we ambushed the train. So yes, I would be happy to meet him."

"And Victor, I too need some help from you. The last time I was here I explained that I needed a German officer uniform for Père Louis, and you were able to provide me with a perfect pair of boots. I was hoping that we could get the necessary material through the new German commissary in Brive, with the intention that Brother Martin, the tailor at the monastery, would make it. However, we have not been successful. I need to find an alternative source. I know that every German officer has his own uniform made to measure, so there must be tailors in Paris making them, and there must be somebody out there that you could trust to help us."

The very next day after Henriette had returned from Mass at the new church of St-Pierre de Chaillot, Therese gave her the news. She'd invited Georges to dinner that evening, and in the late afternoon, Victor would come home and take her to meet a tailor at the famous clothing workshop of Cifarelli on the Faubourg Saint Honoré.

It was after hours when they arrived, and so had to ring a bell and wait until a bald-headed man with a tape measure around his neck and rimless glasses perched on the end of his nose, let them in. Uncharacteristically, there was no greeting other than a "follow me please." Taking them to the third floor where there were only two people working at long tables surrounded by fabrics of every design and color, he mumbled, "so you're looking for an officer's uniform. *I only make officer's uniforms*," he snapped, and drew back a curtain along a wall revealing eight or ten German uniforms in various stages of completion. "What exactly do you want?"

Briefly Henriette tried her best to explain what was needed but was unable to provide all of the details. "Wait here," he said irritably," and hobbled off vanishing inside a darkened office. Seconds later he emerged thumbing the pages of a "Manual for German Uniforms." He suddenly stopped and showed the page to both of them, "there it is, but are you sure that it's exactly what you want?"

"Oh, yes," she blurted out, "and of course whatever the cost…" She did not get to finish her sentence.

"I have one here that is very similar, and it's almost finished," he muttered, "all I need now are the actual measurements."

"I am so sorry, but I don't have them," she said apologetically beginning to feel quite inadequate in front of this morose man. He didn't lift his eyes from the pictures in the book. Quickly gathering her thoughts, she suggested, "My friend here is very much like him but perhaps the officer is a little taller, maybe he could model?"

"Well if you have nothing else," he retorted, then addressing Victor, "come with me," and taking him behind a screen said, "let me measure you, take off your coat and jacket and your pants, and stand on this stool."

Twenty minutes later he silently led them to the front door. "It will be ready in three days, pick it up here at the reception at 4:00 P.M., it will be addressed to Francois Gardin," and with that opened the door for them, turned on his heel and vanished.

They didn't talk on the way home, but later over a glass of wine seated in the lovely airy lounge, with long deep windows looking over the Paris skyline, they shared their thoughts and experiences. "Well, what a strange man indeed," said Henriette. "He was almost rude. But from what I saw, he is certainly a good tailor, and I imagine that working at Cifarelli he must be."

"That he is," replied Victor. "I have absolutely no doubt that he'll produce a quality uniform. However, there is one thing I have been holding back from you, Henriette. The man that you met is the head of a Maquis cell that works out of the Cifarelli workshop, right under the noses of the Germans. He has worked there for so long, he's almost like a permanent fixture, but do not judge the book by its cover. It's better that I don't give you any further information about his activities, the less you know about him the better. We just cannot be too careful."

Dinner itself proved to be something of a letdown for Henriette, as Georges Guingouin appeared to be guarded and ill at ease throughout the meal. Conversation was stilted and difficult no matter the topic, as if he suspected that he was being watched and the conversation being recorded. It was not until they were seated again in the lounge enjoying an after-dinner drink, that he began to relax and talk more freely.

"You did a wonderful job with the ambush Henriette," he began, "I received a full report from my cell in Brive, and they thought that the planning was excellent. I'm just amazed that nobody was shot or hurt. I hope that we can work together again in the near future."

"Well, I too heard about your sabotaging the rubber production plant at Palais sur Vienne," she replied, "it was a major blow to the Germans. And how long will it be before it's operational again? A year? I also heard a rumor that one of your groups completely destroyed the subterranean cable linking the submarine base at Bordeaux with Berlin. Is that a fact or fiction?"

"No, we actually did it," he said with a smile, "and that's one of the reasons I wanted to meet with you. We're planning to follow up quickly on your train ambush and hit the Boches hard. It's not safe for me to give you all of the details just now, but it could involve a complex system of explosives and I need somebody who can set it all up. I know you have an expert on your team, a woman trained by the British, and I'm hoping that we can borrow her services. If you can allow her to work with us for a few days, and if she sees the plan as feasible, she'll then be able to give you all of the details. You can then decide if you want to be a part of it or not."

There was a lull in the conversation as Henriette reflected on the proposition and request.

"If it will help the cause, of course you can use her services," she exclaimed, "and you are correct, she is extremely well trained, knowledgeable, and is quite fearless when it comes to preparing and managing explosives. When will you need her, as we also have some new plans we are working on? It's my intention to sabotage the Ratier Aero factory in Figeac where Heinkel bomber parts are being produced."

"That's very interesting and I hope that you can do it," he replied, "but if possible, could I have her next week?"

"Then call me on Monday evening at 5:00 P.M. sharp and simply say, "the sparrow needs to fly." I will have my driver take her to the Catholic church in Uzerche Tuesday morning, and my car will be waiting outside, it's a late model Citroen, burgundy colored. Have somebody there at precisely 10:30 A.M. Wait for the people to come out from Mass; she'll then exit my car and enter the church. My driver will leave. A few minutes later she will come out and your people can meet her and take her to your car. When her work with you is completed, just call me at 5:00 P.M. any evening and say, "the sparrow needs a nest." Have her back at Uzerche the following day at 10:30 A.M. in the same place, and she will know what to do."

"That sounds like an excellent plan," he responded, "let's hope our collaboration will result in causing the Boches some real heartache." Then suddenly looking at his watch said, "My goodness, if I'm to beat the curfew I really must go," and with that thanked his hosts and turning to Henriette, "you should be very proud Peacock in what you are doing, and I'll call you on Monday as agreed."

As always on these visits, she needed to meet with Charles, Père Louis's brother, not only to share news about the monastery but also about Maquis activities. Phone calls between Charles and Henriette were always short, in code, and dealt with business. Meeting face to face was always a pleasurable experience and gave both of them the opportunity to relax together. After knowing each other for twelve years, if truth be told, he acted more like the brother that Henriette never had.

"We have so much to talk about," he began, as they were enjoying a lunch time aperitif on the patio. He had called in the early morning to see if she was free to meet with him. "You must give me all of the details about the ambush," he said, "I know it was a great success, but I was so worried for Louis, terrified that something would go horribly wrong and that he might get shot."

"I understand completely," she answered, "and when he is actively engaged in our operations, I spend so much time on my knees, just praying that he will be safe, I cannot tell you how I feel during those times." Charles was an attentive listener as she recounted Père Louis' recent activities, including his two trips down the Comet Line.

"That's one item I wanted to discuss with you, Henriette. Ever since the major round up of the Jews last July, and their being held at the Vel d'Hiv center here in Paris, deportations have continued. Did you know that thirteen thousand adults were held there and four thousand children? It's shocking that the Vichy government without even waiting to be asked by the German authorities, began harassing and arresting large numbers of Jews including women and children.

"Yes, I am aware of that," she replied sadly, "it's such incidents that give me incentive and energy to do Resistance work."

"As you know, I'm now one of the Paris leaders of the Comet Line," he continued, "and have been sending allied airmen to the Chateau, and thank God all have made it into Spain with big thanks to your and Louis' help. But there is a small shift in our plans. The Comet Line in Belgium was infiltrated by a man called Jacques Desoubrie using the name Masson, and a huge number of arrests have been made by the Gestapo. Our Belgian operation has been decimated. It has now moved to Paris and we are not yet fully organized. In addition, we've been asked to assist a small group of Jews that are hidden in our safe houses. I wanted to ask you face to face if you'd consider helping us."

"Charles," she replied looking at him intently, "I will need more information before I could make a decision. It may sound unfair, but before I agree, I should first discuss it with the rest of my team. We will certainly not be able to handle families or women and children. It is becoming just too difficult and dangerous moving people to the border, simply getting people into and through Brive is almost impossible. The local Milice have been formed, and are on a determined path of infiltrating and destroying Maquis groups all over our area"

"I thoroughly understand, Henriette," he replied, gently reaching out to touch her hand. These are really difficult times for us all. However, it just so happens that we have four Jewish men in various safe houses that we need to get to Spain. Two of them are engineers, the other two are scientists, and we believe that London would want them. Every day we hide them here it's a strain on everybody, and yet more people keep coming. We have been sending some to Marseille where an alternative route over the Pyrenees has been developed, but it's not totally secured yet. Some Jewish families were captured last week and interned by the Spanish border guards, who handed them back over to the Germans."

"Well I think that the answer will be yes, but why don't I give you a phone call after I get home and have spoken with the group. You do know that it will be Père Louis who will have the final say, since he'll be wearing his new uniform. You know the code, and if they agree, we will keep to the same train schedule. I will pray about it."

Standing to leave, Charles gave her a hug and kiss, saying "you're a wonderful lady, Henriette and I'm so thankful that my brother has you to protect him."

"No," she quickly responded, "not me, just thank God."

As the servant brought in the package and placed it on the dresser, all three of them, Therese, Victor and Henriette, rushed to examine it. The box itself wrapped beautifully in unique black and blue paper only used by the Cifraelli brand, and tied with silver ribbon, looked like a work of art itself.

"Shall we open it?" asked Henriette.

"Of course, the others chimed in together. We want to see it."

They were all stunned with what they saw. It was an immaculate major general's uniform complete with correct crimson arabesque collar patches and shoulder boards of the Veterinary Corps. Included was an array of decorations and ribbons including iron cross, cross of merit for meritorious contributions to the war effort and the blue 25-year service award. It was a stunning piece of workmanship. In addition, there was a new officer's cap.

"What can I say?" gasped Henriette holding up the jacket so they all could examine it, "it's amazing, and how on earth did he get these decorations and medals?"

"I agree," said Victor, "but look at the detail on this cap," holding it out so the others could look at it, and then trying it on his head for size. "This is perfect," he said, "but just don't ask me to wear those pants," he joked. "Isn't it great to have the right kind of people working with us? And what's even more incredible is that we don't know the name of the tailor, how he was able to get the correct insignia, and even more amazing is that there will be no charge to us. It was all done courtesy of the Cifarelli house."

"Well Victor, if thanks have to go to somebody, please let them know just how grateful we are. I hate to even touch this uniform as it represents so much pain and fear, but it will also help us a great deal with the Comet Line. I am sure that if any adjustment is needed," she said, as she was folding it back into the exact shape in which it had arrived, "Brother Martin will be able to take care of it. I am almost at a loss for words."

It felt strange for Henriette to hear air raid sirens on her last night in Paris. Therese explained that this was typical recently and that the Allies, the British RAF, was bombing locations on the outskirts of the city. It was a far cry from the peace and tranquility of the Chateau de Comborn, and Henriette realized that it really was time to leave.

Calling a meeting the day after she arrived home, Henriette presented to the group the issue of using the Comet Line to escort four Jewish men to the border. There was very little discussion and the final decision was left to Père Louis. He had nothing to add except to give his full consent. She had also privately shown him the uniform, but not having time to try it on, just held it against himself saying that he thought that it would fit. "Then let me call Charles, immediately," she said, "he needs to know right away, as he already has these people waiting in the safe houses."

Leaving the salon, she went to the hallway and called Paris. "This is Peacock she said using a monotone voice, "it will be fine if you send me the four male chickens you talked about. They will be collected at the usual time and place the day after tomorrow. Also, the Bull does not need any further treatment."

"Let's all be ready to receive them," she told the group. "Once they arrive, we will need to evaluate them as to when they will be ready to cross the Pyrenees. Père Louis will check them out physically. But first we have a terrible situation we must deal with. Jules, perhaps you can explain to everybody, please."

"Yes, of course," he said standing up and eyeing everybody. "Sylvie was picked up by the Milice two days ago." He spoke in a hesitant and subdued voice. "I knew that the Gestapo had been watching her for weeks, suspecting that she was part of a Maquis cell operating out of the General Hospital, which of course was not true, so she had no information to give. However, travelling up and down from Brive to the border on the Comet Line and then occasionally missing work, had put her on a "watch list." With nothing else being discovered, the Gestapo gave the list to the Milice as a possible suspect, and as you all know they've only just been formed here, but they're a brutal group." He paused and wiped his brow as he was perspiring heavily, then continued. "As far as I have been able to discover from one of my men who was in the building, Sylvie was interrogated for less than an hour and gave up no information. But I imagine the Milice saw her as a petite woman who would not physically have the strength to resist. Apparently one of them hit her hard across the head with a baton, that knocked her over backwards and the chair to which she had been tied. Her head hit the floor and she never woke up. They murdered her," he said, his voice shaking with emotion. There were gasps all around the group as Jules sat down looking exhausted and on the verge of tears.

Clotilde gave a stifled cry and started to weep silently.

There was a long silence as the rest of the group hung their heads, afraid to look at each other.

"There is nothing more to be said," exclaimed Henriette,

sensing the mood and taking control. "It also should remind us that we have to be extremely careful in everything that we do. Hopefully, Sylvie never mentioned our group, but in any case, we cannot be sure, so let's be ready just in case. One final item I should share, is that in Paris I met with the leader of the Maquis of Limousin, Georges Guingouin, and he has requested assistance with a potential major operation, but at this point in time I have no further information. He only mentioned that he wanted to build on the success of our train ambush and needs an expert in explosives and knew about our Sparrow. He asked if she could assist him with the planning. Of course, I said yes," and then looking at Simone, "he will call me on Monday to confirm the details."

Chapter 14

Confession

Thursday evening came around all too slowly for Marta as she just wanted to hold Lucien and make love to him. For him it was filled with a mixture of excitement and apprehension. The memories of the picnic and the powerful emotions he had experienced, were forever etched in his mind, but he now knew that the relationship could not continue in this way. He could no longer lead a double life with her, he must tell her the truth; she deserved to know he was a member of the Maquis.

As they held each other, passionately kissed, and made love, she sensed that something was troubling him. "What is it my darling?" she whispered in his ear, "please share it with me, we promised that there'd be no secrets between us."

"Marta, you know that I want to be with you forever, and once this war is behind us, no matter how long it takes, I want us to live together, to have a family of our own."

"And I too," she replied earnestly, "you know that I'll do anything to help that dream come true. We were made for each other, and nothing must come between us."

"Then I must tell you something," he began, as he held her tightly and with a voice that quivered and shook, "I'm a member of a Maquis group, and our goal is to help liberate France and make life for the German occupiers as difficult as possible. We want them to go home."

For a short while, she said nothing. "Please Marta," he begged, "say something, tell me that you can still love me, don't ask me to leave you."

"No Lucien, "she whispered, "I still love you and I don't

want you to leave. I knew from the start that our relationship would have its challenges, and I didn't want to look too closely at them. I was, and still am so much in love with you," and reaching up with both hands, pulled his face down to hers and smothered it with kisses. "I have a job to do and nothing changes that, and you have yours," she continued in a matter of fact voice. "The people are right; we Germans do not belong here. If I can help in any small way to end this war, then we will all benefit, and it will bring you and I closer to that life together, that we've talked about."

The following day, Lucien arrived at the town hall with a dozen eggs, and watched as Marta blushed, and tried to hide her face, wishing that he could just reach over and take her in his arms. "There is one small favor you could do for me," he asked quietly, "here's a bar of soft soap," and he slid the small package under some papers on her desk. "Keep half for yourself and with the other could you make me an imprint of the stamp you use when making a travel pass?"

Chapter 15
Smugglers

"**M**adame, it's a call for Peacock," said Clotilde entering the small room at the end of the hallway, used as a study by Henriette.

"Thank you, Clotilde," she replied walking briskly to the antique dresser with its centerpiece of flowers, a photo of her husband and the telephone.

"How can I help you?" she said in a guarded and steely tone, always taking the utmost precautions when her code name was used. A man's voice calmly replied, "The sparrow needs to fly," and the phone went dead.

"Would you please have Simone come to my study for a moment?", she asked Clotilde who had followed her down the hallway.

"Of course, Madame," and turning around she slowly climbed the stairs stopping halfway up to catch her breath.

"Simone," Henriette explained, "I am sure you remember, when I came back from Paris, I mentioned that the Limousin Maquis needed your help regarding explosives and the design of another ambush. Well, I have just received a phone call. They would like to meet you tomorrow at the Catholic church in Uzerche; I will give you details of how to proceed during dinner. You will be away for two days and Bernard will drive you there and back. But for now, just prepare your overnight bag."

"Thank you, Madame," she replied, "I'll be happy to help them in any way I can."

Simone arrived back in time for lunch, and Henriette and Serge were already seated and deep in conversation. "Welcome back," they greeted in unison. "Please join us," Henriette said pointing to the chair opposite hers, "do you think you were able to help Georges and his team?"

"I think so," she replied. "The Germans are arranging another train carrying supplies and about two hundred conscripts from Limousin to Ussel in a few days, and Georges wants me to blow up the locomotive on the Bussy-Varache viaduct. As far as we know from George's intelligence, the carriages with the conscripts will be at the rear of the train."

"Is it possible to do this?" Serge asked, "without killing anybody."

"If I do my job right," she answered back calmly, "the only lives lost will be those of the engineers, and possibly some German guards. There are soldiers guarding each end of the viaduct but nowhere else. They'll be handled by a cell from George's Maquis. There were only two guards on duty when we checked out the site. I was informed that the train itself will be driven by German Reichsbahn railway engineers, who've been brought into Limoges due to the amount of sabotage taking place. However, so much will depend on where and how I place the explosives. As the railway line approaches Bussy-Varoche, the train has to cross a viaduct composed of twelve stone arches, each about fifty feet high, and ten by four feet wide. I intend to blow out the two center arches and the engine will simply fall. The couplings then will snap, but with their forward motion three or four carriages carrying freight will also fall and the remainder will derail. The conscripts should be free to escape."

"That sounds very dangerous," said Serge, "will you have sufficient protection from the Maquis?"

"I think so, and what makes this a little different, is that all of my work will be done the night before. As far as we know the train will arrive mid-morning and should be at the arches between 11:30 and 11:45. All I have to do is to push down the detonator, wait for the explosion, pick up my equipment and run.

I'll be well hidden and a long way from the explosion itself, which will create a huge amount of noise and destruction. Georges is very thorough, and I'm confident in the escape route he's prepared for me, we actually physically went over it together. It really does sound like a solid plan."

"You talk as if you enjoy doing this kind of work," Henriette quizzed, and took a sip of wine.

"Enjoy is not the word I would use," argued Simone, looking her directly in the face, "but I was professionally trained for this, and I know I'm good at it. It's one reason why I enjoy being here."

"Then we are so blessed to have you working with us, Simone. I must find more work for you," said Henriette with a smile.

On the March 13, 1943, the Bussy-Varoche viaduct was dynamited by the Limousin Maquis and two of the main arches completely destroyed. Typically, with German efficiency, and with increasing frequency using their own engineers and rail workers, derailments often proved to be a minor inconvenience and were repaired within days. The destruction at Bussy-Varoche was so extensive, and severed the tracks so successfully, they could not be repaired or used for the remainder of the war. All the conscripts escaped.

*****

"Well, what do you think Père?" asked Henriette, as he descended the staircase and she waited anxiously at the bottom to hear his verdict. She had left a message for him after the morning Mass and he had come over to the Chateau in the early afternoon.

"Everything is looking good," he replied, "whoever made that uniform must be an expert. I tried everything including the cap and they fit perfectly. I had already checked the boots which are fine. I will feel very uncomfortable but also confident dressed up as major-general."

"Then Père, I will keep the uniform here so that after Mass in the morning you can come here and change. But please do come and sit down for a moment, there are some other issues we should discuss," she said, leading the way into her office. "Did you notice that I also placed a rucksack on the bed? It is also for you and can be used for carrying your work clothes. When Jules picks you up, he will keep it for you until you return. You will be able to change at his home or at Serge's office on your way back to the monastery.

"So, what are the travel arrangements?" he asked.

"Your brother wants to send four Jewish men the day after tomorrow. I know that this is most unusual, but when I was in Paris, he told me just how difficult it was to help them, since so many of the support groups had been infiltrated. Each of these men had somehow managed to avoid the round ups, and have been in hiding for months, but the daily situation is critical, and they need to be moved on. In addition, clothing like many other items in Paris, is at a premium and it's difficult getting suitable items for them so that they look like workers. One of them was also refusing to have his beard cut short as being against his Jewish beliefs, so we will need to watch him closely. In any case Charles will call me again this evening with more details. When they do arrive, their physical fitness will need to be assessed, since they will now have to take the mountainous route. I am sure your Brothers will also take care of getting them used work clothes, a warm jacket and boots."

"We will be ready for them," Henriette, "just let me know when they arrive. They will stay in the guest house with Brother Roger, he is so reliable and will have no problem taking care of them. Also, if you could contact Raymond and have him think about train tickets, today is Tuesday and we might be able to leave early on Saturday morning. With the multiple arrests of Maquis, and Milice activity in the Saint Jean de Luz area and the loss of several safe houses, you are correct, we will now have to move inland and take the train instead from Bayonne, to Cambo Les Bains. It's a spa town and so less dangerous, and there are two safe houses and Basque smugglers, ready and willing to take people into Spain if the price is right."

"I am so afraid for you, Père," Henriette exclaimed fidgeting with her hands and unable to look him in the face, "I will contact the Maquis down there so that they will be ready for you, but promise me that you will not take unnecessary risks and will abort the mission if you feel it's too dangerous."

"Of course," he replied, gently placing a reassuring hand on her shoulder. "But I really must go now, it's almost time for afternoon prayers."

The four Jewish men looked frightened and insecure. After a midday meal at the Chateau, they walked, accompanied by Lucien to the monastery guest house. Seated at a small table, they looked lost and bewildered, as the guest master explained that each one would be given a physical examination by Père Louis the next morning, and that he was a doctor. They would also be taken to meet the tailor and monastery cobbler. This afternoon they would all get a haircut as they would be accompanying a German Officer on the train and, were supposed to look like conscripted Polish workers and not like unkempt French peasants. Two of them had beards. "Your beards will be shaved tonight and then for the next three days you will not shave," explained Brother Roger. "You must understand that the Gestapo and the Milice are searching intensively for Jewish people and are arresting anyone they think even looks like a Jew in their estimation. Each of you has his own room and can visit the chapel at any time or walk as far as the farm buildings, but do not talk with anyone. If you need anything at all just ring that bell," he said pointing to a small hand-held bell next to the kitchen serving hatch. "The times of meals are posted on the notice board. Do you have any questions?" he asked.

The man with the longer of the two beards, sunken eyes, and

yellow skin, spoke up immediately. "I'll not allow my beard to be removed," he stated firmly, "I'm proud of being Jewish, and my religion will not permit it."

"That's just fine," replied the monk softly as he moved to-wards the interior door, taking out a key on a long chain from deep inside his robe. "We do not wish to force anybody to do anything against their conscience." Momentarily the man looked relieved, then as the monk opened the door, he looked back and said, "there will be a train leaving for Paris in the morning, I'll make sure you'll be on it."

Over the course of the next few days this same man, Eli, caused concern by arguing on religious grounds that he could not eat the rich country food that was offered. Brother Martin, however, made it clear to the group, that there were no options. "The journey across the Pyrenees will be extremely difficult, physically taxing, cold and wet and some people do not make it. The rest in the monastery is to also help build up your phys-ical strength, so eat well and be thankful. There are people all over France who are almost starving. If you're unable to keep up with the Basque guides," he explained, "you will be left be-hind." He also later informed Père Louis that this man, Eli, might be problematic.

The group began to look more like workers, with close cropped hair, unshaven faces, and now all four wearing typical dark blue and dirty jackets and pants, over undershirts that were once white. The four men sat at the breakfast table in the Chateau being fed by Clotilde, waiting for Père Louis to arrive. Suddenly the door opened, and Madame entered, elegantly but simply dressed in a cream colored, long sleeved blouse fastened at the throat with a diamond pin and wearing a pleated calf length black skirt. The men were visibly taken back, shocked by the unexpected sight and presence of this beautiful and impres-sive woman. None of them spoke. It was Clotilde who intro-duced her; "This is Peacock, she is your host and is responsible for your passage to Spain."

"Good morning," said Henriette to the men, "I hope you had a satisfying breakfast."

"Yes, thank you Madame," they answered together, "good morning."

"Let me explain what will happen today," she began, moving closer to the table and taking a seat at the head. "You will travel in the van to Brive with Lucien. Three of you will be in a hidden compartment and one of you will sit in the front. All of you had your photos taken at the monastery and now have authenticated travel passes, so who will sit with Lucien and Père Louis?"

A sullen looking man slowly raised his hand. "Good, and once Père Louis has transferred to the police car, and you have cleared the check points, Lucien will drive you to a lumber yard. There the three of you can come out of your hiding place and sit in the back of the van. At the station in Brive, you will wait with Lucien until Père Louis indicates that you should follow him. You will walk together behind him and will not talk or look around. Keep your eyes down and look at his heels. If there's any single mistake here, you all could risk being shot."

At that moment Père Louis entered the room dressed in his major general's uniform and was not immediately recognized by the men. A look of total consternation and fear came over them until they saw the face of the doctor who had examined them. Henriette too was shaken with his complete transformation, and a wave of conflicting emotions swept over her. She was proud of his courage and bravery, but terrified that something bad might happen to the man she had such deep feelings for.

Two miles outside of Brive, Lucien pulled the van off the road and into a secluded wooded area. Jules was already there sitting in a black police car. It took just a minute for Père Louis to leave the van, remind Lucien to follow them closely, then throwing his backpack behind Jules' seat, jumped in beside him.

"Good morning Jules," he said, "is everything in place?"

"Yes Père," he replied, "Raymond has taken care of the reservations. I have the tickets here and will give them to you when we get to Serge's office. And Père," he added, "you look so convincing it almost made me jump a little."

"Well let's hope that it remains that way, we still have a long way to go."

They crossed two check points into Brive, first the German military who snapped to attention and after a sharp Nazi salute and "Heil Hitler" waved them through. The military barely looked at the passes offered by Lucien, and the van quickly crossed to the other side of the barrier. The second with the French police who recognized Jules, raised no suspicions. After stopping and rolling down his window he joked with them, letting them know that the van following him was to be allowed through, as it was being used for a police exercise.

Once in Serge's lumber yard, the men came out from the secret hiding place in the van and two sat in the front and two in the back. Jules turned over the rail tickets to Père Louis and gave him an embrace. "Be safe Père, and I'll meet you at the station tomorrow. If there's any delay or for whatever reason, you can leave a coded message for me at the police station, you have my number."

The railway station as usual was swarming with military personnel of all kinds, and people carrying packages and suitcases looking for information, or simply waiting to make sure that they would have a place on the train. Since the Armistice, and now more especially because of the invasion of the Free Zone, Brive had become a major railhead, junction and assembly yard for trains traveling all over France and even into Germany.

Stopping his car directly in front of the heavily guarded main station entrance, a gendarme immediately saluted Jules, and opened his door. Père Louis exited the car on the other side, holding his gloves and briefcase in one hand, while two soldiers on guard saluted and moved people out of his path. Turning around, he looked at the van that was now being surrounded and scrutinized by four soldiers holding their rifles at the ready, and barked out, "Those men are my workers, on a special assignment, bring them out, and let the driver go."

As the men descended from the cab, Lucien went around and opened the rear door. The men walked in pairs as they had been instructed to do and followed Père Louis. Once inside the building, he stopped, looked around imperiously and giving Jules a casual salute with a "thank you very much," marched stiffly on to where he could see Raymond waiting nervously for him.

"Good morning sir," he said, "I'll escort you to your carriage." With another casual salute, and an authoritarian wave of the hand, Père Louis signaled Raymond to continue.

The carriage, compartments and corridor were already filled to overflowing with military personnel and as they squeezed through the bodies, soldiers were apologizing and attempting to give a salute. In the compartment itself junior officers were laughing and joking as they struggled to place luggage on the racks and find an unoccupied seat. From the sounds of their conversations they were travelling to Biarritz for a few days of rest.

Raymond was about to intervene holding the seat reservations in his hand when he felt a grip on his shoulder. Père Louis pulled him aside and moved into the compartment. "Who authorized you to take MY seats?" he brusquely asked the group in a commanding German voice." Their faces registered shock and panic. At first nobody spoke, then one officer started to say, "I am so sorry sir…" but got no further, "then get out NOW" Père Louis shouted, before I have all of you thrown off the train, and make it quick."

Within minutes they were gone, mumbling to themselves about the arrogant and self-important SOB of a major general.

As they settled into their seats, watched jealously by the soldiers crammed into the corridor, Père Louis carefully placed his gloves, briefcase, and cap on the seat next to himself and sat back. One of the Jewish men was seated directly opposite him, and as the train began to pull out of the station, he shouted at him for the benefit of the officers staring into the compartment, "Move your ass, I need that space." And as the man quickly moved to the opposite side, Père Louis stretched out, and crossing his legs rested his boots on the vacated seat.

The journey continued almost without incident. An SS Soldier performing a ticket check and travel pass control took one look at the general, and with a quick salute, moved on. Suddenly, Eli, stood up and facing the window, started to rock back and forth, and began murmuring some prayers in Yiddish. Hoping that none of the Germans in the corridor had noticed, Père Luis who had just started to doze, quickly sprang to his feet and in one lightening fast movement, grabbed him by the shoulder with one hand, spun him around and with the other hammered his fist into the man's face. He dropped to the floor as if he were dead. "Do you want to get us all killed?" he hissed through clenched teeth. We should have left you behind." The other men looked terrified and bent down to help Eli back to his seat, who now had blood pouring from his nose and a cut at the corner of his mouth. He was starting to moan, and whimpered "it's the Sabbath, it's the Sabbath."

"No leave him there," Père Louis whispered, "we are being watched, and he turned, stretched to his full six feet height and gave the officers in the corridor an icy stare.

From Bayonne, the line branched along the Pyrenees and the group was en route to the spa town of Cambo Les Bains, just seven miles from the Spanish border where they would be taken to a safe house, before meeting with their smuggler. The increase in the number of troops was very noticeable with the German 7th army moving eastwards and occupying what was formerly the Free Zone, and there were additional controls on the train. Several local Maquis groups had been infiltrated and large number of members arrested. Both the Milice and the Gestapo were determined to capture and slow down anybody trying to cross into Spain, and to eliminate what had been for the locals, a way of life as far back as people could remember, smuggling.

Père Louis was asked by an efficient but nervous looking SS corporal if he could see the passes of the four men. "Is that really necessary?" he asked with an enquiring voice, "they are employed by the Reich and work directly for me. They are Polish volunteer workers and have been assigned to my unit."

"Yes of course, Sir," he replied hesitantly, "I'm just doing my duty, Sir, I want to do it correctly, Sir, I would not want to be seen to be negligent, Sir."

"Yes, of course, you're doing an excellent job, soldier, and should be commended, "Heil Hitler," gave a sharp salute and in a commanding voice said, "and now leave us."

The station in Cambo Les Bains was crowded as hundreds of German military descended on the little town, to benefit from some recreation and enjoy its several spas. In addition, there were many workers and laborers taking seasonal advantage of some work. This was one of the principal reasons why Père Louis had selected this place to hand over the group; there would be less chance of them being noticed. After their documents were checked at the exit, Père Louis gave a scant glance at and returned a perfunctory salute to the sentries.

An older man and younger woman who looked like father and daughter, conversing intently, were waiting for them. Introducing themselves using their almost unpronounceable Basque names, they laughed, and the woman said in French, "you can just call us Jacques and Berthe, we are Maquis and work with the local Mugalari (smugglers). Peacock told us you were coming."

"The men will come with me, Bull, and yes, we know who you are," said Jacques looking directly at him. I'll be in charge of them from here." And with that told the men to follow him. "Good luck," said Père Louis, turning to the group, "and travel safely."

"Père, you must come with me," said Berthe, "we're just going to cross over the road to the church where our priest is waiting for you. Please let me carry your briefcase, nobody here will think that this is unusual. High ranking officers come here with women all the time to enjoy the spas."

"Thank you Berthe," he replied handing it to her, and followed her as she led the way towards an old but beautiful church built in the seventeenth century, although he learned that it was actually constructed on a Catholic shrine dating from the twelfth. It was also one of the stopping places on the pilgrimage road, from Le Puy to St James of Campostella in Spain. Turning past a sign board that read 'Eglise Saint Laurent,' showing the times of services, they passed through a small overgrown graveyard where most of the headstones were old, and many were lying at odd angles. Banging on a heavy weather worn door with the palm of her hand, Berthe shouted in Basque, "Abbé open the door, I am hungry."

"I'm coming." a pleasant Basque voice replied, and as the door opened a smiling middle-aged man wearing the traditional beret, and a well-worn and threadbare black priest's robe, open at the throat revealing a hairy chest, welcomed them in. "I heard the train arrive and was just making sure the food was ready, welcome Père and of course my little sister Berthe. Are you ready to have some 'marmitako'? "But first let's have a glass of txakoli, we make the best in the region? Ah," he exclaimed, "I am so bad mannered, please excuse me Père, my name is Intaxausti and I'm the parish priest here, I'm also a member of the Maquis. It's a pleasure having you stay with me."

"My name is Louis," he replied, "thank you for helping us."

"Père let me explain what will happen with your group," it was Berthe taking over the conversation while they were relaxing after a huge meal and several glasses of wine. "Tonight, I'll meet with Jacques and the two 'mugalari' who will take the men over the border, it's very close to here, only about two miles, after the village of Ainhoa, and I'll pay them the money. I'm sure that you have brought it. They're very reliable and experienced, but for them it's also a business."

"Yes of course," he replied, "let me give it to you now," and walking over to where he'd left his briefcase brought it over to the table. "It's all here," he said taking out the money, "do you wish to count it?"

"Of course not, Père," she laughed, "and they won't count it either. We have an unwritten code of conduct and trust among all of us who live and work in this region. Tomorrow they'll leave very early on bicycles to Ainhoa, and from there they'll hike across the border. I noticed that each man had a warm jacket and they'll need it since there will be a very difficult climb through the high pass, and it can be bitterly cold. We'll also provide each person with a pair of rope made espadrilles which are much more suitable and quieter than boots, we make them right here in the village. Look," she said, holding out her foot, "I'm even wearing mine now. You must pray that they will all reach San Sebastian safely. There are still many Spanish border guard patrols who will turn over to the Germans anyone who is caught."

"But Père, let me show you to your room. If you need anything at all you must ask me," said Intaxausti, it's rare that I have a brother priest as a guest. Your train leaves at 7:15 in the morning and I'll have breakfast ready for you beforehand. Berthe will carry your briefcase for you, as she is a good distraction for the guards, although I'm not sure that you will need any help."

At Bayonne, Père Louis used the station master's office to telephone Jules saying that "the Bull was healthy and would be delivered on time." As he passed through the various check points and didn't have his ticket or pass examined even once, he realized even more than the previous day, that his uniform commanded immediate respect without question or comment.

After being driven by Jules to Serge's lumber yard, he changed into his usual monastery work clothes and waited for Lucien to arrive with the van.

"And how was the journey, Père?" asked Lucien after they had passed through the final check point on the road out of Brive, "were there any problems?"

"None whatsoever, thank God," he replied wearily, "but I will be happy to get back to the monastery."

Chapter 16
Lysander

"**M**adame," it was Simone trying to get Henriette's attention as they were having breakfast. Both she and Clotilde had just returned from Mass at the monastery and were engaged in deep conversation. "I have some very important news that I received last night, and I need to share it with you."

Turning towards her and holding her bowl of café au lait with both hands, she sipped the steaming drink, looking attentively over its rim directly into Simone's eyes.

"Well, what is it?" she asked inquisitively.

"After I had transmitted our messages, SOE in London said they would like to send a Lysander in three days-time with arms, explosives and two radio operators. They wish to know if this can be arranged and are also asking that we help transfer the agents, one to Clermont Ferrand, the other to Paris."

"Well, we could certainly use the supplies," she responded, "but the other request might be very difficult. Do these operators speak fluent French, and have they been here before?" She paused to take another sip. "I have to assume that they are well trained and know how to survive on their own, but we only know how to manage our own area, and once outside of that we have little or no control."

"So, are you saying "no" Madame?" Henriette did not respond but continued thinking.

"The Milice are on a witch hunt now for anyone remotely associated with the Maquis, are even using teenagers to infiltrate cells, and of course the Gestapo are constantly setting up new roadblocks everywhere, often in unexpected places. And it is not even a question of having the right documents. Any foreigner coming in would need to be able to pass as a genuine French man or woman. However, my biggest concern would be the weather, it's been raining almost nonstop for almost a week now and I'm wondering what the meadow will be like. What do you think?"

"Yes, Madame, I too have been thinking about that. Even if the weather clears, will the Lysander be able to land? Do you think Bernard could help us; he knows the meadow so well?"

"I agree," replied Henriette, "that's a very good suggestion," and turning to Clotilde, "could I ask you to see if Bernard is free to join us please." Getting up from the table, she quickly left the room and returned almost immediately with him dressed in his Sunday clothes.

"Good morning Bernard, how kind of you to come at such short notice," Henriette said, rising to greet him and giving him a kiss on both cheeks. "Please join us," indicating a chair next to Simone. "Would you like some coffee?"

"No Madame, thank you, I had breakfast a couple of hours ago. How can I help you?"

"Simone has just received news from SOE in London, requesting help with an air drop." Then turning to her asked that she share the details with him.

"So, what do you think, Bernard?" asked Henriette once Simone had finished. He paused for a few seconds, then in the inimitable manner and accent of the rural people of the Midi, softly replied, "it will all come down to the condition of the meadow, Madame. Will it be able to hold a plane or not?"

"Yes, Bernard, both Simone and I have the same concerns. What would you suggest?"

"Madame, today is Sunday and we only have essential work, so why don't I take Lucien and we'll go over there and look at it? It shouldn't take us long."

"Great!" she replied, "and it is generous of you to do it on a day when you should be resting."

"Not at all, Madame," he responded, "it's thanks to your generosity that we enjoy such a good life here." And with that he stood up, wished them a good day, and strode purposefully out of the door.

"The meadow slopes severely and at the bottom there's now a stream of water at one end about knee deep." They were gathered in the salon in the evening, enjoying a glass of wine and Lucien was providing a detailed description of the conditions of the runway. "We walked the whole way down, from the normal approach line to the bottom of the meadow, the ground is extremely wet but firm, until the last thirty yards where the planes normally turn around. If the rain continues today and tomorrow, I suggest that the flight be cancelled as it's too risky."

"And if the rain eases off, what should I tell them?" asked Simone.

"It will still be risky," Bernard interjected, "but could be possible. London would need to know that a great deal will depend on the weather and consider the additional weight of the aircraft since it will be carrying weapons and explosives."

"Then I think we can agree, Simone," it was Henriette who took up the discussion, "if there's no rain for the next two days, SOE can make the call as to whether the operation is a "go" or not."

"Very good Madame, I'll send that message tonight."

London had decided that this mission was of the highest priority, and despite its additional dangers were willing to take the risks.

Serge, Jean Luc, Henri, Bernard, and Lucien took up their usual positions in the meadow, in the form of an inverted letter L with their flashlight at the ready, waiting to hear the first sounds of the Lysander. The night was windy, with small dark clouds scudding across the sky passing in front of the almost full moon, creating their own form of Morse Code. The faint hum of a plane could be heard coming in from the north west, and then its dark outline suddenly appeared, low on the horizon. It descended over the flight path, flashed its code sign, then banked to the right making a tight circle before coming in at tree top level and quickly dropping into the meadow. As it landed, in the glow from the marker lights, large spouts of water could be seen shooting up from the wheels. No sooner had it stopped, when two packages were thrown from the rear cockpit, followed by two people climbing down the ladder fixed to the side of the plane.

Men from the Maquis ran forward, collected the packages, and quickly off-loaded more boxes from the plane's cargo hold. They were rushed to several vans waiting with engines running, on the cart path at the side of the meadow. Calling out to the two passengers, Serge helped them pick up their suitcases and ran with them to his own truck. The whole action took less than seven minutes.

With engines revving, the plane moved slowly forward beginning its turn-around in preparation for takeoff. Suddenly the noise of the engines increased, but the Lysander did not appear to be moving. Rushing over, and using his flashlight, Serge could immediately see that the front wheels had sunk deeply into the mud. The plane was stuck. The cockpit cover was thrown back, and the pilot shouted in English over the noise of the engine, "it's over, it won't budge." Seconds later the engines died to whisper and then just silence. Jumping onto the wing and then to the water-logged ground, a young pilot stepped down and in broken French announced, "we'll need to leave it, there's no way it will fly out of here. Have everybody stand back and I'll try to destroy it." Bernard noticed that he had a pistol in his hand and waved everybody away.

"Bernard, I must go," said Serge, "we need to get these supplies to the safe houses as quickly as possible. Have Lucien stay with the passengers, then take them and the pilot to the Chateau. But you must move quickly, you don't have much time."

Once everybody was at the trucks, the pilot began shooting at the plane, hoping to set it on fire. Even after emptying his pistol, he was unsuccessful. "We must go, we must go now," Bernard shouted, "the Boches or some local farmer might soon be here," and grabbing the pilot by the arm, pulled him into his own truck.

Back at the Chateau, the atmosphere was somber and depressing. Clotilde had the cook prepare a spread of cold cuts and cheeses in the salon had brought in several bottles of their own wine. But most were not eating.

"First things first," said Henriette, dressed beautifully but casually for the evening. Standing in front of the group, she announced in English, "my name is Peacock, and this is my home. You'll all be staying here for a few days, perhaps a little longer. With the plane being left intact, the Gestapo and the top authorities will be delighted and most certainly will want to keep it, but more importantly for us, the whole area will be crawling with military and Gestapo looking for the pilot and the plane's cargo. We will need to let things cool down before we decide what to do with you. And," pointing to the pilot, "your name is...?"

"Just call me Sandy," he replied with a sullen voice. Then in a more demanding tone said, "I must let London know tonight what has happened, I can't possibly stay here, you need to get me back home as soon as possible." An eerie silence followed, and nobody said anything.

After rearranging several bracelets on her wrist, Henriette looked directly at the pilot, then moving slightly towards the two agents, said in a quiet but firm voice, "I will only say this once, so please listen carefully. You are guests in my home and are very welcome, and we'll take good care of you. If you need anything at all, please ask Clotilde," waving a hand in her direction, "she manages everything in the Chateau. However, it's not for any one of you to tell us what to do, when or how to do it regardless of your skills or expertise. Your lives are entirely in our hands; you will not ask any operational questions of my staff, which includes our radio operator, and you will not be using your radios, we'll keep them safe until you leave. We will share information with you on a need to know basis. Do you have any questions or comments?"

"Yes," said one of the agents, "you'll need our information if you are talking with London."

"Of course," she replied, graciously, "kindly give your codes to Sparrow here," pointing to Simone who was pouring herself a glass of wine, "she'll be communicating with SOE later tonight."

With all the weapons and explosives hidden in safe houses outside of the town, an emergency meeting was called very early in the morning at Serge's office to discuss the situation. Raymond, Jules, Henri, and Jean Luc all agreed on one thing, they could not let the plane fall into German hands. It was Jules who closed out the meeting. "The plane has not yet been found otherwise I would have heard about it, so why don't I get back to my office and let you know when I hear of any development. I'm sure the atmosphere will soon be buzzing with excitement."

"Before we separate, shouldn't we let Henriette know what our thinking is?" asked Jean Luc.

"Absolutely we must," replied Serge," I'll call her as soon as you leave."

Remarkably the gun shots from that night were not reported until the morning, and it was not until almost nine o'clock that the plane itself was discovered. Colonel Otto Kreips had immediately contacted Berlin who quickly responded saying that they were sending aircraft specialists to prepare it for transportation to Germany. Meanwhile it should be towed to a secure place.

The German authorities in Brive were ecstatic with the news

that they now had a complete Lysander that could be examined, something the Luftwaffe had wanted since 1939 and the outbreak of war. They had no comparable aircraft but knew about its advanced wing technology, and ability to operate on very short runways. In addition, with every pound of nonessential equipment stripped out of it, the Lysander's range was dramatically increased, and with an auxiliary fuel tank underneath the fuselage, could cover a round trip of about twelve hundred miles.

At precisely eleven o'clock, Serge's phone rang, and Jules using code suggested they meet immediately, and that Raymond should be invited. Ten minutes later they reassembled at Serge's office and were seated around his desk. To everybody's surprise, they found Henriette already engaged in conversation with Serge, and Bernard sitting in a corner.

"Good morning Gentlemen," she said greeting each one with an embrace, "this is such a critical issue I felt that I should be here to support any plans that can be developed. In addition, I now have two guests we were expecting at the Chateau whom the Gestapo do not know about, and also an unexpected third, we have the pilot. If the Gestapo know he's alive they will certainly want to find him. We know they will put all of their resources into searching for him."

They all responded warmly, "good morning Henriette", and Serge continued, "you know that we always value your opinion, and yes I too have been thinking about the pilot and what we'll do with him." After greeting each other, Jules immediately reported back from the top-level meeting with the German authorities. "A small team has already been assembled, and they'll tow the plane from the meadow to the airfield at Brive La Roche, where it will be kept for the time being. There's a protective hangar there. I've been asked for a police motorcycle escort and will detail one man to ride in front who will control any traffic. However, the road is only lightly used by a couple of surrounding farms one of which my team uses as a safe house."

He paused to see if there were any questions. And since there were none, he continued. It had been explained in the meeting with the authorities that without its heavy cargo and extra passengers, the Lysander was a relatively light aircraft weighing in at about two tons, thirty-one feet long and with a wingspan of fifty feet. Towing it to the airfield would not present any major difficulty, other than the challenge of the narrow country roads that were almost single lane, with low hedgerows on either side. The plane's wings would easily clear them, but there would be the question of navigating the railway crossing at Allanac on the main Brive-Bordeaux line.

"Do they have any time frame?" asked Serge.

"Yes, they do," replied Jules, "three engineers and a Luftwaffe pilot had already assessed how they would tow the plane using a military five-ton truck with a winch on the front, to help extract it from the meadow. Once on the path they estimated it would take them about four hours to negotiate the thirteen miles of country roads to the airfield.

The German sergeant engineer who inspected the plane, anticipates that they'll have the Lysander out of the meadow and at the railway crossing by about three thirty, and at the airport by about five o' clock. A reception committee will be there, with all of the top officials and the German press and information services. They intend to make a big show of this trophy."

"Then, this falls right in my territory," chimed in Raymond. "If we cannot take back the aircraft, then perhaps we can prevent them from enjoying it."

"What do you mean, Raymond?" asked Serge, lighting up yet another Gauloise.

"Well what if we were to destroy the plane?" he replied, "and what if the plane never reaches the airport?"

"Oh my God," replied Jules, "you must be out of your mind, Raymond, how can we do that and at such short notice?"

"You both know that my cell covers this area, and that there are many cheminots who are Maquis. This is what I propose," he explained asking Serge for a sheet of paper. In a few minutes he had drawn a sketch of the road from the meadow to the airfield and also marked the railway line from Brive, showing the railway crossing. "It'll take some serious coordination, but it could be done," he said pensively. "What if the Lysander gets stuck at the crossing while a freight train is traveling through?"

"Tell me more," said Jules incredulously.

"Well at 3:25 every day a freight train leaves Brive and reaches the Allanac crossing at about 3:40. The controller in Brive calls the crossing immediately the train leaves the station or the marshaling yard. At the side of the crossing you may have seen it already, there's a small house where the man who works the barriers lives. He has to close and open them by hand every time there's a train. A signal down the line is fixed with a red light, but once the barriers are closed to traffic, the mechanism changes the signal to green. In this way, the locomotive engineer can tell at a glance that the barriers are down, and that he has a clear way ahead.

The guardian of the barriers is Jean Paul, and he's a member of my team. Once the train has passed through, he calls to the next crossing to let them know. I also have two cheminots who can easily fix the signal in the green position."

"And what else do you propose, Raymond," asked Jules, "all of this sounds very interesting, but also extremely dangerous."

"We'll need help from two other sources. The first will be the police escort; can you assign an officer from one of your cells, Jules? But let me explain. The nearest farm is owned by André, who's also in my Maquis group, and I'll get a message to him, to take his horse and cart filled with mangel beets, which are now being harvested all over the area, onto the narrow road. At three twenty he will be positioned on the other side of the railway crossing about fifteen yards away, where the road turns sharply to the right. He will not be seen from the crossing. He'll dump a heap of beets on the road as if they have fallen off his cart. Shortly afterwards your police escort will arrive, Jules, and he'll start helping André remove the blockage by throwing the beets into the cart. If the Germans live, they'll report that your policeman was most helpful! Meanwhile the German truck will have pulled over the crossing and only then will the soldiers see the obstruction in front of them. They will stop their truck and will not even be thinking about the barriers. The Lysander however will be stuck in the middle. A minute or so later, the freight train which will be travelling at about forty miles an hour will crash through the barriers, completely destroying the aircraft and probably dragging the truck with it. Whether the soldiers and pilot will have the presence of mind to jump, is anybody's guess."

Nobody spoke for a moment they were too taken aback by this seemingly impossible, foolish yet perhaps feasible plan.

"Then we must take our chances, and there's no time to waste, "said Serge.

"Are we all in this together?"

A unanimous "yes" came from the others. "Then let's synchronize our watches said Raymond, "timing is going to be everything."

"Before I can say "yes", it was Henriette calmly intervening, "I suggest that we ask ourselves if we really want to do this? We all know what this means not only for the German Administration in our area or even in France. This will have major repercussions I would imagine right up to Hitler himself. If they succeed it will not only make news all over Germany, it will boost their morale and give the Germans new technology that could help them win this war. If we succeed, it will have negative repercussions such as Brive has never seen or experienced before."

Her somber tone caused some immediate reflection, until the

silence was broken by Jules asking, "what if the Germans do not arrive at the crossing, what's our back up plan?"

"There is none; time is against us," answered Serge quickly, "we simply have to make this work."

"Then you have my full support," announced Henriette, "and no matter what the result, please call me this evening, Serge."

"Of course, I will," he responded, "and Jules, put your most trusted man on this if you can. Let him know that timing is critical."

The two cheminots walking alongside the rails with tools and rope in their hands drew no attention whatsoever, to a casual observer they simply appeared to be doing routine maintenance. After fixing the signal in the green position, they continued walking to the gate keeper's house where their friend Jean Paul lived and worked. Happy to see them, he knew that their presence meant Maquis business, and they quickly explained what was about to take place.

"But what about me, what about the Boches, they will be out for revenge when this is over?" he cried.

"Don't worry," the older of the two said, "once you've received the call from Brive that the train is on the way, we'll tie you up and put a gag in your mouth. When the Germans find you, it will look like you were innocently beaten up as you were doing your duty."

At that moment, the phone rang, and Jean Paul answered, "Thank you," and hung up. Looking anxiously at both of his friends he said, "that was the call, let's do it. The train is on its way." The cheminots moved rapidly, one of them dragging a chair into the center of the room. "Sit down Jean Paul, we'll tie you to the chair, do you have a handkerchief or a towel?"

"Yes, I have both, here take this," pulling a white square of material from his pocket, "you'll find a small towel in the washroom over there in the corner."

It took just minutes to tie him securely. Then after stuffing his handkerchief into his mouth they tore up the towel and created a blind fold. "Jean Paul, I am sorry to do this, but you'll thank me later," said the older cheminot who suddenly clenched his fist and punched him hard on the nose which immediately began to bleed all over his shirt. Seconds later they were gone.

Getting the Lysander out of the mud did not present any problems but getting it out of the field did. Using its front-end winch, the soldiers spent time ripping out a section of the hedgerow to create a sufficient space for the plane to pass through. Once on the narrow road, with the pilot steering it, the plane was towed at a very slow speed. It had only taken the pilot a few minutes to figure out the essential controls but explained to the soldiers that as they towed, they must give him some slack initially so that he could test and dry out the braking systems, since they had been sitting overnight in water. With some trial and error, the tow eventually went without incident, until they reached the railway crossing. By that time, the two German soldiers and a sergeant were all feeling confident and happy with the project. They were laughing and joking about the unique and amazing mission they had been given, and how their families would see them on German Newsreels and in the Press.

The police motorcycle escort drove slowly but kept advancing and returning, after checking the road in front, especially where there were blind corners. From the crossing André had left a trail of fallen mangel beets, and eventually the policeman found him staring at a huge portion of his load that he had deliberately spilled onto the road.

Together they began throwing the giant beets into the cart, just as the German truck completed crossing the tracks, and as anticipated, on seeing the obstruction stopped, leaving the Lysander in the center of the two barriers. The sergeant quickly got down and started shouting abuse and gesticulating at André in German and broken French, to move his stuff quickly and get out of the way. André looked at him and just threw up his hands as if not understanding, and slowly continued throwing the beets into the cart, helped by the police. In the distance, a train let out a loud whistle as it usually did when approaching a railway crossing.

What happened next took place so fast, nobody afterwards could give a clear picture of events. The sergeant ran back to the truck shouting in German to his driver that they must use their truck to push the cart away, but as he started to climb up, the train was less than fifty yards away. He decided to jump, just as it ripped through the barriers, tore through the Lysander, and dragged the truck down the tracks. He never made it to the roadside. With its fuel tanks still half full, the plane exploded almost on impact, sending up sheets of flame and smoke that spread for almost one hundred yards before the train, now completely derailed, came to a stop as freight cars piled up on top of each other.

At the sound of the whistle, André had grabbed his horse's halter and ran with it down the road as fast and as far as he could, but the blast from the explosion knocked him flat on the ground. His horse spooked by it but unhurt, galloped off at full speed shedding the remainder of the cart's load. The policeman had time to kick start his motorcycle, accelerate past André, and eventually got back to town to give his report to Jules.

Jules, however, was not in his office, he had been ordered to be present with the German dignitaries at the airfield, waiting for the much-anticipated arrival of this amazing catch. It fell to the deputy chief of police to break the bad news and when he did so, Colonel Otto Kreips immediately called for an emergency meeting at his office. Shouting and screaming almost incoherently, both the Gestapo and police were ordered to work through the night and have some answers as to the culprits on his desk by 9:00 in the morning.

"We know that there are Maquis groups among the

cheminots, and even among the railway administration. I want them all. We also know from a spy in the Francs Tireurs group about a leader in the area called Peacock and another named Bull. Find them or I'll send all of you back to the Eastern front. If they're leaders then they have to be involved in this. Do you realize what this has done to our credibility in Berlin?"

Jean Paul was eventually found and rescued by the SS Soldiers and commended for his courage and commitment to duty. The escort policeman was also commended by Jules for his service, and for bringing in news of the disaster in a timely fashion. André found his horse and they both still work together.

Neither the German pilot nor any of the soldiers survived.

The pilot who flew in the Lysander was kept at the Chateau for two weeks, much to his annoyance, and was later escorted to the Spanish border by Père Louis. He eventually reached London and continued to fly Lysanders until the end of the war.

The two agents did not reach their destinations. The one bound for Paris was caught within four days. A mobile German radio detector unit pinpointed his location while transmitting to London from a safe house on the outskirts of the city. It had already been infiltrated; five Maquis were captured at the same time, taken to Fort Mont-Valerien, and executed. Fortunately, a woman escaped with the code books and other incriminating documents.

The other agent never reached Clermont Ferrand. Unable to adequately answer questions by the Gestapo on the train during a ticket and travel pass inspection, due to his imperfect French. He was taken to the SS Headquarters in Ussel. His radio set and code books were captured, was convicted for espionage, and forty-eight hours after leaving the Chateau, was shot. The loss of the code books caused untold harm and seriously jeopardized the Maquis operations in the Auvergne and eastern Correze, since it took weeks before London became suspicious of and then aware that their transmissions were being intercepted and compromised.

The railroad tracks between Brive and Bordeaux were not able to

be used for almost twelve days, which caused a serious disruption in
materials being shipped to and from Germany. Fearing that the local
cheminots would not repair the tracks properly, the repairs had to wait
until a German crew arrived from Limousin.

The Gestapo, the SS and the Milice were not able to discover
the people responsible for the planning and execution of the disaster. However, they did bring in for questioning many suspected Maquis, most of whom did not know anything about the
specific event. But several cheminots under torture admitted to
being part of a cell led by Raymond. Convinced that the Peacock
was responsible and that he must know him, Raymond was tortured day and night for almost a week to divulge this information. He did not. The SS had also heard without any proof, that
Bull might be a priest in the Brive area and that he too was involved. Finally, Raymond broke down and admitted that Bull
was the old priest at the parish church of St Martin.

Six days after the destruction of the Lysander, Raymond and
eleven cheminots, none of whom had actually participated in
the incident, and the old priest were taken to a field on the outskirts of town and executed by firing squad. His wife, Claudine
accused of being an accomplice, was quickly tried by military
tribunal, found to be guilty and sent to Ravensbruch concentration camp.

Throughout the war, the Germans were eager to capture a Lysander
but never succeeded. This was their one opportunity, but in their ea-
gerness to benefit from it, and to publicize their success, they failed to
consider that the country was still in a state of war and that the Maquis
might intervene.

Chapter 17
Betrayal

Distraught and concerned at the loss of Raymond, Henriette, invited the team to a special lunch at the Chateau. She had several issues to address with the group, not the least being the news she had received through a Maquis cell and confirmed this morning by a phone call.

By eleven thirty they were all present, Serge, Jules, Bernard, Lucien, Henri, Jean Luc, Simone, and Père Louis and after an aperitif in the salon, Clotilde shepherded them into the dining room.

"Thank you all for coming," Henriette said, "I know that it is increasingly dangerous and difficult to travel around and especially passing through the check points. Thank God you are all safe."

They were now all seated at the dining table in the large formal dining room, where in each place setting was the finest Limoges china, set on a beautiful table cloth made of white Tulle lace, surrounded by real silverware, each piece bearing the Chateau crest. In front of each person were three delicate crystal wine glasses, engraved with the outline of the Chateau and the name Lastiere du Saillant. Both Serge and Henriette were seated at the ends of the table so that they could see everybody's face.

Clotilde poured everybody a red wine from the Chateau as the maid served each person a traditional Limousin hors d'oeuvres dish, of black sausage and baked apples.

"Well I would like to begin with some bad news, before we get down to discussing any future plans," Henriette began, "I've just received the sad news that Jean Moulin is dead. I spoke with

Lucie Aubrac from the Clermont Ferrand Maquis this morning. He was the Prefect of Chartres for quite some time and in fact he was the youngest holder of that office in France. That was where I first met him.

"By November 1940, the Vichy government ordered all elected left-wing officials be fired. Moulin was himself dismissed from his post. From then on, he devoted his time to resisting the Germans, and in September 1941 was smuggled out of France and taken to London to meet with General De Gaulle and other exiled French leaders."

Henriette paused to take a sip of water. Meanwhile the group following true French custom were served their vegetables before the main dish: glazed carrots and creamed spinach. Clotilde walked around the table pouring both red and white wines, that Bernard had brought from deep in the Chateau wine cellar.

De Gaulle sent him back to France as his formal link to coordinate the eight major *Résistance* groups into one organization. Moulin got their agreement to form the "National Council of the Resistance" that held its very first meeting on May 27. But just a few weeks ago on June 21 he was arrested with several Resistance leaders in the home of Frederic Dugoujon in a house in Lyon. Lucie Aubrac's husband was one of those taken."

"They were all driven to Montluc Prison where Moulin was detained until the beginning of July. Tortured extensively on a daily basis by Klaus Barbie, the head of the Gestapo there, and later more briefly in Paris, he never revealed anything to his captors. The last time he was seen alive, he was in a coma and his head was yellow, swollen and wrapped in bandages.

She paused briefly again as her voice shook slightly, and then composing herself continued. "He is believed to have died near Metz on a train headed for Germany, from injuries that were reportedly sustained in a suicide attempt. In my phone call with Lucie Aubrac today, she said that the group had been betrayed.

"This is terrible news," said Jules, "and it confirms what we also are experiencing, that the Gestapo and especially now the Milice are really searching for Maquis members and are trying every method they know to infiltrate our cells. We have already lost Raymond, who will be next?"

"Please do not talk like that, Jules," answered Henriette. "We cannot afford to have a defeatist attitude, especially now."

"I agree," interjected Serge, lighting up a Gauloise, "let's stay positive and look forward. There's still so much work to be done."

As the main course of mustard rabbit was served, Simone commented, "This is probably the most amazing meal I have had ever had. Your cook is extraordinary, Henriette."

"Thank you Simone, I'm happy we can still provide good food, I know that those of you living in the town are not so fortunate, which is why I wanted to do something a little special today. It's also a token of my thanks for all that you are doing for France."

"However, we need to talk about our own business and two people, one of whom has been strongly recommended to us, and the other one we already know," she continued. "But first about Beatrice. She is employed at the Ernest Rupine Museum, in Brive, is twenty-nine years old, single, and lost her husband who fought with the 9th Army in 1940. She works with teachers from all over the region and has spent her time as a Resistant distributing copies of the Maquis newspaper *Liberation*. Jean Luc, you are the one who is asking us to consider her as member of this group, do you have anything to add?"

"I agree with everything you have shared, Henriette. I met Beatrice through a group at the Catholic church, that was attempting to distribute food for poor people. Over a period of weeks, I got to know more about her, and she told me about delivering the *Liberation* newspaper. Apparently, they just appeared at the back door of the museum one morning and she hid them at first then started to distribute them. Politically she definitely thinks like us, and she asked me how she could get in touch with the Maquis. I like her and think that she'll fit in well. Furthermore, she wants to be a writer and mentioned to me that she would like to start another underground newspaper."

"Does anybody else have any questions?" asked Serge.

"Before we bring her here," it was Bernard who broke the silence, "I think that a couple of us should meet with her in Brive, just as an additional precaution. With so many cells being infiltrated, we can't take any chances."

"An excellent idea," replied Serge. "Why don't Lucien and I meet with her the next time he is in town? I'm sure you can arrange this, Jean Luc."

"Yes of course, I can. But when will that be, Lucien?" he asked, looking at him across the table.

"Tomorrow I will be done by one thirty. Perhaps we can meet in your office?"

"No, that will not work, but what about in the park opposite my office? There are benches where we can sit, and also control our surroundings. What do you think Serge?"

"Its fine by me, so let's do it."

The conversation moved around the table, as people shared small talk with each other. After being presented a selection of local cheeses, Creme de St Laurent, Cantal and the Gour Noir black goat, they rounded off the meal with a traditional Limousin desert, a black cherry clafoutis. Henriette gave them time to relax and enjoy the meal, then gently brought them back to Maquis business.

"Let's move on to the next item," she suggested. "We should talk about Raymond's replacement. I think that most of us, except Simone and Henri, have met Pierre Michel. He was working under Raymond and I can only assume that he has passed the scrutiny of the SS and the Gestapo, otherwise he would not have been promoted to Railway Chief."

"What I learned," interjected Jules, "was that he was not in the area when the Lysander was destroyed. He had left on vacation several days previously and was actually in Bayonne with his family."

"Well we definitely need his help," said Henriette, "and I know that the numbers of Maquis among the cheminots is growing, even if the majority are communist. I learned from the Clermont Ferrand group, through Lucie, that the head of SNCF (French Railways) Albert Guerville is helping form an underground group for his workers called *Iron Resistance.* Jules, will you be able to reach out to Pierre, and let him know that we would like to invite him to the next meeting here?"

"Yes, of course, I think he'll be very happy to take a leadership role."

"Wonderful," she replied, "then can I suggest that we regroup here in one week, but let's make it a morning meeting, and hopefully if approved, both Beatrice and Pierre will be able to attend."

"And Henriette," it was Serge speaking, "on behalf of our group I would like to thank you so much for this wonderful food and wine. This was an exceptional meal. And you are correct, it is so rare these days that we get to fully enjoy the food from our own region."

"Yes, indeed," echoed the rest of the group.

The following day Lucien registered his goods at the Administration and brought Marta some food, even as they struggled to hide their affection for each other. "Shall we meet tomorrow night," he whispered, "same time, same place?"

"Yes of course," she replied.

*****

After they had made love and were holding each other, Marta reminded Lucien that Saturday was not only her day off, but that she did not have to return to work until Monday. He had promised to take her on a mini vacation.

"Yes, my love, I have not forgotten. In fact, I have planned for us to stay in Rocamadour. It's an amazing place and has been an important pilgrimage destination for a thousand years. It's built on the site of a shrine to a Black Maddona that became famous for its healing powers, and soon became a stop on the pilgrimage path to Santiago de Compostela in Spain. The medieval village is amazing, with just one narrow main cobbled street, and clings to a steep cliffside above the river Alzou. It is so picture perfect, it's quite breathtaking. We'll be staying in a hotel that has been caring for customers as far back as anyone can remember. It has now been renovated and modernized and has its own restaurant. I'm sure you will like it."

"Oh, darling, it sounds absolutely wonderful. I can't wait to go there," she cried, reaching for his head, and giving him a long kiss.

"And before I go, I have something for you," and reaching into her purse brought out a small package. "Here," she said, "let me give you your soap back. I did not cut it, so I made two impressions of the stamp. I hope that they will help you. Is there anything else I can do?"

Pausing for a moment, Lucien quietly replied, "Yes, there is. We know that the Administration is going to issue a new ration book, and if it is anything like the new travel pass it could take months before everybody gets one. If you could get me a copy of the new one, I just need it for a few days, then I'll return it to you."

"I'm sure I can do that for you, my love. I'll bring one with me on Saturday."

"Then I'll meet you at the same place but a little earlier this time. Let's agree on 8:30 A.M. then we'll have more time to explore the area around Rocamadour, and don't forget to bring an overnight bag.

On Sunday evening as he prepared to drop off Marta behind

the church, after a romantic and love filled two days, she suddenly turned to Lucien and clinging to him like a child, cried "I don't want to leave you." As tears ran down her face she whispered "You make me so very happy, we need to be together. I want this weekend to last forever."

"I know my love," he whispered, "but we must be patient. We're already hearing that the war is beginning to turn in favor of the Allies. I'm sure your own intelligence knows that the British, the Americans and the Russians are preparing a major push to take back all occupied lands. It's all a question of where and when, but one day it will all be over. Meanwhile, we have each other and we just have to wait."

*****

The meeting at the Chateau was a lively event and the group was delighted to meet Beatrice, whom both Lucien and Serge believed would be a strong addition to the team. Pierre Michel the new railway chief introduced himself to everybody and spoke briefly about the strength and willingness of the cheminots to disrupt German rail traffic.

"Please, help yourself to the wine and cheeses," said Henriette pointing to the trays of food and the wine sitting on the dresser. And let's hear what Beatrice has to say about producing an underground newspaper."

"Oh, Madame, please don't call it a newspaper."

"Beatrice, my name is Henriette or between Maquis cells I prefer you use my other name, Peacock."

"Well, thank you Henriette, but I was thinking of just a single sheet of paper to begin with, printed on both sides that could be distributed all over this area. Until I learn more about the Maquis, I would have little to say. And in any case, I would have to find someplace where it could be printed."

"Well, perhaps I could help you with that." a deep voice from the corner of the room interjected. It was Père Louis, sitting quietly but observing the proceedings. "I'm sure that Brother Pascal could take care of that for you, but you and I should first talk more about it, then you can come over to the monastery and meet him. And what about your distribution, have you considered that?"

"As a matter of fact, I have, Père. I have other friends, all school-teachers who are already helping me, and they are prepared to distribute anti-German material through all of the schools as far south as we can go."

"Well that's wonderful, and I'm sure the other Maquis groups will lend a hand once they hear about it."

At that moment, there was a banging and shouting outside of the front door. "Monsieur Bernard, Monsieur Bernard, Monsieur Bernard, you must come quickly."

Clotilde moved quickly followed by Bernard and as she opened the door a workman shouted so loud everybody could hear. "The Germans are coming; the Germans are coming."

"Calm down now Thomas," said Bernard gently, "tell me what you have seen."

"Monsieur Bernard, I was down on the south side watering the vegetables, and I heard the sound of a truck that was not ours, changing gears. I looked down and at the entrance to our road I saw a large German truck, it has the Swastika on the side, and in front is a black car."

"Well done Thomas," said Bernard, "please find Basil and the two of you close the main gates into the courtyard. Then wait there. Go quickly."

"Yes sir," he replied.

Everybody had now gathered anxiously around the front door and it was Henriette who took charge. "We cannot take any chances," she announced in an unemotional voice, "we must assume they are Gestapo. Père Louis please leave us immediately and take the back path to the monastery." Without a word, he turned and left the group. "We will have about ten minutes at the most before they arrive, so we must all move quickly. Simone, remove your radio and any documents according to the emergency plan we put together, then meet me here as soon as you can. Turning to Clotilde she said, "please have the maid and the cook help you tidy up everything in the salon, remove any trace of the meeting and smoking; open all the windows. The rest of you will go to the winery with Bernard and wait for Simone. He'll explain where he will take you. Don't worry, it will be safe but a little frightening."

"Henriette," it was Serge moving towards her, "I can't leave you on your own," he said solicitously, "I'll stay and help you deal with this."

"You will do no such thing, Serge, you are a leader and must be kept safe. Please," she urged, "go with Bernard. But before you go, give me your packet of Gauloise and matches."

Moving inside, Henriette helped her staff re-arrange the salon and placed the packet and matches on the round table. Then rushing upstairs quickly, returned with a purse which she placed on the dresser in the hallway next to the telephone.

As Simone came down the stairs, Henriette gave her a questioning look. "Yes Madame, everything is taken care of. I lowered the radio and suitcase with all of the papers from the window and released the rope. They are now safely hidden behind the wood pile."

"Then come with me," she said, and led the way to the winery. "Bernard will lead you out of the Chateau, through the old tunnels," she explained to everybody looking at her nervously, "just trust him and follow his instructions exactly. Once you exit, he'll show you the path following the river and you will be able to easily reach your vehicles. Bernard will return with Simone. Meanwhile I'll try to buy time for all of you. May God go with you."

"Lucien," Henriette said "you will stay with me and open the gates with Thomas and Basil once I give you the signal. It will not be long before they arrive. I will be waiting outside of the Chateau."

Climbing up the steep, narrow, twisting, and uneven track to the Chateau took the Germans a little longer than ten minutes.

Standing at her front door, Henriette listened to the banging on the Chateau gates and the shouting in French with heavy German accents. The gates were ancient, made of solid oak and had withstood stronger challenges than a few military fists. She nodded to Lucien who shouted out loud, "we are trying to let you in, please wait." Then Henriette turned and went into the lobby of the Chateau where Clotilde was waiting.

A black Citroen entered the courtyard, and three men almost identically dressed in plain clothes and wearing black fedora hats, got out. They were followed by a five-ton truck carrying eight soldiers. Once the soldiers had got down, they formed up in two lines of four. An officer, a Gestapo Major, also stepped down and marched stiffly and quickly to the front door of the Chateau, followed by the three men who in turn were followed by the soldiers. He banged on the door with his swagger cane, while shouting in French to "open the door, this is the Gestapo."

Clotilde opened the door, and before she could say anything was sharply and suddenly pushed aside, and as she fell to the floor, hit her head against the wall. Letting out a little cry of pain, she held her head which had started to bleed. Coming face to face with Henriette, the major announced in a contemptuous voice, "we will search this Chateau, you are accused of sheltering Maquis and a radio operator. Let me pass."

Neither flinching nor retreating, Henriette, exuding an intimidating power, looked him directly in the face: "Major, you will do no such thing. You are rude and uncouth and should be reported for your behavior."

Not accustomed to such a rebuttal, he hesitated, then suddenly found himself starring into the dark, steely, unwavering eyes of a beautifully dressed and dignified lady. Turning to the men behind him, he ordered them to take the soldiers and examine every room starting with the top floor. He himself would conduct a search of the ground floor.

"Are you sure you want to do that?" Henriette asked in a cold and contemptuous voice, "your superior officers may not agree."

"What are you saying you stupid woman. My superiors have sent me here. You are high on our list of suspects. Move out of the way and let my men pass."

"You are very mistaken, Major, and if you continue, you will probably lose your rank and be sent to the Eastern Front for intruding into my house, physically abusing my staff, and accusing me of working against the Reich. Then slowly stretching out her hand, without taking her eyes off him, reached for her purse on the dresser and took out a small card. "I suggest that you make a phone call to this person before you make any more mistakes. Either you can call him, or I will," and moving just a step backwards, lifted the telephone receiver holding it out to him. "We have a very particular relationship," she said coquettishly, "and we recently travelled to Paris together. He will not be happy when he hears of your blundering escapade, and how you have mistreated both me and my staff. Here is his card, please make the call."

Seconds later the Major's face turned ashen when he read the name on the card, and turning to the three men in plain clothes, speaking in German explained, "we have made a huge mistake, this lady is a personal friend of Lieutenant General Karl Bomelburg. Our information sources have deceived us. What shall we do?"

The first thing you will do is bring a chair for my poor staff whom you have assaulted. "You," she said pointing to one of the plain clothed men, "go into this room" waving her hand in the direction of the salon, "bring one out, and quickly." The man obeyed without saying a word and on his return helped Clotilde who was sitting on the floor with her back to the wall, stand up and then sat her carefully down.

"It's alright Major, you can now speak freely, I understand German perfectly," she explained," but I insist, please make the call, I would like to hear what the General will have to say."

"Madame if you will please excuse us, we are extremely sorry, we have made a terrible mistake and we apologize for the intrusion into your home."

"You say "we" Major, but aren't you in charge? No, I am sorry, your apology will not suffice. I need your name and the name of your commanding officer." And then speaking in fluent German said, "please call your own commander now. I need assurances from him that this will never happen again. He can submit an apology in writing to me and also include the promise, that from here on out my household will be left in peace. Nothing short of that will do. I will be travelling to Vichy soon, and I am certain Lieutenant General Bomelburg would not like to hear how you have insulted me and my household and subjected us to such unprofessional and ill-bred behavior."

The phone call was short, and Henriette could almost hear the gasps at the other end as the Major explained to his superior officer what had happened. Profuse apologies were expressed, and assurances given.

"I will thank you for returning my card, Major," she said holding out her hand, and sheepishly almost obsequiously he offered it back to her with a slight bow and click of his heels.

"You may go now," she said dismissively, and waved her hand towards the door. Following him out Henriette waited until the sounds of the car and the truck had faded before re-entering the Chateau. Clotilde stood up as she entered, and the two women held each other in a tight embrace, the old woman unashamedly crying on her shoulder.

Lucien, understanding the danger and stress of the visit, did not even knock on the door but came in and seeing the two women consoling each other, quietly asked if he could help in any way. Gently disengaging herself, "yes" replied Henriette, "go to the monastery and ask Père Louis to come quickly, tell him that Clotilde has been injured and has a head wound."

Moving into the salon, Henriette helped Clotilde into an easy chair, then calling for the maid, asked that she bring two bottles of wine and some glasses.

Twenty minutes later as Père Louis arrived, Bernard also appeared with Simone and reported that all the group got away safely, long before the Gestapo had descended the Chateau hill on their way back to Brive. On their return to the winery, they had made sure the Germans had left before coming out. There were hugs all around, and once he was finished with Clotilde, whom he described as having a nonserious wound but would need a sedative, he asked Henriette to share in detail what had taken place. When she had finished, he stood up, called her over to him, and peering intensely into her eyes asked how she was feeling. For one fleeting moment she thought about responding stoically as a leader should, but instead just stood there, and as she looked up at his face, tears began streaming down her cheeks. Père Louis reached out and pulled her tightly close to him, as she collapsed in his arms.

Chapter 18
Discord

The line was full of static, but the message was clear: "I have four more chickens for you, but one is a little sick. They will arrive tomorrow at the same time and the same place."

As soon as Charles had hung up Henriette knew what to expect. With four birds (airmen) arriving tomorrow, and one of them injured she needed to let Père Louis know right away. After Mass the following morning, she spoke with him and asked at what time he could come to the Chateau to examine the injured airman. They had decided some time ago, that all physical examinations would be done there, where there was more privacy and less disruption to monastery life. The airmen would of course be lodged in the guest house.

"Lucien will pick them up in the van at 9:50 A.M. so any time after 11:00 A.M. would work just fine Père. But your time is precious, so you tell me when we can expect you."

"I think about noon would work out fine, Henriette."

"Wow, what a smell!" Getting through the checkpoints at Uzerche railway station and then again on the road to Brive did not present any problems. Lucien had put three airmen in the secret compartment of the van, and the other rode in front with him. This airman, the oldest of the four, was Polish and spoke fluent English, good French, and reasonable German. It was one of the two American airmen who was now complaining about the smell of the truck. All four looked around in amazement, as they found themselves in the Chateau courtyard and were greeted by Clotilde, with her head still bandaged.

"Gentlemen," she said, "you're all very welcome. Do come in," and led them into the salon where some food and drinks were laid out on the large round table. "Please help yourselves and take a seat, Madame will be here shortly." She noticed that the Polish man was translating into English for the other three, and so assumed that they didn't speak French. She also noticed he was holding his right arm in an unnatural position, walked rather stiffly, and wondered if he was wounded.

"Good morning gentlemen," all heads turned towards the door where Henriette, dressed in a navy blue, long sleeved, turtleneck blouse, and a striking white skirt with hidden pleats, was entering the room and greeting them in English. They couldn't help noticing the regal way she carried herself, that she wore a sparkling broach on her left shoulder and a large diamond ring on her left hand, together with a plain gold wedding band.

"Can I assume that you all speak English," she said jokingly. "My name is Peacock, and this is my house, and I am a leader of the Maquis in Brive La Gaillarde. You're all welcome here and we'll take good care of you. My sole responsibility is to make sure that you reach Spain and hopefully get back to England. I know that you have already met Lucien and you are aware that his English is very limited. Clotilde here who manages everything here at the Chateau, only speaks French. Do any of you speak French?"

"Yes, Madame," it was clearly the oldest member of the group who answered. "My name is Tomas Feric and I am Polish, but I speak English, French and some German and of course my own language."

"And what about you three?" she asked looking at the others.

"We two are Americans, Ma'am," a thin and tall man answered softly rising to his feet and nervously pointing to his neighbor, a little bit in awe of this strikingly beautiful and commanding woman.

"And I am English, Madame," a young airman who looked like he should still be in high school, stood to attention as he addressed her with a very educated accent, "I speak just a little French."

"Wonderful," she exclaimed as she moved towards the center of the room still speaking in English, "please make yourselves at home and enjoy some refreshments. Once Bull gets here, we'll explain what will happen during the next couple of days, and you'll have the opportunity to share a little about yourselves."

At that very moment Père Louis arrived and was greeted by Clotilde who led him into the salon.

"Ah, here he is now," Henriette exclaimed cheerfully," walking over and giving him a kiss on both cheeks, then greeting him in English with a "good morning, Père."

"Good morning, Henriette," he replied in French, "I am sorry I'm late, but I needed to take care of Brother Alphonse, he has taken a turn for the worse and I am sure he will not last much longer." Then turning to the group, said in English with a heavy French accent, "good morning everybody, I hope you are well,"

"So, Père, I know that you will not eat," said Henriette," but please do enjoy some wine," and moving towards the table, and knowing his preference, poured him a glass of red.

The airmen watched in amazement, shocked at the presence of this impressive figure of a monk dressed in medieval robes, and yet clearly comfortable in this sophisticated setting. Sensing their unease, Henriette quickly regrouped everybody and asked them to drag their chairs into a circle. "Why don't we briefly introduce ourselves, then we can discuss the program. Père, would you please start for us?"

"Of course," he replied with a smile "and I'll do it in English. My name is Bull and I am the Abbot of the monastery of Notre Dame de la Paix, which is a half- mile from here. We have thirty-eight monks there. I am from Alsace, speak fluent German, was trained and practiced as a doctor, am a member of the Maquis and will be escorting you to the Spanish border."

"Thank you, Père," said Henriette, "why don't we just go down the line, starting with you?" pointing to the airman next to him.

"My name is Gerry Wilson and I'm twenty-four. I was the co-pilot of a B-17 bomber and we were shot down over Belgium returning from a raid on Hamburg. I've been flying for about a year and half."

"I was the navigator on that B-17, and we believe we are the only ones who survived. My name is Harry Oldhouse, I'm twenty-three years old, from San Francisco, California. I've been flying for about ten months.

Suddenly the door opened, and Simone entered, looked around the group and after greeting Henriette and Père Louis, said "Good morning everybody."

"Allow me to introduce Sparrow, said Henriette, "she is a key member of our team, who also speaks English and handles all of our communications. London already knows that you were coming here, and tonight we will give them your name, rank and serial numbers and let them know when you reach the Pyrenees."

"And what about you?" she asked, pointing to the-oldest man in the group.

"I shall speak using my limited English, Madame. I already introduced myself, but I am Tomas from Jaroslaw in Poland, I have been flying for thirteen years and am a squadron leader. I was flying a Spitfire escort to the Rhur valley and with my plane on fire, almost made it as far as Bruges before having to bail out."

"My Spitfire was also damaged on the way back from Hamburg and I had to parachute out over Liege. My name is Colin Harvey," said the last man in line, "and I've been flying for four years and am a pilot officer."

"Well, thank you all for sharing your information," said Henriette. But based on what you have told us, both of you, Tomas and Colin, survived the Battle of Britain."

The two pilots briefly looked at each other, "yes Madame," replied Colin, "I was scrambled forty-nine times."

"And I went up twenty-two times," added Tomas with a smile, "it could have been more, but the RAF were afraid to trust us Poles with their precious planes."

"But we were told that one of you is wounded, who is that?" she asked.

"It is I, Madame," replied Tomas, and it was only then that she noticed he was holding his arm rigidly down by his side and grimaced each time he tried to move.

"Then perhaps, if you are ready Père, you can examine Tomas in the small salon next to my study."

After having the man remove his jacket, shirt and undershirt, Père Louis was shocked at what he saw. He had second degree burns from his upper chest down to his waist on his right side and there were burn sections along his arm. Two issues flashed through his mind: I don't have the time or the materials to treat these wounds, and this man will never make it across the Pyrenees and into Spain.

"Tomas," Père Louis began, speaking in French, "it doesn't look good. These burns need special treatment, as I'm sure you are aware. We are fortunate that I recently received medical supplies from London, so I can cover your wounds with clean, sterile bandages. I'll change them twice a day as it looks like there are sections of blisters that are ready to burst. I can also give you something for the pain. But my main concern is how you'll manage crossing into Spain, it will be physically terribly difficult."

"Père," Tomas replied emphatically, "I have been shot down twice, and I'm still alive. I'm also a Polish Catholic and I *will* survive. I'll not be any trouble to you or any other person helping me."

"Then this is the plan," explained Henriette, once everybody was back in the salon. "You will all stay at the monastery guest house for two nights, Bernard will drive you there, or you can walk with Père Louis. You will be fitted out with better clothing and a warm jacket as well as a pair of boots. In this area and as you travel further south, a new type of pass is needed, but these also will be provided at the monastery. Père Louis will tell you what your role is, and it will be critical that you follow his instructions to the letter. This is not Paris; you will be subjected to many check points in the towns and on the trains, and your documents will be scrutinized. You will need to be calm and controlled at all times."

Two days later following the exact protocol that they had used with the Jewish group, Lucien drove the airmen into Brive and they eventually took their place in the carriage at the front of the train with Père Louis. At breakfast that morning, they had been shocked to see the monk transformed into a German major general, sitting down with them, and giving final instructions for the journey.

"I will not go over all details again, I've covered them several times with you," said Père Louis. "But Tomas," he continued looking at the older man, "I need you to take the lead right behind me as we march through the station and especially as we enter the carriage. It will be crowded with military and although we have reserved seats, I want you to jabber away in Polish to the other three and they need to look as if they understand you. Don't forget all four of you are supposed to be Polish workers. Am I clear?"

"Yes, Père," they responded in unison.

The journey itself was uneventful until changing trains in Bayonne for Cambo Les Bains. The group had to move to a different platform in a station crowded to overflowing with Milice and SS troops from the "Tetenkopf" or "Death Head" 3rd Panzer Division, that carried a skull and cross bones emblem on their uniforms. They had been transferred from the North to Bayonne just two months prior due to the huge amount of Maquis activity in the area. They were notorious for their brutality and were at the station in force. The previous night telephone lines all around the city had been cut and a series of consecutive explosions had shaken the town, one at a bakery where the Germans purchased their bread and the owner was a collaborator. In addition, the doors of the town hall had been blown off and a bridge on the main road to Bordeaux had been dynamited. General Herman Preiss who had only recently taken over command, was furious and demanded that the culprits be quickly found and punished.

Leading the way to the adjacent platform, Père Louis exuding military precision and authority, marched the group forward, giving perfunctory salutes to the many soldiers who were snapping to attention. As they squeezed through the crowd, Tomas accidentally stumbled and trod on the boot of an SS Panzer soldier who immediately screamed at him in German and hit him in the ribs with the butt of his rifle. As he fell to the ground, Harry, the American navigator reached down to help him up, and was himself met by a rifle butt in the face, as the German called both of them "dumb asses."

Père Louis hearing some commotion, was turning around just as Tomas was falling, and in a flash pushed everyone aside and glared at the soldier. Then holding himself inches away from his face, he shouted at the top of his voice, "you bumbling idiot, these are my men you have hit, I should have you court marshalled. Is this the way you treat workers of the Reich? I should have you horse whipped. Now pick them up, pick them up," he yelled.

More worried about his two airmen than the commotion itself, Père Louis commanded the soldier to "call somebody and help these two men to my compartment." An SS soldier close by responded immediately and Père Louis then marched through the hushed crowd that seemed to melt away in front of him, intimidated by this imposing major general.

Once inside, it was obvious Tomas was in severe pain and seconds later as the train started to pull out of the station, he threw up on the floor. Harry sat in a corner with blood pouring from his nose, a cut on the side of his lip and what was quickly turning into a huge black eye. Standing up to his full height with his back to the compartment door, Père Louis shouted so that everybody in the corridor could hear, "you filthy swine, look what you have done to my compartment, I should make you eat it," then whispered in English, "hold on for another thirty minutes and we'll be at the safe house." And seeing the look of fear on the faces of the other two, added, "you will all be fine."

Then suddenly leaving the compartment he looked in at the adjoining one which was full of young officers chatting and laughing, clearly looking forward to some relaxation and recreation in Cambo. Seeing the General, they all jumped to their feet and snapped to attention with a "Heil Hitler salute." Stony faced as if he had not heard them, and with a perfunctory salute he sternly ordered, "everybody out, I am taking over this compartment." And with that he turned on his heel returning to the airmen, and after picking up his briefcase, cap, and gloves, signaled to them to follow him, making his way into the vacated compartment without as much as a glance at the officers now crushed together in the corridor.

The group was clearly happy to see two smiling faces greet them at the station in Cambo, as Jacques and Berthe gave them a warm welcome, even though the airmen did not understand much. Explaining quickly about the incident, Père Louis suggested that only Gerry and Colin go with Jacques to the safe house and that Tomas and Harry come with him to the parish house.

"Good afternoon Père," greeted the parish priest, Abbé Intazausti. "It is so good to see you again. Peacock told us to expect four of you."

"Thank you, Abbé, but this time I have two men who need medical attention. They were beaten by a soldier in Bayonne, and one already has serious burns, I must treat him right away."

"Père I can help?" said Berthe, "I'm used to giving first aid and helping people who injure themselves in the mountains."

"Wonderful," he said, "then please help Colin with the bleeding. I brought some first aid supplies with me. Tomas, please take off your shirt, I need to see your wounds, but first Abbé, could he have a glass of water to help rinse out his mouth."

"Of course," he responded, and walking to his kitchen quickly returned with a jug and a glass.

As he gently probed with his fingers and ran them over his ribs, Père Louis' face looked serious. "Tomas," he explained, "I came prepared to change your dressings, however, it looks like you now have a cracked rib, the area is very tender and badly bruised. It's not serious in itself, but it is questionable as to whether you can make the climb across the Pyrenees."

Before he could finish, Tomas responded sharply, "Père, I have come this far, I'm not going back, even if it kills me."

"Then tonight you must sleep here where I can watch you. I'll rest in the chair, then in the morning I'll change your dressing again. I'll also bind your ribs tightly and with God's help you'll make it into Spain."

"Abbé," I think that everybody should have some txakoli to kill the taste of your food," joked Berthe, after what was an excellent dinner.

"Of course, of course," he said apologetically, "how bad mannered of me. But what do you think, Père? Will it harm our patients?"

"No, not all," Père Louis responded, in fact I hope it will make both of them sleep tonight, they'll need as much rest as they can get. Please pour each of them a stiff drink! And Berthe,

I know that you will be meeting with Jacques later, would you please let him know that Tomas will be staying here with me and why." Then walking over to where he had left his briefcase, he opened it and gave her the money with a smile saying, "I know that you will pay the 'mugulari' (smugglers) tonight, that you will not count it, and neither will they, but trust me it's correct."

Berthe burst out laughing, "Well Père, you really have learned our custom, all you have to do now is to learn how to speak some Basque. Colin and I will now go and meet the others."

The following morning after Père Louis had prepared Tomas as best he could, Jacques and Berthe arrived with the other two plus two Basque guides. "I wish you well and a safe journey," he said. "I look forward to hearing from London that you have arrived safely."

"Thank you for all of your help," the airmen said together.

*****

While his thoughts on the way home were at first regarding Tomas, the closer he got to Brive, he could not stop thinking about Brother Alphonse, one of the original founders of the monastery. Old age, hard work and a life of austerity were finally taking their toll, and his heart could simply take no more. Père Louis wondered just how much longer he would last. The minute he entered the cloister and heard the monks in the chapel singing the Prayers for the Dead, he knew that Alphonse had died. After a quick shower, he sat in his choir stall looking at the two monks kneeling in vigil one at each end of the coffin set in front of the altar, as they would until the burial, and quietly shed his tears for the saintly man and friend. Alphonse was one of the four monks who actually knew to what extent he was involved with the Maquis. He had little time to reminisce, as he had promised to meet with Beatrice and introduce her to the printer.

It was Jean Luc who drove her to the guest house where they were first met by Brother Roger, who then scurried off to find the Abbot. Père Louis arrived together with Brother Pascal who managed the monastery printing presses. It didn't take long for them to agree regarding the kind of publication needed. It was decided that initially it would be a twelve by twenty-two inches news sheet and printed on each side. Five hundred copies would be produced each month. Beatrice as the editor and principal writer, would evaluate the circulation after six months. Once printed, it would be delivered by the monastery van on its trips into Brive and dropped off at Serge's lumber yard for collection.

The following morning, at the early Mass, the funeral of Brother Alphonse, officiated by Père Louis, took place. He had no family except his religious Brothers, but all of the Chateau staff attended the service led by Henriette who looked completely distraught. She'd known him for thirteen years, and as a founding member of the community who had lived in the Chateau, felt a particular attachment to him. As the monks carried the body out of the chapel in a simple open coffin, it was Bernard who reached out to her, putting a comforting arm around her shoulders now shaking with grief. This was the fourth funeral she had attended since the founding of the monastery, but none meant as much to her as the passing of the monk she considered to be a very dear friend.

Following the funeral, the Abbot, Père Louis held a Chapter meeting which was typically held periodically before or after a significant event or if there was an important topic for the whole community to discuss. At these meetings, a section of the Religious Rules was usually read followed by a sharing of any pertinent information affecting the whole community. Père Alberic was concerned about hiding allied airmen in the guest house and preparing them for their journey into Spain. Should this information somehow ever become known he asked, "what would happen to the monastery?"

Both Père Anthony and Brother David made long statements about the role of the monk which was to pray for the world and not to be involved directly in any community action. Several others expressed fear of reprisals from the Germans if it was discovered that the monastery was forging travel documents, ration books and now was about to start printing an underground news sheet.

Père Louis realized that by allowing the monks to hear the news on the radio and himself giving almost daily updates from German radio and the BBC, it was affecting the community in a manner that he had not quite foreseen. In many ways far from helping the community stay informed, all of these issues combined to create an atmosphere of anxiety, tension, and division. Knowing that he had to address them, he decided to take a risk and reach out to the strength and support of the group.

"Brothers," he began, "I hear and understand your concerns, but let me share with you the daily reality of the villages and towns surrounding us. People are hungry and cannot get sufficient food even for their children. It's almost impossible for families to get clothing, and there is no fuel or coal for heating their homes. People are abused daily and treated like animals. Young men are taken from their families and forced to work in Germany. People are arrested for trivial offences or simply on suspicion, are tortured and sometimes shot. The Gestapo and the Milice are committing murders and atrocities all around us." He paused to look around the group, but most were sitting with arms folded in their robes, their heads bowed as if in prayer. He was unable to read their body language or receive any sign of encouragement, but still he was determined to continue.

Then taking an even bigger risk, he began, "What I am about to say you must keep under your strict vow of silence. I'm a member of a group that is working to liberate France and send the Germans home and the work we are doing here in the monastery is to support it. When I am absent some of you must be wondering where I go. I'm either helping people who need a doctor, working with a Maquis group, or helping Allied airmen get to the Spanish border. Do you have any questions?"

There was just silence. Then one of the younger monks asked, "Père can I join you; can I help this group?" Before he could answer, three others expressed similar desires. But it was Père Clement, the most senior of the monks who finally replied. "Let me speak on behalf of all of us, Père, and say first that the country needs the power of prayer more than ever at this time, and we monks are a living reality to that. We need to be here and pray for the world. Secondly, we do not judge your activity outside of the monastery, for only you can reconcile that with your God, but know that we trust you and value your leadership and guidance. However, we also now have the added burden and concern of knowing that you also might be putting your own life in danger. And finally, understand that each one of us will sacrifice our lives rather than reveal the information you have shared with us today."

"Thank you, Clement," said Père Louis, "for your honesty, frankness and brotherly concern." Then addressing the community, he continued, "I am touched and moved that some of you would want to join me in my external activity, but that is not possible. I'm also so grateful that some of you have been working with me for many months. However, I want to leave you with a lasting thought, one that we all need to wrestle with as we go about our daily lives and especially as we spend time in prayer. All of the produce and livestock that we sell is requisitioned first by the German army, very little reaches the ordinary people, so we are literally feeding the occupiers, the torturers, the abusers, the murderers. And yet the revenue generated allows us to maintain our chosen and undisturbed lifestyle."

The four airmen all reached London. Both Gerry and Harry after a short rest in the English countryside were re-assigned to a new bomber wing flying B-17s and they were both killed five months later after their plane was shot down over Berlin. Colin was assigned as a Spitfire trainer based at RAF Grangemouth near Falkirk, Scotland, and remained there until his demobilization in 1946. As a result of his injuries, Tomas never flew again.

Chapter 19

Unexpected

Although he saw Marta every other day when he brought the milk and farm products into Brive, Lucien was looking forward to spending even more time with her. They wanted to be together, but the situation on both sides was extremely difficult. Given her position with the German military, and the prohibition regarding intimate male relationships, time together would necessarily be secretive and limited. She also knew she would soon have to face another reality. For his part Lucien was aware that as Catholics, his family would not only disapprove of his courting a non-believer, and especially a German woman in this time of war. They would simply not comprehend why he would be doing it. But above all, he understood that Henriette would never tolerate such a relationship, not just from the perspective of her faith, but it would be seen as a betrayal of everything she stood for as a leader of the Maquis. It would be out of the question for either of them to think that they would ever visit the Chateau as a couple.

They met as usual on Thursday evening at Jean Luc's office. As they were cuddled together just holding each other, he said, "are you alright my love. I get a sense that you have something on your mind that you're not telling me?"

There was a pause as she looked at him and hesitated, "I have something very special to tell you my darling."

"What is it my love?" he asked gently, kissing her on top of her head.

"Well I'm not sure how you will respond. I lay awake all night, thinking about how I would tell you."

"Please, Marta, there is nothing I can't handle when it comes to the two of us."

"Lucien," she whispered, "are you ready to become a father? I am pregnant."

There was a long pause as Lucien's face registered shock, surprise, and disbelief. "What shall we do? he stammered. "What will happen to you? I am afraid for you."

"I too am afraid. In about four months I will have to deal with my commanding officer and in all probability, I'll be sent home in disgrace, and dishonorably discharged from the army."

"Oh, my love, that is so terrible, and I am the cause."

"But since Hitler is promoting and protecting Aryan births, I will be fine. My family will support me, and I can stay with them."

"And if the Authorities ask who the father is?"

"I will tell them that I have slept with several men and have no idea who is responsible."

"But Marta, Marta," he cried, "what about us?" He paused to catch his breath, his heart beating so fast he felt that it might burst out of his chest. Then breaking into tears implored her, "please don't leave me. I'll never survive without you. I love you so very much. I want to be a father to our child."

"Yes, you will," she responded, taking control of the conversation. "And let's make a solemn vow right now, that we'll each wait for the other, no matter what happens. Once this war is over, we will be together, I too want to be your wife. So now every day will have a special meaning, and we must enjoy them as much as we can."

There was such a rush of conflicting emotions and thoughts running through his mind, that Lucien felt as if his legs would not support him. In a complete daze he just wanted her to hold him, to let his tears flow and express the deep pain inside him. He was frightened and excited at the idea of being a father and devastated with the thought of her not being here, of not being able to make love to her, of losing her. He was at a loss for words.

As she stood up rearranging her uniform, and getting prepared to leave, Lucien pulled out the ration book she had given him some weeks ago and said awkwardly, "Thank you for this, my love, it has really helped us."

Chapter 20
The Pig

Brother Gaspard stood looking over the wounded pig pondering his options. One of his pigs, a breeding sow had gone lame after breaking out of its pen and falling into a deep hole. There was the possibility that the leg was broken. Knowing that the Germans would not accept such an animal in the market, he could butcher it and send some meat to the Chateau and some could be smoked or cured and saved, but there would simply be too much remaining. It was Lucien who came up with a solution, albeit an illegal one. What if he took it to Henri the butcher who could then dispose of it? Gaspard would not need to know that it would be sold on the Black Market.

Realizing that he could make a great deal of profit, and quickly, Henri did not hesitate to accept it and in one day it was all sold. Some meat went back to the Chateau and Lucien himself took a nice portion and gave it to Marta. Brother Gaspard was satisfied; Henri was pleased with his sales and everybody seemed happy with the outcome.

Marta was delighted to receive a nice piece of pork since she had not had any meat since her arrival in Brive, and her landlords simply could not believe their good fortune. That evening the old lady told Marta that she would make a typical Limousin dish with mushrooms served with a "facidure", a spicy savory tart with grated potatoes, onions, garlic, parsley, salt, and pepper. It all sounded wonderful and to cap it all, Marta brought out a bottle of white wine that Lucien had given her some weeks previously. It was a special occasion and for the first time in many months, they all went to bed with a feeling of satisfaction and contentment.

Three days later the Gestapo arrived at the house in mid-morning and questioned the old couple about the cooking that had taken place earlier in the week. They had received an anonymous letter about unusual cooking odors coming out of the apartments and in fact the person had traced them to their door and had heard people enjoying a feast. Under questioning at the SS headquarters, they in all innocence not only told the authorities where the meat came from, but shared the fact that Marta routinely brought home produce that could not be bought in the shops. That they had sometimes wondered where she was able to get cheese, butter, and eggs when none of their friends or neighbors had any. The interrogators allowed them to go back home, but immediately sent two staff to bring in all five of the German BDM women for questioning. After an hour of interrogation, Marta admitted that she had a source for getting produce through the black market but would not reveal any names. However it was one of the other women who stated that she had noticed a certain young man, whom she was able to describe since she thought him to be very handsome, coming in every other day to register his produce and waiting until he could be served by Marta. Perhaps he might be the source.

Nothing more was done that day and the women went back to work, but the SS simply waited until Lucien showed up, and since Marta had not been able to communicate with him, he was arrested as he was talking to her and had in his possession a big piece of cheese and a half dozen eggs. Marta watched in horror as he was marched off and taken to SS headquarters, knowing that he would be questioned for hours and possibly tortured.

Under interrogation and later beatings until his head was a bloody mess, he finally admitted that he had been stealing produce for months from his employers and been giving some to Marta. Not satisfied with his answers he was subjected to torture with his hands being beaten with a hammer until he could no longer use them. They especially wanted to know "where did the pork come from?" Lucien failed to give them any information and realizing that he was stubborn, the SS tried a different tactic. They decided for the moment to throw him into jail and pursue potential sources and an obvious one was the local butcher, Henri.

Ever since the train ambush, the Gestapo, SS and Milice had been looking for Maquis cells all over Brive. It happened purely by chance that a German officer went into Henri's butcher shop to buy some meat and was offered some from the black market. Without his knowing, the Milice then set up a spying system and within a few days noticed two men enter the store just before closing time and they did not come out. Shortly afterwards with the help from the SS, the Milice forced their way in and captured the three men. Each of them broke down quickly under questioning by the Gestapo and admitted to being in the Maquis. Two of them pointed to Henri as the cell leader. They had little information to give the authorities since they only knew about their own cell and their primary function was cutting telephone lines and painting anti-Nazi graffiti. They were later found guilty of crimes against the Reich sent to a labor camp in Germany.

Always terrified of the "Boches," Henri had previously given significant information to the Gestapo. He was assured that if he could provide details and names of people, he would be well paid and also not just allowed to operate as a butcher but also as a mole. His first confession was to being a member of the Maquis and then working with the leader Peacock. He provided details of meetings and especially her participation in the ambush, and the fact that she was harboring an English radio operator called Sparrow.

The subsequent joint SS and Gestapo raid on the Chateau turned out to be an embarrassing 'bust' and Henri was threatened with punishment and pressed for more information. He identified Serge as a leader, but a search of his lumber yard turned up no evidence of illicit activity, neither did a whole morning of interrogation.

Having participated in Lysander landings, Henri then gave precise details of the times and places of the landings and especially the responsibilities of his own cell. The safe house where some of the munitions were stored was identified, as was the member who owned it, Lawrence Boyer, a farmer living on his own in a small hamlet called La Prodelle.

Two trucks with ten soldiers and a car with three Gestapo agents arrived at Boyer's farm early in the morning just as he was finishing milking his three cows. "Where are the armaments?" an officer screamed into his face while waving his pistol at him, "we know they are here."

Realizing that he was outnumbered and that it was inevitable that the arms would be found anyway, Boyer led them to a large barn and told them to look under the hay, that there was a secret hiding place in the floor. The SS officer was excited with the huge amount of armaments stored there, and had the soldiers start loading boxes immediately. While this was taking place, the Gestapo were ransacking the house but found nothing, and Boyer was taken inside and asked if he had any other weapons and illegal goods.

"No, you have everything," he said.

"Good, then we will take you with us to Brive where you will stand trial for working against the Reich."

"I am old man and I need to shit before I go," he said, pointing to an old wooden outhouse close by the main building, "let me take care of myself first."

"Ok," replied the officer, 'but make it quick."

The old man shuffled off, while the troops having finished loading the cases of arms and boxes of volatile explosive material, climbed into their trucks and were ready to depart. The officer stood waiting for Boyer, talking with the Gestapo who stood around their vehicle, smiling, and laughing about the great stock of material they had recovered.

Suddenly the outhouse door opened, and Boyer appeared with a Sten Gun in his hands and almost before anyone could move, gave several bursts into the trucks which immediately erupted into a ball of flames, and then a gigantic explosion blew them apart. Walking slowly towards the Gestapo, he gave several more bursts into their car killing all three agents while shouting "take these bullets with you as well, you filthy Krauts." The SS officer, wounded in the leg, was able to pull out his pistol and screamed, "you bloody fool, you are a dead man," and shot Boyer twice in the head.

News of this event and the loss of so many men, travelled quickly throughout the area and was printed in several underground newspapers, including the new *Brive Liberty* edited by Beatrice.

Furious at this disaster, the SS called Henri in and interrogated him regarding the black-market pork that Marta had been given. Turning against his friends, he identified Lucien as a member of the Maquis and the one who had brought the pig to him in the first place. He also explained that he had given some portions to Lucien for himself and in all probability, he had given the pork to Marta.

More importantly, Henri identified the monastery as the place where the pig had come from in the first place, and that yes, Lucien had stolen it. However, he also explained that the Abbot was a leader in the Maquis whose code name was *Bull*, but whose real name was Père Louis, and that he helped downed Allied airmen cross the border into Spain.

"But how is that possible," the SS interrogator asked, "we have already executed Bull, he was the priest at the local Catholic church.

"No," replied Henri, "he was working in my cell, but he was not the leader. The person you really want is in charge of the monastery. And you should know that you will not surprise them with an early morning raid, these monks will have done a day's work before you will have gotten out of bed. They get up at 3:00 A.M. to pray."

"This time your information needs to be correct, and you had better not send us on another wild goose chase," the officer said emphatically, "or there will be dire consequences."

Not knowing exactly where the monastery was located, the SS officer asked Jules the chief of police for an escort to be ready the following morning at 7:30, to lead two army trucks together with twelve soldiers, an officer and two Gestapo agents and their sedan. Shocked at how the SS could have obtained any information about the monastery, he immediately called Henriette who in turn called Père Louis. At the same time, he informed her that Lucien had been arrested and tortured by the Gestapo, but did not know why, and was now in jail. Since the French police were in charge of all prisoners, he would try to make sure that Lucien received food and water and would keep her appraised of any future developments.

Before the monks retired for the night, Père Louis called in to his office all of those who were playing a role in helping the Maquis, and discussed with them how they should hide any trace of work for the Allies. There were now eight of them. Three young monks who worked primarily on the farm were excited about the opportunity to support him, and had a proposal of their own, just to make it difficult for any vehicle to reach the monastery. Breaking all the rules of silence they were huddled together chatting quietly. "Père, we all also have a suggestion."

"Yes, what is it Brother?"

"We think that if we open the sluice gates on our lake, it will flood the meadow and wash out the road to the monastery. If nothing else it will slow down the Gestapo advance and give us even more time to prepare for their visit."

"Good idea," replied Père Louis with a smile. "Then you

must take care of it. There is a full moon tonight, why not start now?"

"Thank you, Père," they responded, "we will be done before our morning prayers."

"And what about the print shop Brother Pascal, what are your plans?"

"Père, we have already decided that with your permission we will move everything temporarily to the Chateau, the Gestapo will surely not go there again. It will take us just a couple of hours and I have three Brothers who will help me."

"And you, Anselme, will you be able to conceal all of your forgery equipment?"

"Yes, Père," he replied, "and I too would like to move it to the Chateau. I'm sure Madame Henriette will oblige us."

"Yes, I'm sure it will be fine," he replied, "but let me call her now, it is not too late for her." Minutes later it was all arranged. "I have one issue for myself, Brothers. The Gestapo will be looking for me, for Père Louis, and I too have a suggestion, I will ask Brother Alphonse to look over us and help us through this crisis. I know he will not mind if I make use of his name. God bless us all, and now let's get some sleep before our guests arrive."

Seeing the road suddenly submerged by what appeared to be a huge lake, caused the convoy to stop and an irritable discussion took place with the SS officer and Gestapo. He decided that one truck should try to cross first. Once all of the soldiers stepped down, the driver inched forward and slowly entered the water. About halfway over in about three feet of water, with its wheels spinning, it settled in the mud. The driver stood on the running board shouting to the officer that he could move neither forward nor backward. Fortunately, the second truck had a winch on the front, and the driver took off his boots, waded out and tied a cable to its rear hitch, then returned and slowly pulled the truck back to dry land.

All of this had wasted two hours and since the monastery

was in plain view, if there was to be any element of surprise, it was long gone. The issue for the group was how to proceed. After another hotly debated discussion, the officer in charge removed his boots and rolling up his pants, waded into the thigh deep water, followed by the soldiers and Gestapo. As they regrouped, they were not only wet and mud covered, but had lost much of their initial excitement, enthusiasm, and German assuredness, at being able to capture Bull and his clandestine operation.

Banging repeatedly on the front door, it was finally opened and Brother Roger the guest master stood there looking at the bedraggled group and asking innocently how he could help them.

"We are here to arrest Père Louis and to make sure that there are no activities against the Reich taking place. My men will search every room." And waving his hand, signaled for them to spread out and begin.

"Stop," shouted Roger. "This is a house of God. Are you all heathens? Are you all pagans? Take off your dirty boots and leave them here. There is no need to break down any doors, wait just one minute and I'll have several escorts for you who will take you wherever you wish to go."

Shocked at first by the monk's affrontery, the officer finally nodded in agreement.

After vanishing through a cloister door for a few seconds he returned with four monks, who led the soldiers after removing their boots, but still dripping water over the stone floors, into the cloister and the workshops.

While this action was taking place, Père Louis entered the lobby with two other monks. With shaved heads dressed identically in their Trappist robes and all almost the same height and build, it was difficult to differentiate who was who just by looking at them.

"How can I help you officer?" greeted Père Louis. "And disdainfully eyeing the Gestapo up and down, asked "who are these other gentlemen, they must be here on important business since they troubled themselves, like you, with crossing the lake?"

"They are looking for Père Louis, he is believed to be a leader of a local Maquis group and the head of your monastery."

"That's just not possible," he replied, "he could never do such a thing. Our monks are bound to stay inside the cloister and only go out to work on the farm. There is much false information being spread these days, I would suggest that you verify your sources."

"That is for us to decide," the officer said dismissively, "let's not waste any more time here, "take us to Père Louis."

Then please follow us," he said softly, "and you will forgive us officer, but we would like to pray as we go along." The officer, the Gestapo and two soldiers put their waterlogged boots back on and with the monks leading, went out of the front door, and walked along the outside of the chapel until they reached the cemetery. It was its own separate area of about a quarter acre, surrounded by a white picket fence. Entering inside, Père Louis stopped before a grave that had been newly filled in. There was a simple white wooden cross as a marker. "Here is '*Père Louis*', he said sadly, we buried him two weeks ago. He had been sick for some time."

"Then who are you," the officer asked in frustration, what is your name?"

"Oh, I am only the acting Abbot, the community has yet to decide who the next leader will be. My name is Père Bertrand. Would you like to see my identity card?"

"No, that will not be necessary," he snapped back angrily. But we must now meet with my soldiers and see what they have discovered."

Once assembled in the lobby, Brother Roger invited everybody into the dining room for a drink of cold water. "Well what did you find," barked out the officer, "is there anything here that shows action against the Reich?" Nobody moved or said anything. "Then we are wasting our time here, let's return to Brive. And after pulling on their boots again they exited the monastery and prepared to slog through the mud and water.

Unhappy with the raid, and especially so since the officer in charge had announced to his superiors that he was about to arrest Bull, who had evaded them for so long, he immediately called for Henri. This time the interrogation was short and to the point. He had again provided inaccurate information to the SS and the Gestapo, and they had not only wasted time, it had been both a shameful and embarrassing operation. Showing up in wet and filthy uniforms, having to step out of their boots and execute a search barefooted was both humiliating and belittling. But above all there was not a single shred of evidence that Père Louis was active, in fact he had been dead for some time, nor that the monastery was engaged in any clandestine work.

The military court quickly established that Henri had provided misleading information to the Reich on two occasions, that he himself was engaged in illegal black-market activity and had already confessed to being the leader of a Maquis cell. Needing to show retaliation for the disaster, loss of soldiers at La Prodelle, and to get maximum publicity, the German authorities planned on having several public executions on the next market day in Brive. Together with three members of the Francs Trieurs group that had recently been uncovered, they were marched from their jail cells around the market place, taken to the courtyard behind the Administration building, where people would be able to hear the shots, and then executed. Henri died ignominiously begging for forgiveness from the Germans and shouting out that he would give them inside information regarding the Peacock, if only they would spare his life.

Lucien remained in custody for another week and underwent continuous interrogation and torture, but the Gestapo were never able to extract any information from him. Other than dealing in the black market and accused of stealing a pig, none of which charges were ever brought against him by the owners, the authorities were forced to release him. Even the accusations of him being a member of a Maquis group were never proven, so he returned to the Chateau. It would take many months of care by Père Louis before he would be well enough to work and have some use of his hands again.

Marta was also accused of dealing in the black market and was reprimanded by her commanding officer. Her lodging was changed, and she was forced to live with a couple who were self-declared paid informers. Working alongside her colleagues was almost intolerable, knowing that they had contributed to her being questioned both by the military and the Gestapo. She continued at the Administration but never saw Lucien again, and had no idea what happened to him until several weeks later. The produce was being brought in, unbeknown to Marta, by Lucien's father, Bernard, and then one day she found a note slipped onto her desk among several other papers. In it Lucien described what had happened to him, reminding her that he would always wait for her.

For her part, Marta was terrified of trying to get any message back to Lucien, knowing that her every move was being watched. It was almost four months later that she took a risk. Knowing that she would be sent back to Germany in disgrace, the day before she had decided to tell her commanding office of her pregnancy, she waited for Bernard to come into the office and slipped him a message written on the back of a receipt for his goods. It was only when he was in his truck that he realized what he was holding, and for the very first time learned that his son was about to be the father of a German woman's child.

Discovering that Henri had been a mole greatly disturbed Henriette and she called a meeting at the Chateau so that the team could regroup and reorganize, not knowing how much information he had divulged. Jules, Serge, Jean Luc, Bernard, Beatrice, Père Louis, Pierre-Michel and Simone were all present as was Lucien, albeit still very much recovering from his injuries. Meeting in the salon where they enjoyed Clotilde's hospitality, Père Louis gave a detailed account of the SS and Gestapo visit to the monastery and assumed that it was Henri that had provided the information. He also shared that the visit had only served to harden the resolve of the monks to support the Maquis, and especially his own work.

Jules was eventually able to confirm that Henri was the mole and had tried to satisfy the authorities who were desperate to arrest both Henriette and Père Louis. He also confirmed that Lucien did not divulge any useful information and had suffered the consequences. But it was Bernard who silenced the group and who since his return from Brive, had not given the note to Lucien.

"I need to share some terrible news," he began, "and I'm an old man and don't know where to begin. So, I'll ask Lucien to tell you what he has done and what has happened."

Taking his time and speaking slowly through a broken jaw, Lucien explained in detail what had transpired, that his relationship with Marta originally encouraged by Serge, and through which he had been able to get the official stamp and ration book, had turned into a genuine love affair. "Then you must read this note before you continue," Bernard insisted and passed it over to Lucien.

It took just a minute for him to read it, and looking up he announced to the group, "Marta is pregnant and carrying my child."

There was a stunned silence, but it was Henriette who spoke first. "Then you must have had a place where you could meet. Is that correct?"

"Yes, he replied, "we used to meet every week at Jean Luc's surgery after he was closed. We also went away and spent some weekends together."

"So, you obviously condoned this behavior," she asked with pursed lips, pointing at Jean Luc. "Did you not think about the risks? Where was your head? Must I now start to have doubts about you?"

"And what of the shame to my family and to this Chateau?" cried Bernard. If news of this were ever to get beyond this group, I would not be able to live with myself. Getting an unwed woman pregnant is not a good thing, but a German woman is unbearable."

"And what will happen to this woman now?" Henriette asked.

"Her note says that she and my child are being sent back to Germany this week. She will receive a dishonorable discharge from the army," explained Lucien, "and I want you all to know that I am in love with her. She is not just any woman, and I will wait for her as long as it takes."

"Well I will deal with this issue as it stands," said Henriette rising to her feet and looking around the table. "And regardless of how Lucien feels, he has shown a remarkable lack of discretion and judgment, and in my estimation should be excluded from any further discussions of this group. He will no longer be considered a member of the Maquis."

"But Henriette, is that not too harsh," interjected Jules. "Let's not forget that I witnessed some of the torture he went through, and yet he gave nothing to either the SS or the Gestapo. What do you have to say, Lucien?"

"I can only add that you all know that I am committed to this group, and I'm sorry for the upset and shame I have brought to you all, and especially to my family. Let me prove to you that I can learn from my mistakes." And turning to Bernard he said, "Papa I need your forgiveness, I need to know that I can still live in your house."

"Forgiveness is something we all need at moments in our lives," he responded and getting up from his chair, Bernard walked over and embraced his son.

"And I too, agree with Jules," said Père Louis as all of the heads turned in his direction. "Lucien is young, impetuous and emotionally immature, but he is also loyal and proved his love and trust in us by being able even under horrible conditions, to keep his mouth shut and not betray us. That cannot be said for Henri. Let this be a learning experience for him. And let's also remember that he did obtain the new travel stamp we urgently needed and a copy of the new ration book."

"Then let that be the last word," said Henriette. "And as far as the pregnancy is concerned, it did not happen. The woman is no longer in France."

Chapter 21
Sabotage

Despite the many successes of the Brive Maquis group under the leadership of Henriette and Serge, 1943 was in many ways a disastrous year and really spoke to the multiple factions and differing goals, especially among the larger Maquis organizations. In that year, the Germans achieved their greatest successes. They infiltrated the Spindle group and arrested its leaders including the SOE agent and radio operator. They were able to do the same with the ORA organization. Together with several Maquis members, General Delestraint, the head of the Secret Army was arrested, taken to Dachau, and then executed by the Gestapo. In the summer, SOE's largest network Tranmere was eliminated, and several other groups were compromised including Archdeacon and Mithridate.

The seriousness of the situation was such that Henriette and Serge attended a meeting in Limoges with the Maquis leadership, to discuss security issues and the fact that cells were being infiltrated so easily. With so many people wanting to join, it was impossible to screen everybody and keep the double agents out. They themselves had discussed this months ago in a meeting at the Chateau with the many young men trying to avoid conscription into the German volunteer work force, by joining the Maquis. Without the means of vetting them all, they had in fact referred some of them to other groups.

One of the worst mistakes that had occurred, was the use of the same radio operator by several resistance groups. It was Henriette who raised this issue since she had been approached by the Francs Tireurs cell from Uzerche, and several others who had lost their radios with no other means of contacting London. Since there were many networks but few radio operators, this meant that the ones that had been infiltrated by the Germans could compromise the others.

On the British side many errors were made. Radio operators were given special code signs to insert into their messages that would tell London if they were under German control, but often these checks were treated as simple transmitting errors by the operator.

With their newly captured radios and code books, the Germans created phantom Maquis groups and communicated with London for months causing untold damage. Multiple Lysander drops were planned and executed, and all the arms and explosives were delivered directly into German hands. In preparation for the invasion of France that was already in the planning stages, SOE began sending over huge amounts of money, and on six separate occasions it never reached the Maquis cells. But worse was yet to come; over a five- month period, twenty-one agents were either dropped by parachute or brought in by Lysander, and all of them were captured and dead within a matter of weeks.

Throughout the winter Simone, in addition to her daily radio reports, worked with Jean Luc and several cells, destroying telephone communications between Bordeaux and Brive. They also caused a landslide that blocked the rail tunnel near the town of Martel and prevented freight trains from travelling through for a week.

In late 1943 Harry Rée, an SOE agent, witnessed an RAF bombing mission on Peugeot's automobile factory in Sochaux/Montbéliard. The factory had been taken over by the Germans in 1940 and switched from making automobiles to producing tanks and armored cars. It employed 60,000 workers. As many bombs missed their target, damaging houses and killing innocent French civilians, he was aware that it could turn public opinion against the Allies. After discussing the idea with the authorities in London, he approached one of Peugeot's directors and made him an offer: "Agree to have your vital machinery sabotaged or have the factory destroyed by British or American bombers." To help the director decide, he was offered compensation by the Allies after the war. He agreed to co-operate and gave Rée the plans for the factory, suggesting the best places to sabotage the factory by selectively placing plastic explosives. The Peugeot machinery was effectively destroyed on November 5, 1943 and output never recovered.

The Michelin family were approached with the same offer concerning their factory at Clermont Ferrand, France's largest tire factory and a major resource for the Wehrmacht, but they declined. In March 1944, the RAF bombed it using newly developed precision techniques, destroying the workshops, but left the restaurant next to them standing.

As a result of this success, SOE set up a *Blackmail Sabotage Committee* which targeted over thirty French factories. London sent a message to Henriette asking if Simone could help sabotage one of them, a factory in Tulle where sub-machine guns were being produced for the Germans. That same night a second message came in asking if the Peacock group could also assist a newly arrived SOE agent, George Hiller, working in the Lot region, with a raid in Figeac.

"So, Simone," asked Henriette as they were sitting together enjoying a glass of wine before dinner, "what shall we do?"

"I'm not sure," she replied. "I would need to have a lot more information before I could give you a professional answer. Sabotaging a factory, even where the owner is supportive, may not always be feasible, I would need to see the place for myself. Destroying machinery in the Armament Factory itself might not be too difficult, but Tulle is crowded with Germans and especially SS, and simply getting into the town with sufficient explosives could be very difficult. I really need to think this through. I also need to know how large the machines are, and how many of them are in use."

"Yes, I understand," she replied, "and that makes perfect sense. But if I can get you all the information you need, would you consider it then?"

"Of course," she said, "if the Maquis there can develop a safe and feasible plan. I'll sit down with them beforehand so we all know precisely how it will be executed."

"Well, I have an idea", replied Henriette. "What if you went there with Beatrice? It might give her an opportunity to visit some schools along the way where she's developing distributors for the newspaper. You could meet with the Maquis and decide if you're comfortable with the plan. I have friends where you could both stay the night; I could have Bernard drive you in the truck. In the meantime, I'll get in touch with the Tulle Maquis and get the information you are asking for."

"Fine, then I'll talk with Beatrice and see if she's interested and can get the time off work to come with me."

Four days later Simone had everything she needed, and Beatrice had agreed to go with her. Visiting the various schools was a new experience for her and she admired the methodical and organized way Beatrice managed her distributors. It was also clear that with more demand for copies, she would have to talk with Brother Pascal about an increase in his print run.

Meeting at the safe house with a group of local Maquis in the late afternoon, Simone modified their plan, deciding to split up the explosives into five individual packages. The Maquis would act as mules and deliver the packages to five workers, who the following morning would take them into the factory hidden in their lunch bags. Already familiar with the same military personnel checking them in, security was relatively lax and only ID cards were examined. Once inside they would immediately go to the manager's office where the explosives would be hidden. He had agreed to leave a rear door unlocked once work was finished for the day. Lack of electricity and the need for total blackout prevented the owner from having a late shift.

The following morning, the two women had time to see the town. Simone especially wanted to visit some homes where the famous Tulle lace was still being made. They were able to walk in the district of Le Trech with its picturesque old houses, typical stairs and Romano-Gothic cathedral crowned by the highest bell tower in the Limousin.

Timing her arrival to coincide with the end of the workday and posing as machine repair men, two Maquis drove a small van through the factory security check point with Simone hidden under some sacks surrounded by impressive looking toolboxes. Slipping through the rear door she collected her materials from the office and quickly set up her charges. They were all time sensitive and set to explode during the night. Working quickly, she finished sooner than anticipated. There was still plenty of daylight, so she decided that it would be better if they went back to the Chateau and avoid the curfew. Since Bernard knew many of the backroads, they would be able to avoid some of the checkpoints.

From all accounts the factory machinery was destroyed beyond repair. Henriette had just returned from Mass at the monastery when she received a phone call, and while they were at breakfast, gave them the news. "It appears that you did excellent work again, Simone, but I'm not surprised. The SS and the Gestapo will be furious that it's taken place right under their noses. But what it does mean, is that the Germans' primary source for obtaining sub-machine guns is no longer available".

"I'm happy about that," Simone replied, but I'd like to discuss with you the other request we've received regarding the factory in Figeac."

"Yes, let's do that, but first I want to hear from Beatrice how the distribution is coming along."

"Well, Madame Henriette, it looks like we'll have to increase our production. I'm finding that among many teachers, there's a real willingness to learn what is happening around them, and they in turn are recruiting others to help with delivery. Will it be possible to let Brother Pascal know about the additional copies needed?"

"Of course,", Henriette replied. "If you write down how many you require, I'll leave the message myself in the morning. Once they are ready, I'll have Basile, who's now driving the produce into town until Lucien recovers, bring them to the back-door of the museum."

"Thank you so much Madame Henriette."

"And what about the request to help with Figeac?" Simone asked again.

"It seems to me that you are eager to help out," Henriette replied, "there's an insistence in your voice. Is there something you're not sharing with me?"

"Yes, Henriette," she responded, slowly sipping her café au lait, "there is something you need to know. I have met the other agent London mentioned. In fact, it was during my training. His name is George Hiller and he was parachuted with his wireless operator Cyril Watney into the Lot area in January. We are similar in some ways; whereas I had a French father and an English mother, Hiller had the opposite. He was also trained almost two years after me, with no military experience, and was a consular officer at the start of the war. He is not trained in explosives and radio, which is why they sent an operator with him. His skillsets are in organizing groups, and based on other communications I've received, I believe that's why he was sent to the Lot region. You and I both know that there are so many Maquis factions out there, squabbling with each other. However, he's just received instructions to sabotage the Ratier factory in Figeac. It is the chief producer of aircraft propellers for Focke-Wulf and Heinkel aircraft and he is requesting assistance. Some weeks ago, you will recall, we too had discussed plans for destroying it."

"So, what do you propose?" Henriette asked.

"There are just so many unknowns: what size is the factory, does the group already have explosives, if so what kind; how is the factory guarded; do they have Maquis on the inside?" And I would need lots more details before I could help plan a raid and sabotage operation. I would suggest that I meet with him and have him share with me all the information that he has. If we can agree on the plan, then he can inform London of the operation."

Henriette looked lost in thought for a moment, then said, "You are of course correct. I am just worried about you travelling alone, and especially now with so much SS and Milice activity everywhere."

"Well, Henriette, would you consider this idea? Beatrice wishes to expand her distribution network and if we travel together again, she could visit some schools on the route where she has already made contacts. If you would allow Basile to drive us in the truck, that would be a safe option. We would of course ask Hiller and his team to house us for the night."

"I'm still unsure," she answered, and turning to Beatrice asked, "Do you have any thoughts about this?"

"Yes Madame Henriette, I do. I think that it's feasible, and it will certainly help me expand our readership. I'm not afraid".

After pausing for a moment, Henriette quietly spoke directly to Simone, "I trust you to make careful arrangements and to take care of Beatrice. Let me know when you've finalized things with Hiller, and I will talk with Basile."

Four days later, they were on the road south heading for Figeac. Beatrice was delighted with the reception she received and was able to set up potential distribution centers in Cressensac, Souillac and Payrac. These schools alone would probably double the circulation of the paper.

Hiller was excited to meet with Simone and introduced his radio operator Watney, who being new to SOE and to France, peppered her with technical questions. It appeared that the local Maquis had done their homework and Hiller planned the next morning to drive her around the factory perimeter. In fact, she learned that there were two factories. A small one near the center of town that had been functioning for many years but was now producing bicycles, and the other, outside of the town, built just six years prior, was so extensive it covered several acres. It was clear that it could not be destroyed by sabotage alone. The plan that Hiller had devised, based on inside information, was to destroy key machines and equipment. The good news for Simone came from Watney, who told her they had received two Lysander shipments including a huge quantity of explosives. After quizzing him on the specifics, she soon realized that he had little knowledge about them, and so had to graphically describe what was required. A date was finally set, and Simone agreed to come the day beforehand, by train, to supervise the preparations.

The return journey to Brive was uneventful until they stopped at the tiny village of Nespouls just to break the monotony and enjoy a drink. Outside of a small café they noticed a German motorcycle with a side car, belonging to two young soldiers. They were seated inside talking loudly with each other. It was obvious they had been there for some time, as the old lady behind the counter had not yet cleared away their dirty plates and a line of empty bottles. They were drinking beer.

Basile said that he would rest in the truck while the women enjoyed their drinks. Sitting just across from the soldiers they ordered glasses of wine and quietly chatted with each other. In broken French, the soldiers tried to make conversation with them, saying, with other flattering remarks, that they had not seen such pretty women in a long time. The women ignored them at first, but the men were insistent on talking with them. Leaving their table, they came over and sat down, one on each side of the women. Clearly having drunk too much, Simone was extremely watchful and remained cold and distant. Conversation was stilted and given their limited French and the effects of the alcohol, mostly incoherent. But the women learned that they were carrying special mail from Pau to Bordeaux.

Without being asked, the soldiers ordered more beers for themselves, and wine for the women. One of them was focused on Beatrice and began pawing her arm even as she cringed and tried to draw herself away. Suddenly one of them asked the old lady where the toilets were. She pointed outside and indicated that they were behind the building. Both soldiers went out together.

"Let's go now," said Simone, and immediately got up from the table and asked for the check.

"I need to use the toilet before we leave," said Beatrice, "but I'll be quick." The old lady told her it was also outside.

Before Simone had received her change, she heard a scream and Beatrice calling "Simone, Simone, please…." Then the sounds of her voice were muffled.

Rushing around the building, she saw a soldier holding Beatrice with one hand and the other over her mouth. The second soldier had his pants around his ankles and was starting to drop his underpants. Without a moment's hesitation, Simone reached into her coat pocket, took out her Ibberson gravity knife, grabbed the soldier from behind, pulled his head backwards with one hand and with the other in a single lightning-fast move, slit his throat. As he fell to the floor, the other soldier totally shocked, released Beatrice and before he could make another move, Simone chopped him with all her force across his Adam's apple with the side of her hand. He dropped to the ground as if he had been shot, grasping his throat, and mouthing as if he was screaming but no sounds came out. Pulling Beatrice by the hand she ran with her to the truck.

"Drive, drive as fast as you can Basile," she demanded. "we need to get as far away from this place as possible." Struggling out of her jacket that was splattered with blood, a few miles down the road she asked him to stop when there was no traffic, and quickly threw it away behind a stone wall. Since the bar was in the countryside and more than seventy miles from the Chateau, Simone doubted very much that the old woman, if questioned, could give an accurate description of them, and certainly she had no idea where they had come from nor where they were going.

Nothing was said for quite some time, and Simone calmly thought back to the hand to hand combat training sessions she had received in Scotland, in which she had excelled. Her sergeant she mused would be very proud of her now. She was also thankful for the standard issue knife given to all SOE agents.

"Are you alright?" she asked quietly. It was only then that she realized Beatrice was crying and shaking like a leaf. Pulling her close, she held her saying, "I understand, that was a horrible experience, but you're safe now."

"Yes, I know," she whispered, "but if you hadn't been there, I'm terrified even now at the thoughts of what might have happened. Thank you so much for saving me, I had no idea that you could do what you did, and so quickly, you're an amazing woman". She paused and then between her sobs asked, "weren't you afraid?"

"We are trained for many things," Simone replied in matter of fact tone, "and in some situations there is no time for fear, our reflexes simply take over. Do you want Basile to take you home or would you like to come back to the Chateau and rest for a while? I'm sure Henriette wouldn't mind."

"Oh, yes, I would like that," she murmured, "and I could also tell her about the new distribution centers that can be developed".

It was after dinner that night, while they were sitting in the salon enjoying a digestif and Beatrice had gone to bed, that Henriette spoke her mind.

"Thank you, Simone, for taking such good care of Beatrice. I knew that she would be safe with you, but obviously did not anticipate what happened at the café. She's a good worker and dedicated, but going forward, I feel she should not be out on her own. Today's experience will have shaken her up terribly, and I don't want her to lose confidence or be too nervous around the military. I'll ask Jean Luc if he will work more closely with her, after all he brought her to us. And you, are you alright? How do you feel?"

"Thank you, Henriette, I agree, I like her very much as well, she's very motivated and all of this activity is very new for her, but she's a fast learner. Working together with Jean Luc might be just what she needs right now. As for me, I'm just a little tired, but nothing that a good sleep won't fix."

"And you have no feelings about possibly killing two soldiers?"

"I think you know how I feel, Henriette, so why the question? We don't play games with each other. I volunteered to come here and work with you in any capacity I can. You understand I'm not a simple radio operator, I can do much more, and if that means killing Germans, through ambush, sabotage, shooting or any other means, I will do it. So no, this is wartime and I have no compunction killing German rapists and will do it again if I have to."

"Then we are lucky to have you with us, Simone and I will continue to pray for you each day at Mass."

*****

Arriving in Figeac, Simone was met at the train station by Hiller. He carried her suitcase which was not just an overnight bag but contained timing devices and fuses she had brought along, just in case. All the explosives themselves were hidden in the garage of a Maquis in Saint Cere about thirty miles away.

Based on previous instruction from Simone, Hiller had selected what she required and transferred them to a bakery in Figeac that was located on the side of the town facing the factory. It was also a safe house.

During the afternoon, she worked on the charges, together with the timing devices but the problem was how to load them into the van that would take them to the factory later that evening. The town was heavily patrolled by German military and French police, and vehicles were regularly stopped, and their cargo inspected even between check points. It was the baker, however, who came up with a very risky but novel idea. They first agreed to hide the vehicle near some houses on the other side of the military check point, closer to the factory. Twice that afternoon, the baker dressed in his white coveralls and hat, carried a tray on his shoulder with the explosives, covered with a white cloth together with some freshly baked pastries, through the check point. Each time the soldiers made jokes with him, asking him to give them some, but they also waived him through. The second time he did not return but remained with his three Maquis companions in the van. They then drove to the factory that was very heavily guarded. With especially forged clearance passes from the Luftwaffe, they drove through the guard post and parked the van at the back of a building to which they had been given keys by a foreman. After depositing the explosives in his office, they departed leaving the door unlocked.

Later that evening Hiller left the bakery with Simone and a senior Maquis. Posing as French machine quality assurance inspectors with all the appropriate documentation, they were quickly ushered through the controls and drove their small car inside the factory perimeter. Simone was hidden in the trunk.

Working fast under her direction, following a map of the buildings with the specific machines for sabotage clearly identified, the three of them completed the placement of the charges, without interruption.

"Hiller, I want you to take me directly to the railway station please," she said when they were back in Figeac. I have all my papers with me. You can keep my suitcase," she said laughingly, "I'll spend the night there and intend to take the train back to Brive at 6:50 in the morning. By that time, all hell will be let loose and I don't want to be around for the repercussions."

"Of course, Simone, it's your choice and I can do that. Whatever you prefer, but also know that you can stay safely with us if you wish."

Dropping her off in a dark alley, she made her way to the check point at the station and was confronted rudely and angrily by the French police who demanded not only to see her papers but were ready to arrest her for breaking the curfew. Playing the poor damsel in distress, she begged them to let her enter, explaining that she had to get back to Brive where her grandmother was dying, that she was not used to traveling. She was afraid she would miss the early train, so was going to sleep at the station. Since people sleeping at the station was a very common occurrence, the police eventually let her enter after giving her a lecture on breaking the law and its possible consequences. Just in case she might need it, she created an alibi for herself by chatting several times throughout the night with a lonely policeman from Cahors, who was ready to talk with a pretty woman as he was missing his wife and children.

At precisely 6:00 A.M. the whole town was rocked with a series of huge explosions which woke up everybody. Looking at her wristwatch, only she knew what had happened.

Later that evening in a coded phone call to the Chateau, Hiller gave Henriette a brief report of the damage. Although the factory was on the outskirts of the town, the blasts were such that it seemed that every house had its windows blown out. Several factory buildings were in flames and later burned to the ground completely. All the essential machinery used to produce the precision blades for aircraft propellers was destroyed.

The Ratier factory never reopened. In July Hiller and his associates, including Andre Malraux (the famous author and Maquis) ran into a German roadblock near the town of Gramat. They were both injured in the ensuing shoot-out and Malraux was taken prisoner. He was later freed from prison by the Free French forces in 1944. Hiller was more seriously wounded but managed to escape. Despite the presence of many Germans in the area, the radio operator, Watney, was able to summon an emergency RAF supply drop that parachuted in essential medical supplies which saved Hiller's life. Shortly afterwards, a second Lysander operation successfully transported Hiller back to England for surgery. He never returned to France. Watney remained active in the Lot region until liberation.

Chapter 22
Carpetbaggers

"We need to find another landing strip and quickly," commented Henriette. Both she and Serge were holding their first general meeting at the Chateau in a month. The weather had been so bad with snowstorms, freezing rain, and high winds, that Maquis activity had been greatly reduced. Gathered around the fireplace in the large salon, the mood of the group was both somewhat anxious and anticipatory since Serge had sent out the message that everyone who could, should attend. He had briefly coded to each one, that there were significant items to be discussed.

"Help yourselves to the refreshments," said Henriette, waving her hand towards the large round table containing trays of cold cuts, pate, and assorted pastries. "And my wine remains as good as ever," she joked, taking a sip from her glass, "so please enjoy it."

"We have received a series of critical communications over the past week from London," she began, "and I would like Simone to discuss them with you. And oh, by the way, some of you do not know it, but she played a major role in the successful sabotage of the arms factory in Tulle, and of course, the destruction of the Figeac plant."

There were smiles and congratulations from the group, but Simone waved her hand as if to brush them off.

"Oh, please, Henriette, I'm just doing my job. That's why I am here. But thank you for the compliments anyway. London has been giving us a series of clear messages and the news is very encouraging. There **will be** an invasion," she emphasized.

"There is a huge build up in England of British and American forces. No dates have been given yet, but I think we can safely assume that it will not be in the winter or spring as the weather in the English Channel will be too unpredictable. In any event these are the instructions we have received. London wants to arm all of the principal Maquis groups in the whole of France. Our role will be to make the German retreat as difficult as possible for them, and once we learn where the invasion will actually take place, to prevent German forces and supplies from getting to the front. In addition, London has asked me if I can give weapons and explosives instruction to some of the other groups, and I have agreed. They will generate a list for me once the Maquis cells have been contacted."

The group was completely silent as they hung on to every word she spoke. After moving to the table to refill her glass, she continued. "Over the next several months the RAF and the USAF will be dropping weapons all over France, and in our area enough for forty thousand men. We need to be ready to manage several Lysander drops containing both light and heavy arms. We'll be receiving some of the usual explosives, but also bazookas and machine guns. All of these will need to be stored until we are told where and when to distribute them. Any questions so far?"

"Yes," Serge quickly interjected, "the obvious one, which Henriette has already raised, where can we find a suitable landing ground?"

"And I have another question," said Jules, "when does London want to start sending these weapons?"

"I can answer that question easily Jules," replied Simone, "they are waiting for us to tell them when we are ready. They would like to start as soon as possible."

"Oh, my Lord," cried Jean Luc, "then we have to move fast. Does anybody have any suggestions where the Lysander can land?"

An embarrassed and anxious silence followed, but it was broken by Lucien who, with his hands swathed in bandages and obviously still in great pain, wanted to show his support. "I know where there's a suitable meadow, but it's further away from Brive and closer to Uzerche. Both my father and I know the farmer well and he's reliable and solidly anti German. I'm sure if we talk with him, he'll let us use it, and will keep his mouth shut." Then turning to Bernard, he asked, "what do you think Papa?"

"I agree, so why don't you and I visit him in the morning?"

"So, now we have a potential drop zone," said Simone, "but there are several other logistical issues. How do we move such large quantities of arms and where can we store them?"

Again, there was silence and Jules reminded everybody of the farm at La Prodelle that had been betrayed by Henri, and the large arms cache that had been destroyed.

"I have a suggestion but let me first tell you what we've been doing at the railway yard," replied Pierre-Michel who was sitting almost outside of the group. Walking to the front, and standing with his back to the fire, he explained, "the cheminots have been really causing confusion and irritation to the Germans. There's a German officer on duty at the yard, but he's more concerned with sabotage to the actual trains than anything else. The traffic in the marshalling yard is growing almost by the day, and frankly I and my deputy are the only people who know what's really happening. There are German soldiers guarding the entrance to the yards, and a couple of German engineers for the engines, but that's all. There are lots of cheminots in the Maquis, however, who are ready to do whatever I ask them. For the past couple of months, we identified freight cars that arrived from Germany, filled with supplies for the commissary and for the troops. They contain everything from weapons, to uniforms, boots, etc. We simply re-label the wagons, and after shunting them onto a sideline, leave them there for a couple of weeks until finally we send them back to Germany. We keep doing this and the Germans have no idea what is happening. They just know that they can't get the supplies they need. Periodically I'll let some through just to keep them happy and stop them from investigating further."

"You are amazing, Pierre," replied Serge, "that's great work."

"And I have a crazy idea that might solve our problem," he continued, "why don't we store the weapons in some freight cars? We have hundreds in the yard, and they are large enough. I could have three or four shunted onto a back line that's rarely used, and nobody will know they're there. We'd be storing them right under the noses of the Germans and they would be none the wiser. There's also an entrance to the yard from the Avenue Guynener, opposite the Ecole Henri Gerard, that's only lightly guarded. The soldiers rely mainly on their dogs and I don't know what they're looking for. Trucks pass in and out constantly. What do you all think?"

"It's innovative to say the least" said Henriette quietly, "but very high risk, and we are still faced with the problem of how to get the weapons into the yard, and remember there will be lots of them. We'll not be able to take truckloads of them from the landing site to the freight cars."

Her comments caused separate discussions and the group divided into smaller units which became louder and louder the longer they continued, until finally Serge called it to order. "It seems to me that we have some good suggestions and perhaps the best one is this. In addition to using some new safe houses, if Henriette can agree, the arms can be brought here to the Chateau directly from the landing site, then every other day when Basile brings the monastery van into Brive with their produce, he could also bring in three or four containers of arms hidden in the secret compartment. Once he's delivered the produce, he'll go to the marshalling yard, contact Pierre, and drop off the weapons. His reason for going to the yard so frequently will be to pick up garbage and broken pallets or whatever Pierre decides. He'll take care of everything in the yard with his cheminots, including a special pass for the van. So, if we can agree on this, the big question is for you Henriette, are you prepared to store the armaments at the Chateau?"

"If the group accepts this idea, then I'll play my part," she replied, "but what do you think Père?" she asked, turning to Père Louis quietly sitting and listening to the discussions.

"Given the fact that so many of the safe houses have recently been compromised," he began, "perhaps this is a creative but dangerous solution. We know the SS, the Gestapo and especially the Milice are currently hunting down Maquis with a vengeance, so I support Pierre's suggestion. They would probably never think of looking under their feet and would need an informer to reveal it. Let's stick to and use our basic principle, especially with the cheminots. The fewer people who know about this the better. Also, should the weapons ever be discovered accidentally, the Germans will never know how they got there, especially if the freight cars are labelled as having arrived from Germany."

"Thank you, Père," she answered softly, "you know I can always count on you to give a balanced opinion. So, once we have the landing site secured and Simone has further information from London, I will send a message to everybody, and Serge will organize the labor and trucks for the delivery to the Chateau."

As they were filing out, Henriette signaled to Père Louis that she would like to talk with him privately. Once Clotilde had locked the front door and bid them both a good night, she invited him to sit down near the fire. Drawing up her chair closer to him, she began to share her concerns for his being in the Maquis, and the danger he would face again in a few days, taking four airmen to the border. Struggling to find the words, she explained what it would mean to the group if ever he was caught wearing a German uniform. She then spoke about the monastery and how worried she was about its involvement in so many aspects of the Resistance. Père Louis sat relaxed and listened intently, rarely looking at her, but stared into the fire as the logs crackled and popped, sending sparks shooting up the chimney.

Unable to say what was really troubling her, Henriette, sat stiffly on the edge of her chair, her stomach churning around as she scrutinized the profile of Père Louis' face, afraid to admit to herself that she had imagined this moment so often. They had never before had any intimate time together alone, and she had played it over and over in her mind as to what it would be like. Now it was here, she was unable to enjoy it, bound by the ties of her religious convictions. Here she was with her friend the Abbot, a Maquis, a person she respected, trusted, and admired. But he was also the one man she deeply loved, and had loved for the past thirteen years, something she could never admit to him. She'd dreamed this scene so many times, with her sitting on his lap, hugging him, being gently caressed by him as he held her in his arms. She knew deep down that this was the only man that could make her supremely happy. Feeling the warmth of his body, the tenderness of his embrace, the beating of his heart as she rested her head on his chest, and experiencing his complete love for her, tears of utter happiness ran down her cheeks.

The silence was broken by Père Louis as he turned towards her, and she immediately took out her handkerchief, discretely dabbing the corners of her eyes, trusting that her eye makeup had not run. Speaking softly, he said, "Henriette, I think that both of us know what you wish to say, and it is truly beautiful. We both know what it means to love somebody totally, someone who is a soul mate and that is God given. But we are both bound, each in our way, by the commitments we have made, you to your religion and me to my vows, and about which we feel so strongly, nothing will come between them. I know that you care about me, and truly love me as I do you, but we both also have to live with the pain of knowing, that the expression of our love will be restricted."

"Oh, Père," she responded, her voice breaking with emotion, "I feel so guilty. Please forgive me. I had no idea that it was so obvious, that you could read my heart so well."

"Henriette, there is no need for forgiveness. I think I know what you would like to say. True love is a beautiful thing, and I have known about yours for many years, so let us rejoice and thank God for the gift of each other. And now I really must be going, it will soon be time for evening prayers," and with that he stood up and walked towards the door. As Henriette unlocked it, he turned to her and briefly, kissed her lightly on both cheeks, and with a simple "good night" strode off into the night.

She stood there watching until the darkness enveloped him, with his words still ringing in her ears. There was nothing to assuage her pain, her sense of loss, not even prayer, nothing to fill the gaping hole she felt inside of herself. Locking the Chateau door seemed to accentuate her feelings of loneliness and separation. Her footsteps rang hollow as she climbed the stairs to her room, and as she lay down, she was overcome by the vivid memories of the sounds of his voice, his gentle touch, and his chaste kiss. She knew it would be a very long night even as she cried herself to sleep.

*****

Five days later the first of the shipments arrived by Lysander. Bernard had persuaded the owner of the meadow, which was ideal as a landing strip, to allow the Maquis to utilize it. It was in a remote part of the region, seven miles from Uzerche, the nearest large town, surrounded only by farmland and dense forest. Following their normal procedures, the plane landed, discharged its cargo and was gone within six minutes.

Two trucks had been obtained by Serge who managed the

whole operation, together with four men and two women from Maquis cells in Brive. All went well until the second of the trucks, on reaching the narrow and steep incline up to the Chateau, could not make the ascent. It took half an hour before Serge realized that the truck was in trouble and decided to drive down and start looking for it. Quickly finding it stranded on the incline, he had to make a decision: either bring the other truck and tow this one to the courtyard or bring the other truck down and off load the cargo onto it. It took all of two hours to complete the latter.

Henriette was furious. Afraid that the truck could have broken down on the open road, or away from the Chateau, once everybody had left and standing outside of the storeroom, with her hands on her hips, she lambasted Serge for his failure to secure reliable vehicles. "Is this how it will be next time as well?" she asked through pursed lips. "Is this how seriously you undertake a major assignment? I understand that accidents can happen, and that in these times it might be difficult to get good trucks, but better to have none, than one that's unreliable and that could jeopardize the whole project."

"I'm so sorry, Henriette," he said apologetically, "you're right, I should have done a better job. Trust me it will not happen next time."

"I have to be able to trust you implicitly Serge," she responded sharply, "and right now that's not how I feel. Your carelessness could cost us lives, and if you believe that the responsibility is too much for you, then tell me now and I'll get somebody else to lead."

"No Henriette, everything you say is true. Please allow me to earn your trust again."

"Then good night Serge," she snapped back, "I'm going to bed. We'll talk again later," and with that turned quickly and walked into the Chateau.

Three days later after Basile had received his military pass for the railway yard, he delivered the first of the arms shipment. Pierre had been looking out for him ever since he received the phone call from Henriette that morning. Getting through the check point at the gate posed no problems, other than looks of disgust from the soldiers at the state of and the smells of the pig manure coming from the van. Pierre climbed into the passenger seat and guided Basile to a remote corner of the yard where there were four older freight cars lined up, looking the worse for wear. Suddenly almost out of nowhere, six burly cheminots appeared, and once the van was opened, removed the crates in minutes and stored them in the first wagon. Pierre put a large padlock on it, and Basile noticed that each of the wagons had the same label stenciled on it: 'Ship to Berlin.'

Over the next ten days all the crates were removed from the Chateau and taken to the railway yard. Simone signaled to London that they were ready for the next shipment. However, before loading then into the monastery van, she opened each one and took out a sample of each kind of munition including a Bazooka. Together with her own supply of explosives, she made sure she had sufficient material for her training classes. Not having transport of her own, at breakfast one morning she asked Henriette how best to manage her travelling to the different sites around Brive. "I would suggest that you talk with Jean Luc," she advised, " as a dentist he has a pass that allows him to travel after curfew, and I assume that some of your meetings will be in the evening. We could pass you off as his assistant, I am sure Brother Anselme could create the necessary document. However, you will need to figure out with Jean Luc, how you'll carry your materials and weapons."

"An excellent idea, Henriette, I'll call him and see how available he is. Then I'll find out which groups London wants me to help."

Later that week Jean Luc came to the Chateau at Simone's invitation, to help figure work out how the weapons would be concealed in his car. It was Basile who found a solution: an artificial floor was created out of plywood for the trunk, then covered with an old rug, creating lots of space underneath for the weapons. He also created additional storage behind the rear seat.

Word came through quickly and messages and meeting places were all arranged by London who clearly wanted to keep a tight control on the procedures. Already aware of the conflict and jealousy between the many different Maquis groups, and the danger of infiltration, they did not want Simone or the Peacock group making their own arrangements, or have the different cells talking or arguing with each other.

The first training took place at a farmhouse in the village of Baretz eight miles outside of Brive where eighteen Maquis leaders assembled. Simone had come into town with Basile who dropped her off at the surgery, and later that afternoon Jean Luc took her to the meeting. She'd developed a careful training plan, and while the Maquis were eager to hold the weapons and the explosives, they were much slower to understand the dangers and care needed to handle them. Teaching men and women how to quickly break down a Sten Gun, how to hold it, shoot with it accurately while running, lying down, or standing, was a tedious and slow process. Explaining the use of, and how to calculate the amount of explosives needed for a particular task, took even longer.

It was late when they returned to Brive and Jean Luc suggested that she stay at his house for the night as he had a small extra room. The evening was pleasant and relaxed but turned into something of a drinking marathon, since after he had prepared a light meal, he asked her to talk about herself and her background. "I've known you for almost two years, and yet I really don't know you," he said inquisitively. "And I'm sure you'll say the same about me. So why don't you start? I honestly would like to know who you are."

Late into the night, after finishing two bottles of excellent wine on top of two local Salers aperitifs each, they learned a lot about each other, but both were exhausted and needed to sleep. When she finally awoke, Simone found a note on the kitchen table saying that he had gone to work, and that he would meet her at noon for lunch. Once the effects of her hangover started to lift, she showered, then looked around his house, basically decorated in a very masculine fashion. Finally settling down with a bowl of black coffee, and a book from his library about the history of Limousin, she waited for his return.

"I know a small cafe where we still might be able to get some real bread and local cheese," he said with a smile, "will that work for you?"

"Of course," she replied, "but I'm not particularly hungry, and I know that there'll be a big meal waiting for me when I return. Also, I wanted to ask you if I could use your phone to call the Chateau and let them know where I am."

"Certainly," he said, "you know where it is."

As it happened, the café had neither bread nor cheese, and they both simply sat for a while chatting about the previous evening and drinking coffee. "Before I take you back," he asked, "would you like to walk with me along the bank of the Canal Des Moines? It's really pretty at this time of the year."

"Yes, I would love to do that," she exclaimed."

As they walked, Jean Luc explained, "The canal is an awesome showcase of the resourcefulness and industry of medieval monks. In the 12th century when the monks of the abbey wanted to irrigate their gardens and fields, they decided to cut a mile-long aqueduct from the cliff face. Almost nine hundred years later here we are, and the conduits still continue to irrigate farm plots in the valley."

Simone was captivated with this man, whom she was now seeing in a completely different and new light. He was no longer simply a dentist and member of the Maquis, but a very sensitive human being and she was beginning to really like him. She was also very aware that as they walked, he had reached out and was holding her hand.

The drive back to the Chateau was uneventful, and Henriette was happy to see them both, but in spite of her insistence he declined to stay for dinner. "I'll see him to the front door," Simone told Henriette, and when they were outside, she said, "thank you for today Jean Luc, it was very special."

"For me too," he replied, "we should do it again," and drawing her close, she responded as they enjoyed their first kiss.

With a full schedule of trainings already established, both Simone and Jean Luc agreed to meet again the following week, but as the number of Maquis increased, and some of the trainings took longer than anticipated, it meant that she had to go to the same group twice, and so it became almost a weekly exercise. Since many of the meetings were in the afternoon and located far from Brive, staying overnight with Jean Luc became part of the routine. It all was going according to plan with one exception, they both knew they were falling in love with each other.

The messages from London were increasing in frequency and since a new landing site had been established, so too had the air drops, but two major changes had been introduced. At the end of 1943, the United States Air force had developed a partnership with the RAF, and combining and repurposing two aircraft groups, created the *Carpetbaggers Squadron* who flew heavy bombers. With a huge cargo capacity its sole purpose was to supply Maquis groups all over France.

The B-24 Liberator bombers used for the flights were modified by removing the belly turret, nose guns and any equipment unnecessary for the mission, such as oxygen equipment, in order to lighten them and provide more cargo space and speed. The rear guns were kept as protection from night fighters. Agents and crated supplies were dropped by parachute through the opening left by the removal of the belly turret gun. In addition, supplies were loaded into containers designed to fit inside the bomb bay and released from there by the existing mechanism. The aircraft were painted glossy black, the best color to evade being spotted by searchlights; and targets were given by exact longitudes and latitudes, thus making precise navigation imperative.

Informed that her next arms drop was by the Carpetbaggers, and that up to thirty containers would be dropped by parachute, created a logistical problem for Serge. More trucks than usual would be needed, and he knew that he had to deliver them. Including two of his own from the lumber yard, and one each from the monastery and the Chateau, he was able to coopt the Secret Army group into providing two additional ones, together with six Maquisards. They were given strict instructions to ensure that the vehicles were in good working order.

Simone had received a new communication instrument herself, and this would be the first time she would get to use it, but it meant that she would have to be present for each flight at the drop site. In the last Lysander flight, she had received a special package and had been instructed to read the instructions carefully. It was named the S-Phone and was completely new technology that would enable a person on the ground to talk directly with the pilot of an aircraft and guide him over the dropping zone. This instrument would be invaluable in the event of bad weather, when typically a Lysander would have to turn back to base. It was a mobile unit worn on the chest with a directional antenna and had a range of thirty miles and could operate up to ten thousand feet. Simone realized that this development alone could transform Maquis groups in preparation for supporting an Allied landing.

*****

When the phone rang late at night, Henriette knew that it had to be something serious. It was Charles, calling from Paris. "Henriette," he said softly, "I have some terrible news, for you. This evening, the Gestapo arrested your sister Therese and her husband Victor, on suspicion of operating a safe house, and took them to 93 Rue Lauriston for questioning. They searched the house from top to bottom but found no evidence. What I do know is that their cell has been infiltrated."

Chapter 23

Armored Car

"**B**less me Father for I have sinned…"

"Yes, what is it Henriette?" asked Père Yves.

"I keep having bad, terrible thoughts about the Gestapo. I want to see all of them dead."

"Tell me more," he said gently.

"My sister and her husband have been taken by the Gestapo and are held at their headquarters in Paris. They've been helping allied airmen cross into Spain."

"Oh, yes, Père Louis told me about your involvement. How can I help you?'

"I don't want to be a collaborator, but I know a high-level Gestapo official who might help me. If I were to approach him it would go against all I believe to be just and honest. This man is a monster and is responsible for thousands of deaths."

"But could you influence this man to prevent the deaths of your sister and brother-in-law?"

"I'm not sure, but I think so, Père."

"Well what's the greater good, that you hold to your values or that lives be saved? You should do everything in your power to save these two people."

Walking back from the monastery, she tried to formulate how she would approach her phone call to Lieutenant General Bomelburg.

"Please give a message to the General," she told the receptionist, "that Madame Henriette, the Countess de Lastiere du

Saillant, from the Chateau de Comborn, wishes to talk with him." Several minutes later the phone clicked, and a familiar voice said, "How nice of you to call, Madame. I remember our last conversation well. And to what do I owe the pleasure of this phone call?"

"I have some business to attend to in Vichy tomorrow, and was wondering if you are available for lunch. You asked me to call if ever I was in the area, and this is the first opportunity I have had."

"Madame, of course, it would be my pleasure. I'll cancel my other engagements. I have my own table at the Alleti Palace Hotel and will make reservations. Could you meet me there at 12:30?"

"Well, yes of course, that's most generous of you General, I'll look forward to it."

As she entered the restaurant dressed in a beautiful Christian Dior navy blue dress and a stunning matching jacket lined with fox fur, with large foxed trimmed cuffs and wearing a fashionable hat, all eyes turned towards her. Henriette paid no attention to their stares. As she was being seated, the General himself entered.

Still wearing her gloves, she removed one as he greeted her and with a slight bow and click of his heels, took her proffered hand, and kissed it. "It gives me great pleasure Madame, to see you again," he said with a smile. Over the next hour they discussed music, the opera, literature, food, and wines in a conversation that was free flowing and interesting. At one level, Henriette realized that she missed having this kind of interaction. As if to mirror her thoughts, he suddenly said, "it's not often I can have this kind of stimulating conversation, and especially with a beautiful and cultivated lady. And if it's not too impertinent, can I ask what business you have in Vichy, perhaps I could be of some help?"

Anticipating such a request, through a friend of hers, she had called a wine distributor and asked if they could meet, if for no other reason, than to hear about the Chateau wines. "I don't think so," she replied, "but thank you. This is strictly business, business concerning our Chateau wines."

Clearly wanting to spend more time with her, he pushed for her attention. "I believe there is a concert this evening, a chamber music recital with a cocktail reception beforehand. Would it be too much to ask if you're available to join me? I know that I can get reservations."

Knowing that he was eager for her company, she took her time responding. Finally, reading his face and sensing that this would be the time to make her own request, she replied, "that's most kind of you General, of course I'd be delighted to attend." "Then it's settled," he said beamingly, his face lit up with expectation. "Where are you staying, I will have my driver pick you up at 7:00 P.M?"

"Right here," she replied, "at the Alleti."

"Excellent, excellent," he responded. "We shall have a pleasant evening together."

Realizing that the meal was almost over and that he was ready to leave, Henriette carefully broached her request.

"General, you told me that if ever I needed your help, all I had to do was ask, is that correct?"

"My dear Madame," he replied, "if I can do anything to assist you, yes, I will do so. How can I help?"

"We live in very difficult times and especially for people, dare I say it, in my 'class.' Many people are jealous and feel that it is not right for some people to succeed. My family is very fortunate in that we have a very strong revenue producing wine business, that helps us maintain a certain quality of life. It appears that some people in Paris are envious of my sister and her husband who live in the 16th district, which as you know is considered one of the most desirous in the city. They have been accused of being involved in some kind of Resistance organization.

They were denounced to the Gestapo. I am devasted that people would do this," she said, chocking on her words, then taking out her handkerchief dabbed the corner of her eyes, "just to harm innocent and good people. I have no idea what you do, except that you told me you had held a high position in Paris. Perhaps you know people who could help rectify this horrible situation."

"My dear Madame," he replied, it grieves me to see you so upset and you're correct, these are troubling times and many innocent people are being denounced. Please give me the names of the two people concerned and their home address. I'll see if anything can be done."

It felt strange being driven in a German officer's car with a swastika flag on the front fender and was curious as to why Bomelburg was paying her so much attention, clearly enjoying her company. She was certain in her own mind and behavior that she was not giving him any mixed signals.

He was waiting for her on the steps of an imposing looking, art deco style building, with a delicate filigree iron work balustrade leading up the steps. He was standing at the curbside, waiting for her, looking impeccable in his dress uniform. Henriette had changed into a white silk satin, slim fitting gown with long sleeves. From the waist up, there was an intricate pattern of cross over pleats. Her hair was styled up in a chignon, held together with a diamond barrette. As he escorted her into an ante room filled with officers, he discretely asked her if she would tell him her first name again. "Yes," of course, "my name is Henriette," she replied."

"Then may I call you by that name," he asked kindly, "I would like it if you would call me Karl."

It was obvious that he was proud of his escort for the evening and delighted in introducing her to his friends using her full French title. Henriette understood that this was part of his game and was prepared to go along with it. Once they had been given glasses of champagne, he gently moved her towards a quiet corner of the room and said, "Henriette, I have something to say to you. I made a phone call this afternoon to Paris and you were correct, a terrible mistake was made. Your sister and husband are innocent and were released with apologies a couple of hours ago."

She did not know at first how to respond, part of her wanted instinctively to hug and kiss him, but common sense and the knowledge that she knew who this man really was, enabled her to remain composed. "That is wonderful news, Karl," she replied, giving him a big smile, "you are so kind and considerate, and you obviously have friends in high places. When I come back to Vichy, perhaps I can take you out for dinner?"

The rest of the evening was something of a blur for Henriette, all she wanted to do was call and talk to her sister. Karl was his courteous and amiable self, attentive to her the whole time. Before she went back to the hotel, he told her that he'd had a wonderful evening, but that he was a very lonely man and missed having such quality company. He asked if she would stay in touch with him, and if she would be coming back to Vichy any time soon. "Yes", she said, "I'll call you, and if we can expand our wine sales into this area, I'll be back soon."

Knowing that she would do neither of those things did not cause Henriette any conflict in her own mind. The greater good had been achieved and people very close to her were now safe.

*****

"We have reached a critical stage," said Serge speaking to a group of Maquis assembled in his office at the lumber yard, the habitual 'Gauloises' stuck in the corner of his mouth. "The news isn't good, and London is pressing us to help. Just in the past two months three air shipments of large amounts of money totaling fifty-five million French francs ($110,000) intended to finance Maquis operations in preparation for the invasion, have been dropped directly into German hands. There's an intensive campaign by the SS, Gestapo and Milice to infiltrate resistance groups all over our area and they're succeeding. It's my intention to reverse this and recoup some of the losses."

"So, what's your plan?" asked Jules, who had arrived late and was at the back of the group. "I see you have a map on the desk."

"Yes, I have," he replied, "and here's what I'm suggesting. Once every two weeks a German armored personnel carrier comes from Bordeaux to the Credit Agricole bank in Brive. Due to the excessive and increased Allied bombings, the Bordeaux military decided to keep their funds there. With true German precision the carrier comes at exactly the same time, on the same day. The next pick up will be in four days, Monday at 11:00 in the morning. It takes the team about forty-five minutes to take care of the shipment and the paperwork, and then at 12:00 noon they start their return journey. There are two soldiers in the front of the carrier, four in the back, and all are heavily armed. A single motorcycle with side car leads the convoy and the passenger is also armed."

For the next hour, Serge went through the details of his plan. A local cell would provide a five-ton German truck complete with military regiment identification, but with false registration plates. Twelve Maquis would be needed, dressed in German uniforms utilizing those collected at the train ambush, plus others stolen from the commissary. As the only German speaker, Père Louis would wear a major's uniform. Everybody would be armed. Finally, he asked Simone, "if the soldiers refuse to open the rear doors, will you be able to blow them off?"

"It will not be a problem," she responded, "I'll be ready, just let everyone know that until the blast is over, they must all stay well clear of the vehicle."

The ambush was planned to take place on the main road

eight miles outside of Brive, and if this was to be a successful mission, then timing and speed would be essential.

Half an hour before it was expected, everybody was in place. Serge had explained the ambush to Henriette and Père Louis, who now looked the part having been brought to the site by Jules. Reversing his police car, Jules had it now pointing back towards Brive to help with a speedy getaway. All the other vehicles, including a second back up truck, together with most of the Maquis, were hidden on a narrow cart path, just a few yards from where the roadblock was being set up. It led to an isolated farm.

Four uniformed Maquis were manning the barrier, and off to the side, Père Louis stood in the shade of a large oak tree, which also concealed Simone.

The motorcycle was heard long before it appeared, roaring around the corner. It came to halt at the barrier, and Père Louis immediately confronted the soldiers, asking for their papers. Whilst pretending to examine them, he announced that there was danger of a Maquis ambush further down the road, that they should go and help investigate. Waved through by the soldiers and with a quick salute, they set off. The armored car was already slowing down as it rolled to the check point. Père Louis, shouted in German at the driver to open the doors, that he needed to inspect the cargo. With no response, he shouted again. Still there was no response. Running from her hiding place at a signal from Père Louis, Simone reached into her satchel, pulled out a lump of Nobel 808 explosive with a five-second fuse which she stuck in the center of the rear doors, and then everybody dived for cover.

Just seconds after the blast, with dust and smoke billowing into the air, the first group of Maquis arrived with Basile, driving the military truck which he began backing up to the armored car. With the rear of the car destroyed, the dazed soldiers were dragged out, their weapons seized, and then tied up on the side of the road. Everything appeared to be going according to plan, and the loading of the boxes of money onto the truck was begun. What happened next was not clear even after the group spent hours recalling events.

Hearing the blast, the motorcycle sensing danger, turned around and headed back to the barrier. Seeing what was happening, the passenger opened fire with his automatic weapon and two Maquis standing guard were shot and fell to the road in a pool of blood. Simone with a Sten gun slung around her neck, instantly returned fire killing both Germans as their motorcycle careened off the road. Meanwhile, unexpectedly a German staff car with an officer and three soldiers arrived that stopped in front of the truck. Hearing the shots and witnessing what was happening, a soldier stood up in the car and opened fire with an automatic weapon. Père Louis standing next to Simone suddenly fell to the ground. The other Maquis quickly returned fire, killing all the occupants.

"Quickly, Jean Luc," Simone screamed as he was supervising the transfer of the boxes," "leave what you are doing. Get your car and come quickly. Père Louis has been shot." Then turning to Jules, she shouted, "Go as fast as you can, find a doctor, tell him we've a person with a serious gunshot wound that we can't take to the hospital, and bring him to Jean Luc's office." Turning to Père Louis, she could see he was delirious and bleeding profusely from a wound on his thigh and another on the left side of his head above his ear. Tearing off a long strip of her blouse, she doubled it, twisted it into a cord, and using her knife as a lever, made a temporary tourniquet around his thigh, making it so tight he groaned with the pain.

"Help me get him onto your rear seat," she shouted to Jean Luc as he drew up alongside her, then jumping in said, "drive, drive as fast as you can to your surgery." As they were speeding away, she heard another round of gun fire, but focusing on Père Louis' wounds, had no time to wonder what was happening.

Wriggling out of her blouse, with her free hand she rolled it into a ball and tried to hold it with as much pressure as she could, against Père Louis' head wound.

Continuing to hold the tourniquet tight, Simone just hoped that he would not go into shock. They arrived just as Jules was getting out of his car with a middle-aged gentleman, carrying a doctor's bag. "Please," she called out, "help him into the office", and while Jules and the doctor carried Père Louis, Jean Luc quickly unlocked the door. Simone only just realizing that she had left her Sten gun on the floor, picked it up and hid it behind the rear seat.

"That was really quick thinking, Simone," said Jules, "it would never have crossed my mind to come here, and fortunately I know the doctor well, he's a member of a cell from outside of the town. Peeking into the surgery room, she saw that Jean Luc and the doctor had the unconscious patient laid out flat on the dentist chair. As Jean Luc later explained, coming to his surgery was a good choice since he himself used nitrous oxide and procaine for some of his patients, and the doctor had brought morphine with him. Using all three, had enabled the two of them working together to anesthetize Père Louis which allowed them to remove the bullet from the thigh. The wound on his head was not deep and had not destroyed any bone, but the doctor was quite concerned about the shock to the brain. He'd given another sedative, and only time would tell what permanent damage if any, might have been sustained.

"I'll leave you with some medication, Jean Luc, and would like to see him again in two days if nothing changes. He's stable and looks to be in fine physical health which will help his recovery. I know you'll want to move him quickly, but he needs as much rest as he can get just now."

"He can't stay here, doctor, we need to get him back to a safe place which will probably be his monastery, thirty miles from here. It will mean crossing several check points so I suggest that we bandage his head to look like he has had major surgery on his jaws and just hope that the soldiers will not be too inquisitive."

"You're taking a great risk even moving him so soon, let alone trying to cross check points, but I do understand." Once they'd finished, the doctor washed his hands and his bloody instruments and said, "just let me know where you are keeping him."

"Thanks, so much doctor. I'll stay in touch," and with that Jean Luc walked him out to the door.

"You are an amazing woman, my love," whispered Jean Luc after removing the blood-stained sheets and swabs from the table and washing his hands. Then holding Simone in his arms, he gently kissed her. "Your cool headedness and decision-making have probably saved Père's life and made the mission a success."

"Well, I hope so my darling," she responded, "I just do what I need to do."

"We need to break this news to Henriette, who should do it?" asked Jules.

"Let me take care of it," said Simone, "I can't imagine what her reaction will be."

Ten minutes later after talking in code, Simone informed them that, Henriette would be there as soon as possible.

"I am really worried" Jean Luc said to Simone and Jules, "although he is heavily medicated, there really is no way he can sit upright. This is too dangerous. We need a better solution."

The three of them stood there looking at Père Louis in silence. It was broken by Jules, "I have a suggestion," he said. "Why don't we take a coffin from Serge's wood shop, put Père Louis into it, and use the van to take him to the Chateau?"

"That might work" they replied in unison.

"I have a special pass as a dentist and can travel anywhere at any time," argued Jean Luc, I can claim that Simone is my as-

sistant. We have done this before without any problems. The soldiers usually think I'm a doctor!"

"We really need to hear from Serge that everything is in
place, and that he agrees with the plan," said Jules, "then we
should phone Henriette. I'll run over to the yard right away
while Père Louis is resting and will be back shortly."

Forty-five minutes later Jules returned. His face was ashen
white and looked close to tears. I have some terrible news. Serge
was fatally shot along with two other Maquis. One of the soldiers in the staff car was only wounded, and as Serge was making sure that everybody was fine, and the first truck was on its
way to the yard, the soldier managed to fire two bursts of automatic fire and he was shot in the head. Two others also died on
the spot. One of our Maquis finally killed the soldier."

Jules paused for a moment. "The group at the yard were very
stoic and were starting to hide the boxes of money as we had
arranged. Basile asked me what he should do, so I told him to
put as many of the boxes as he could into the secret compartment of the van, then gave instructions for the coffin, and asked
him to bring it in the van to the back door of my surgery. The
other Maquis said they'd take the German truck when they were
done and set it on fire. They told me that they were using the
backup truck to carry the four dead Maquis home to their families."

Two hours after the phone call, there was a knock on the
door, and they all knew who it was. Deathly pale and it was obvious she had been crying. Henriette asked quietly where Père
Louis was. She barely took one look at him with his head almost
completely enveloped in bandages and his exposed, heavily
bandaged thigh resting on the table. "Jean Luc," she asked, "do
you think it's safe for me to take him?"

"We already have a plan, Henriette, but the first thing we
need to do," he replied, "is to get him out of this German uniform and into something less noticeable. Let me rush home, it'll

just take a minute, I have some clothes that will work."

Changing the clothes on Père Louis who kept lapsing in and out of consciousness, was not easy. Jules and Jean Luc cut the uniform and shirt off him, then slitting an old pair of pants down one seam to accommodate his now very swollen and bandaged thigh, managed to put them on him. A large, oversized sweater and pair of sandals completed his new wardrobe.

Basile arrived at the back door of the surgery and asked Jules to help him bring in the coffin. Placing it on the floor at the side of the operating table, they made it as comfortable as they could, then together lifted Père Louis and placed him in it.

Despite an increased military presence, and a heightened level of scrutiny at the checkpoints, Jean Luc's papers and explanations worked, and he drove the van to the group's usual secure location. Carefully taking Père Louis out of the coffin, they transferred him to the back seat of Henriette's car where, stretched out, and covered with a warm blanket, she could support his legs in her lap.

Clotilde was well prepared but looked as if she too had been crying, and spoke in hushed tones as Jean Luc, Bernard, Simone, and Basile carried Père Louis to the guest room. Once they had him on the bed, Jean Luc asked the women to leave. The men stripped Père Louis down to his underpants, made him comfortable and invited them back in.

"Père, you must lie quietly for now," Henriette spoke softly, not knowing if he could hear her. "If you need anything at all, Clotilde will be here, she will not leave you. I must call the monastery and inform them that you are here. They know nothing, and I need to speak with Père André."

"I'll come over immediately," the monk replied answering her call once she had explained everything.

"Madame Henriette, if I could speak to you for a moment," asked Basile.

"Oh, my boy of course, how insensitive of me. Thank you so

much for all your help. Are you injured?"

"No Madame, I'm fine, but I've several boxes of money that I need to off load, what should I do with them?"

"Jean Luc, would you please help Basile bring them into my study? When they had finished, she gently told Basile "I'm so grateful for what you have done. Now please go home to your family and rest, we'll talk more about things in the morning."

"Jean Luc and Simone, if I could speak to you for a few minutes, while we are waiting, would you please come into the salon?" asked Henriette. Once they were seated, she broke into tears, her sobbing the only sound in the room. "I need to know what's happened and how serious are his injuries," she cried softly. "I can't bear the thoughts of him dying." Moving quickly over to her, Simone reached out and held her tightly, "Henriette," she whispered, "I know what he means to you, that you really love him. He will need all the love and care you can give."

"His thigh wound is very deep," said Jean Luc, "and we believe that some nerves have been severed but are not sure. He should make a good recovery and hopefully will be able to walk normally again. We do not know about his head wound, only time will tell us how serious it is. The wound is not deep and will heal quickly, but sometimes there is a trauma to the brain, caused by shock waves from the bullet. We can only hope for the best."

For the next twenty minutes sitting directly across from her, Simone gave a detailed description of what had taken place, holding one of Henriette's hands, while with the other she clutched a handkerchief and periodically wiped her eyes. Finally, she told her about Serge's death.

"Oh, my God," she cried, starting to sob again, throwing her arms around Simone, "where will all this killing end?"

When the knock on the door came, they knew it was Père André and they all escorted him to see the patient. He was clearly troubled at seeing him so sick. Both men had more than a simple religious relationship, they shared their innermost secrets and respected and trusted each other like brothers.

Suddenly Père Louis' eyes opened and with a startled look asked in a mumbling voice, "Where am I?" Clearly recognizing André, he whispered, "please bring my medicine bag from my study, it contains a new drug called penicillin." Then he lapsed back into unconsciousness.

"Of course, Père Louis, I'll go and get it immediately," and with that Père André told Henriette that he'd also hold an emergency meeting with the monks to give them an update on the situation.

"Père André," I know that it is an unusual request," whispered Henriette, "but I'd like to keep Père Louis here where he'll receive the very best of medical attention, until such time as the doctor suggests he can return to his community. I know that you'd prefer to have him in the monastery infirmary.

"We trust you implicitly, Henriette, and I'm sure the answer will be yes, but let me first put that question to the monks. I'll be back shortly."

Meanwhile Jean Luc and Simone had a deep discussion with Henriette about Père Louis' care, suggesting that Jean Luc stay a couple of days until the doctor had visited and changed the dressings for the first time, just in case there was an emergency. She agreed. Simone told her that she herself needed to give London a full report of the day's activities but would wait until midnight as there was just too much radio traffic due to the forthcoming invasion.

"The answer is yes, Henriette," said Père André on his return, handing her a leather medicine bag. The monks agree and are praying for Père Louis, now I would like to go and sit with him for a while."

Once he had left, Simone and Jean Luc had a leisurely dinner together, not having eaten since breakfast, recounting the day's events and especially how despite the tragedies, they had worked well as a team. "Each time we are together," Jean Luc explained, "I discover so much about you."

"And can you handle what you are learning?" she asked.

"Yes, of course," he replied, "and when this mess is over, I want us to live together."

Leaning over, Simone reached for his face and after taking it with both hands, gave him in a long kiss. "I love you so very much Jean Luc, that sounds like a wonderful idea."

Henriette had dinner alone, sitting with a tray on her knees in the easy chair close to Père Louis' bed. Even after a long argument with Jean Luc and Clotilde about her needing to rest, that they would take it in turns to watch over him. She stubbornly refused, saying that she needed to be there when he woke up, that she would take care of him. Although this was not how she would have wanted it, in her mind Père Louis was now living in her house again, and this time she could nurse the man she loved without feeling guilty.

Chapter 24
Liberation

In the Spring of 1944 one of the largest Maquis groups, the Secret Army (SA) which was very much in support of General De Gaulle, joined forces with the Francs Tireurs (FT) and the Peacock group. After attending a series of clandestine meetings, Henriette became close friends with Marius Guedin, the leader of the SA, and his field leader, René Vaujour. They knew that when the word came, together they could put almost eight thousand Maquis into action. As London intimated repeatedly, an invasion was imminent, and cells were urged to arm themselves and to be ready for major sabotage.

Communication between groups and cells was always problematic with most having to use a courier system to exchange information. For those without a radio, reliance was on word of mouth and underground newspapers. Beatrice and Père Pascal, supplied with current information by Simone, focused on increasing the frequency of their circulation, and began producing a weekly news sheet.

As the airdrops continued and Pierre-Michel continued to store the arms in the railway yard, Simone supported by Jean Luc, continued to give weapons training to hundreds of Maquis leaders using a "train the trainer" model. "We have so few heavy arms," she confided in Jean Luc, "But even so, I need to show a few people how to use a Bazooka and a machine gun." The problem was in finding a safe site where it could take place. It was the parish priest of Beysac who operated a cell for Henriette, who offered a solution; he proposed a mock funeral complete with casket in which Simone could conceal some heavy arms.

Sixty Maquis attended, and Simone provided an intensive work-shop in the church, finishing with a distribution of some of the heavier weapons that had been dropped, just three days previ-ously.

Two days after being brought to the Chateau, Père Louis was visited by the doctor who changed his dressings and suggested no more sedatives be given. He had not spoken since saying a few words to Père André but had spent most of the time sleeping as Jean Luc had given him additional sedation. He had also ele-vated the wounded leg, supporting it with several pillows to help reduce the swelling. Twice Père Louis opened his eyes and each time they focused on Henriette who, other than for basic necessities and going to daily Mass, refused to leave his bedside. Jean Luc said there were encouraging signs, but for Henriette it was an agony, and she had not cried so much since the death of her husband.

It was shortly after the doctor left that Père Louis' eyes opened and remained fixed on Henriette. "Could I have a glass of water?" he requested in a feeble voice, "I am very thirsty." Al-most fainting with relief at just hearing the sound of his voice, with trembling hands she poured a glass and then carefully held it to his lips.

"What happed to me Henriette?", he asked softly.

"Père, I will explain everything later. You were shot twice, in the thigh and the head and you have not eaten for two days. Would you like some soup?"

"Yes, please, I'd like that," he replied.

Going to the top of the stairs she called, in a voice mixed with excitement and fear, "Clotilde, Jean Luis, please come quickly."

Jean Luc arrived first, followed by the old lady, as she puffed and wheezed her way into the bedroom. He could see immedi-ately that Père Louis was awake and alert, and taking control of the situation, checked his eyes to see if they were reacting to the light, and asked him to squeeze his hand. Satisfied that there seemed to be no obvious problems, he then asked some simple questions: what's your name, what's my name, what's my profession, what year is it?

In a somewhat sleepy voice, Père Louis answered them correctly.

"Excellent," he announced, "I think you will recover well, Père."

"Clotilde," asked Henriette, "would you please bring the Père some soup? And then added, "You will remember that my sister Therese and Victor are arriving today. I spoke with them again last evening and they will stay here for some time. We must help them recover from their terrible ordeal with the Gestapo. Will you make sure the maid has their room prepared?"

"Of course, Madame," she replied, "everything will be ready."

After Basile had brought them from the station and dropped them at the front door of the Chateau, the meeting with Henriette was emotional and intense. Both Therese and Victor looked haggard and tired, and he especially so, with two huge bruises under his eyes and a swollen nose. The three of them stood in the hallway, saying nothing, just hugging each other as they wept. Therese broke the silence, "Henriette, how did you do it? You are an amazing woman."

And how can we repay you?" asked Victor, "you have saved our lives."

"We'll have lots of time later to talk about that," she replied. "All you have to do now is enjoy my home. You are safe here; rest, get well and try as best you can to put the past behind you. I suggest that you freshen up, then join me in the salon for a glass of wine. Clotilde will show you to your room."

Later that evening while Clotilde was sitting with Père Louis, Simone met with Henriette, Jean Luc, and the guests, giving them the latest information from London. The authorities wished to increase the number of weapon drops and were sending in what they called Jedburgh Teams to help organize and coordinate sabotage and guerrilla warfare. The teams consisted of three men: a commander, an executive officer, and a non-commissioned radio operator. Several of these teams would be dropped five days from today, at the usual meadow near Uzerche, and they would need to make their way to the various Maquis groups.

"Then we must act quickly and get messages out to the leaders. I would like to have a meeting here the day after tomorrow. Simone, can you make some coded calls and have Beatrice help contact people?"

"Of course," she said, "I'll take care of it."

In addition to the leaders of the Secret Army, in the meeting were Hiller from the Lot area, and five other SOE agents whom, to Simone's surprise, only spoke rudimentary French. Apparently, London could not find sufficient native or fluent French speakers yet wanted to increase the number of agents to help organize the Maquis groups in order to provide better support for the invasion. Even more shocking, Simone learned that the new agents were not trained in the use of Morse Code and so were accompanied by a wireless operator. She was ultimately proven right in saying that this working in pairs and speaking poor French would only lead to creating a higher Maquis profile. There would be difficulty in finding suitable secure hiding places and make them a larger target for the Gestapo. In less than three months, more than forty SOE agents were captured within just a few weeks of landing. Most were executed, the remainder sent to camps in Germany.

*****

"Ladies and gentlemen, we have several issues to cover today, but please do enjoy the food and wine, it is all produced here, and we are very proud of it," Henriette began. Now fully composed for the occasion, wearing makeup and a lovely white, long sleeved silk blouse tied at the waist, over a calf length pleated white skirt, she looked imposing. The newcomers were all taken aback that this beautiful and sophisticated lady was the head of the Peacock group and Maquis cells all over the Brive area. They were even more shocked when realizing that some of them had difficulty understanding and speaking in French, she immediately switched to addressing them in perfect English.

"But let me start by introducing my sister Therese, and her husband Victor newly arrived from Paris, who as you can see from his bruises, were recently unfortunate "guests" of the Gestapo. They work with the Comet Line and operate a safe house." Then taking a seat facing the group, she continued.

"London has advised us to distribute the money we have, both that which we captured from the Germans and some recently parachuted to us." Then turning to her left addressed the man wearing the chief of police uniform, "Jules, will you please take responsibility for working out a distribution plan for the groups that are not here. You know where the boxes are hidden in Serge's yard."

"Of course, Henriette," he replied.

"We will divide up the ones we have in the Chateau, between all of you before you leave, if you think that this is a good idea?"

There was a moment's silence then Marius Guedin from the Secret Army, spoke. "I'm not sure that that is a fair approach, after all some groups are larger than others, shouldn't it be based on size?"

Then the leader of the FT group jumped up from his seat, "We would never agree to that, we have been fighting since the beginning, the SA are relatively new to sabotage."

"Enough," said Henriette, holding up her hand to stop the discussion. "It is well known that the Maquis groups from here to the border have the reputation for not only squabbling among themselves, but even stealing from each other and generally making the movement look like it is run by a bunch of amateurs. Do you wonder why London wants to send in Jedburgh teams to help provide structure and organization?"

"Well that'll never happen with us!" the leader of the FT group shouted from the back of the group, "there is no way we communists will accept any British people. Just give us the money, the arms and the explosives and we'll take care of ourselves. And remember most of the cheminots are part of our group. We're the ones that will shut down the railways."

"What I said will stand," Henriette said emphatically. "Each group will get equal amounts. This raises the question of weapons. We have several railway cars filled with arms and explosives and we need to get them distributed discretely and quickly. What would you suggest, Pierre? For those of you who do not know, Pierre-Michel," she added, "he's the chief of all rail activity in Brive and operates his own cell."

"I recommend that Basile, using the monastery van take out several boxes every other day and store them at the gate keepers house where the Lysander was destroyed. Jean Paul is the gate keeper and a member of our cell. Each group can be given a particular day to go and collect them. They will need to figure out for themselves, how to cross or avoid the check points."

"Alright," said Henriette, "then let's do that. Simone, would you kindly help by giving each leader a specific day? We can start pulling the weapons from the rail yard the day after tomorrow."

"There is one other item we should discuss, and I will leave it to Simone to explain."

"Thanks Henriette," she said moving to the front of the group. "There will be four days of drops starting next Monday. London will be sending over a B-24 every two days and will parachute in weapons and explosives. They will need to be collected immediately and hidden, and later distributed to the various cells. Typically, you will need at least three trucks, perhaps four. The drop will be south of Uzerche and I will give you specific details. It will be a midnight pick up, and I suggest that the two largest groups collect these weapons, the Secret Army for the first two drops and FT for the second two. I will be there since I now use an S-radio for direct communication with the aircraft. Am I clear?"

There were mumblings throughout the group, but nobody challenged her or offered any alternative. "The allies have a huge bombing campaign underway and this has been going on for some days. They're targeting communication systems all over northern France. I also have received a code sign for the start of our operations. You must listen in to the BBC every day and once you hear the call sign, *"Let the Peacock Sing,"* you must maximize disruption to the enemy's lines of communication. Execute well-timed guerrilla operations, sabotage railway lines, destroy petrol dumps, but avoid any large-scale action that could expose the civilian population to reprisals."

Even before the signal was given, with their new weapons and explosives, many Maquis groups were emboldened to challenge German forces by cutting telephone lines and disrupting rail service. In Montauban, the 2nd Panzer division was preparing for the invasion, which German intelligence also acknowledged was imminent. A seasoned group that had been fighting since 1939 had only just returned from the Eastern Front where they were being refitted. Their atrocious record of brutality and murder preceded them, and they intensified their sweeps of the countryside for Maquis groups. They acted quickly and in the town of Terrou in the Lot, on June 2, twenty-nine farms were burned to the ground in retaliation for a Maquis attack on a bridge. On June 3, in Figeac after telephone lines were cut and an office destroyed by explosives, they rounded up seventy-four people including men and women and shot them on the spot.

One day later in Cahors, a cache of new arms was discovered including a Bazooka, and this time they executed forty-one people; one thousand were sent to camps in Germany.

On the evening of June 5, Simone received her call sign, *"Let the Peacock Sing"*, which was later confirmed by BBC radio. Many men who had been secret Resistants for months, even years, left their homes and their families and began to walk or bicycle to various rendezvous points.

On June 8, two days after receiving the order, the Das Reich 2nd Panzer Division began to move North, arriving in Normandy from Montauban twelve days later. The journey of four hundred and seventy miles with fifteen thousand men and two hundred and ten tanks, would normally have taken seventy-two hours. It was hindered from the outset. The Maquis had destroyed all of the flatbed rail cars used for carrying tanks, sabotaged all of the main lines running north, and blew up several major German fuel depots. The tanks themselves, not designed to run on regular roads, incurred a huge amount of break downs.

The main force consisting of heavy artillery pushed north towards Brive passing through Souillac, Grolejac, Sarlat and Noailles. At each village they were harassed and attacked by Maquis, but not having any heavy weapons, resistance was limited and most fled to fight again later. Where Maquis were captured, they were summarily executed.

At Cahors, the division split with the main group moving north and the tanks moving east towards Tulle. Word had reached the commander, Major Kowatch that the town had been taken over completely by Maquis. From all reports they retaliated against the Germans, brutally treated the soldiers including cutting off genitals and dragging them behind vehicles. But after two days of fighting, the partisans were no match for German fire power. The Das Reich soldiers saw the Maquis as armed citizens, and so under international law could be executed at will. Men, women, and children were shot indiscriminately.

On June 9, one hundred and twenty men were rounded up, suspected of being Maquis. Executions lasted for three hours and the men were hung from trees, lamp posts and balconies. After ninety-nine hangings the process suddenly stopped, apparently for lack of rope. An additional one hundred and forty-nine men were deported to Dachau.

The main force continued to Brive where the FT group and the Secret Army prevented their advance for several hours. But at Uzerche just twenty-two miles further north, it ran into a well-designed ambush.

"Jean Luc you must help me," said Simone. "We know the Das Reich Division is coming up route nationale N 20, so we must try to stop them reaching Limoges. I know that road well and have a plan, let me show you what I have drawn up." With that she opened a notebook and Jean Luc saw an ambush designed with military precision. "We know that we don't have sufficient fire power to out-gun the Germans, so we have to be strategic in our approach," she explained.

"Then show me what do," he responded.

"Nothing just now, but tonight we will go and set things up. Pierre-Michel just called the Chateau to let us know that the Division was resting and being re-supplied in Brive, after their encounter with the Maquis."

Carrying boxes of explosive equipment using the monastery van, they drove to an area two miles south of the town where there was a double bend in the road. It was cut into the side of the mountain with sheer rock on one side. On the other was a dry gully about thirty feet deep that followed the road all the way into Uzerche. Simone had chosen a very high, densely covered ground overlooking the ditch and the road, for the set up. "I am going to blow up the road in two places, about half a mile apart. I will let the convoy pass my first marker, then I will time them, and blow up the road at my second marker. The convoy will have nowhere to go, and as the soldiers exit their vehicles, they will be like sitting ducks. It would seem that their only way to safety would be to run down into the ditch and towards us. We will be waiting for them. The Germans will not be able to follow us, the ground is too steep on our side, and when they return fire it will go over our heads."

"My God, you should have been a General yourself," he joked, "I'm happy I'm on your side." It took just two hours to set up the charges and Simone smiled when she had finished. "This will really shake them up," she quipped.

Returning to the Chateau, she had a strategy meeting with the group that Lucien had assembled from the local cells, composed of thirty-eight men and women, and explained how things would work. The most important thing she told them, was to realize that the strike had to be very quick as these military were professionals and would start firing back immediately, even though they would not be able to see anyone. They should only shoot at soldiers and not waste their shots at trucks or equipment. They must not delay after their first twelve second burst but retreat immediately and run to the trucks. The steep gully would prevent any soldiers from following.

"Remember you all have Sten guns and at close range they will be devastating. Wait fifteen seconds after the second explosion and you will all have easy targets; just one long quick burst from everybody, then run. Lucien, I want you to take a Bazooka, you are now able to use your hands sufficiently, and you too Jules. Target the mobile guns, you cannot mistake what they look like."

By early morning everybody was in place safely hidden and Simone was satisfied that they all understood her instructions. She herself re-checked the detonators, then set up a machine gun in such a way that she would be able to fire along the length of the column.

At 6:20 A.M. the first trucks filled with troops arrived at the first marker. From her position Simone could clearly see her second marker, and as the truck approached it, she hit the plunger and two huge explosions took place simultaneously. Her plan was almost perfectly scripted. The column could move neither forward nor backwards. Within seconds soldiers began pouring out of their vehicles but could only gather on the roadside facing the gully. The noise of the machine gun made German heads turn in the direction of Simone who was well concealed, as she raked the length of the convoy with bullets. Just as the first returned shots were sent in her direction, a sheet of flame came out of the bushes as everyone fired their Sten guns almost simultaneously, emptying complete magazines. Two other major explosions took place, and Simone saw two mobile gun units erupt in flames as she ran back to the trucks.

Back at the Chateau, after the Maquis cells had dispersed, and they'd hidden their weapons, Simone met with the Peacock group in the dining room for breakfast. At that moment Henriette and Therese entered, just having returned from Mass at the monastery. "I am so happy to see all of you here. I have been praying that no one would get hurt. So how did it go?"

Jules took the lead and described how Simone's plan had worked out, and how Jean Luc, Beatrice, Lucien, and himself, together with the men and women, had destroyed a whole section of the convoy. "The planning was amazing," he explained, "and was executed perfectly. I was so nervous firing a Bazooka for the first time, but I know I hit my target."

"The retreat to the trucks was complicated," added Lucien, "even after being given clear directions. I saw three Maquis fall over themselves and one of them obviously had a twisted leg or ankle, so the others had to carry him. Also, one of the small trucks would not start and the cell leader made the right decision I believe, and set fire to it, rather than letting it possibly fall into German hands."

Two months later they were informed that the group had destroyed more than fifty-five vehicles and guns and wounded or killed more than

two hundred soldiers. It delayed the Germans another half a day as
they were forced to create a detour.

On June 10, it was reported that commander of the 2nd Panzer
Reconnaissance Unit, Helmut Kempfe, had been kidnapped by
the Maquis north of Limousin. The General in charge decided
to retaliate and closed off the tiny village of Oradour sur Glane.
Frustrated at being delayed by so many Maquis attacks and be-
lieving that the village had held the commander hostage, he
herded one hundred and seventy men into wooden barns and
shot them in the legs so that they could not walk. The Germans
poured gasoline over the buildings then set fire to them. Women
and children were also rounded up and locked in the church,
which was then set on fire. In all six hundred and forty- two people were massacred.

After the Normandy landings, the Allies pushed further East,
and the Maquis continued to harass the retreating German
troops. On July 26 near Ussel, the Maquis highjacked a train with
37 wagons carrying flour, rice, beans, sugar, chocolate, and blankets heading for Germany as well as 40 trucks. Even as they were
retreating, the SS retaliated by deporting 200 specialists from the
munition factory in Tulle to work in Germany.

*****

At the Chateau Père Louis continued his slow recovery
nursed by Henriette and Clotilde, and after six weeks was beginning to walk with crutches, his head wound almost completely healed. The Maquis were continuing to provide daily
details of German troop movements, and almost every evening
after she had completed her radio messages, Simone would sit
together with Henriette on a sofa in the salon. They had grown
closer over the past few months and as they shared their own
thoughts and feelings, she frequently found herself holding
Henriette in her arms, sobbing as she continued to thank her for

saving Père Louis' life.

"You really love this man, Henriette," she whispered one night. I see it in your eyes when you look at him, I see it in your smile when he enters the room, I hear it in your voice when you talk to him and I have known this for a long time. I assume he knows this, so why don't the two of you get married?"

"Am I that transparent, Simone?" she replied, "is it that obvious?"

"Yes, it is, at least to me. I have loved a man in the past and am now in love with Jean Luc, so yes I understand."

"But what you cannot fully understand, is to feel the pain of loving deeply, knowing that you are loved back, but also realizing that you will never experience the physical expression of that love. Père Louis will never leave his monastery, of that I am certain."

"Then you are an even stronger lady than I imagined," Simone replied.

Since arming the Maquis, the harassment of the Germans continued more openly, and groups had even surrounded Brive itself. An estimated one thousand Maquis and SOE agents were poised ready to take over the city. In addition, between July 14, and August 15, forty-nine German infiltrators had been captured by the Maquis. Lieutenant Colonel Bohmer, the commander of the Brive garrison, was informed that he was facing well organized and armed combatants who would be respectful of the regulations of war if he surrendered. From August 7, through the 14, overtures led by the Prefect of the Region, Pierre Chaussade, the highest-ranking government official, were made to the Germans. It was the leader of the Secret Army, Marius Guedin who was directly involved, that suggested they send for Henriette since she spoke both fluent German and English.

Arriving in Brive on the evening of the August 11, Henriette checked into the Hotel de L'Étoile on the Place de La Gare, downtown. Despite multiple meetings, the process was almost jeopardized on the 13th due to gun fire breaking out at the Pont Cardinal and the Pont de la Bouvie that was started by the FFI Maquis. It was thanks to the Prefect Pierre Chaussade, that a truce with both sides was reached allowing the surrender negotiations to continue.

On the 14th, Henriette arrived at the Prefect's office, elegantly dressed in a striking light blue suit with matching hat, over a high neck aubergine colored blouse. Her very presence added a degree of formality and dignity to the proceedings. The negotiating process was slowed down by the fact that nobody on the French team, other than Henriette, spoke German. She thus spent much time translating, and eventually it became clear that a settlement would be reached. Towards the end of the day, however, the German contingent asked for a time aside so they could consult with each other. Thinking that perhaps they might renege on the proposal, Marius asked Henriette to listen in.

"Walking towards the small group that had moved into a corner of the room, she approached the Colonel directly. Speaking in German, she asked, "could I be of any assistance Colonel? I know that using a second language has its challenges, and perhaps I could interpret for you if you think it would help."

"Thank you, Madame," he responded graciously with a slight bow and click of his heels. "We wish to make three issues clear to the French and are having some difficulty getting them to understand. The first is that the dishonor of surrender would be accentuated by having to do so to the Maquis which is an unofficial military group. Secondly, I am wary of the treatment that might be given to my soldiers, by poorly supervised armed groups who might be quick to take revenge. And thirdly, I will only surrender to an officer of the regular army or one of the British forces."

"I completely understand Colonel, she responded, "let me take your concerns back to our group and then we can reconvene."

"Thank you, again Madame, you are most helpful."

After sharing this information with the group, there was real concern regarding the finding of a military officer, but it was Marius who saved the day. Taking the French team to one side he said, "Colonel Jack" is known to all the Maquis groups in the area and even the Germans. Yes, he is an SOE officer, but he is officially part of the British army. The Germans do not need to know that his real name is Jacques Perrier and that he was born in Paris! I am sure we can get him here later tonight, and everyone can sign the surrender tomorrow morning."

With that proposal on the table Lieutenant Colonel Bohmer agreed to the terms and the signing of the official document.

In the presence of the Prefect Pierre Chaussade, Marius Guedin and Rene Vaujour from the Secret Army, Pierre Jacquot representing FFI, "Captain Jack" representing the British army, and Henriette Lastiere du Saillant, Countess du Chateau de Combon, as translator, at 9:00 A.M. on August 15, 1944, five days before the liberation of Paris, the Germans signed the surrender. Brive la Gaillarde became the first town in France to liberate itself.

Unable to contain her joy, Henriette called the Chateau, and after announcing the news, asked Clotilde to invite all of the workers and their families for champagne and lunch. After a brief meeting with Jules, Beatrice and Jean Luc who had been waiting to hear the news, Basile drove her back home. Jean Luc followed her wanting to share his joy with Simone.

When she walked through the front door, Clotilde burst out crying as she greeted and held on to Henriette, the stress of the past four years finally pouring out. As she entered the salon, a huge cheer went up as people rushed to kiss and hug her, most were crying with tears of joy and happiness. Suddenly she saw Père Louis on crutches near the fireplace, wearing his monk's robes, the first time he had been down-stairs in two months, smiling and holding out his arms. Walking slowly toward him, she reached out and taking his hands in hers, looked deep into his eyes and said softly, "Père it is over for both of us, we can now resume our normal lives again."

Epilogue

After defeating the German forces in Normandy, the Allied armies marched quickly across northern France. The liberation of Paris didn't have priority, because of the risk of damaging the city, and in addition General Eisenhower did not wish to divert essential men and supplies. He had planned that the city would be encircled and liberated later. On August 18, 1944 however, the Allied forces were near Paris, and as word spread, workers in the city went on strike and Resistance fighters began attacking German positions. The German commander of Paris, Lieutenant-General Choltitz, was ordered by Hitler to crush the insurrection and to destroy the city. He had neither the manpower nor the resources to do so, but later in his memoir created the myth that he "saved the city."

Urged by General de Gaulle, Eisenhower sent in the 2nd Armored Division under General Leclerc, and on August 24 it crossed the Seine and reached the Paris suburbs. Just before midnight on August 24, it arrived at the Hôtel de Ville (town hall) in the heart of Paris.

In the early afternoon, the following day, Choltitz was arrested in his headquarters at the Hôtel Meurice and the capitulation was signed at the Police Department on the Île de la Cité. Cholitz was then taken to the Montparnasse station where he ordered his troops to surrender. De Gaulle himself arrived in the city later that afternoon, and on the following day both he and Leclerc led a triumphant liberation march down the Champs d'Élysées.

On August 15th, the Allies began Operation Dragoon with an

invasion of the south coast of France. In just four weeks, they pushed right through Provence to the German border. Effectively, by the middle of September 1944, the whole of France had been liberated.

In Brive, it took three days for a complete withdrawal of the garrison, and all the troops were sent to defend the city of Metz. They were subsequently engaged in a brutal battle with General Patton's 3rd army and surrendered to him on 22nd of November.

*****

Marius Guedin from the Secret Army Maquis group who accepted and signed the surrender of the German garrison in Brive, continued serving in the French army until 1977 receiving several military decorations and awards, eventually becoming mayor of Arcesau in Burgundy. Colonel Rene Vaujour who also signed the surrender document, had a lifelong and distinguished military career serving in Austria, Tunisia, and Algeria. Edmond Michelet who started the very first act of Resistance in the Brive area in 1940, and André Malraux a Maquis and writer, were both later made ministers in the new de Gaulle government.

*****

Clotilde died of old age in 1949 after serving at the Chateau for sixty-five years.

*****

Lucien continued working with his father in the Chateau vineyards and farm. After the end of the war in January 1946, he travelled to Germany to look for Marta. It took two months of searching as her family had moved from Munich, until finally he found her and his daughter in the small village of Auerbach on the Swiss border, living with her sister and teaching in an elementary school. Her father had been killed earlier in an air strike near Berlin. Six months later, Lucien brought her and his child to the Chateau, having been reconciled with their own family and Henriette. Even with post war anti German sentiments prevalent all over France, they felt that the Chateau was sufficiently isolated to offer protection for them from any public disapproval.

His hands never fully healed from his torture, and two fingers on his left hand remained deformed. He worked at the Chateau all his life, raising three girls, until his death in 1985. Marta died in 1989.

*****

Bernard died in 1947 after spending his whole working life at the Chateau and leaving behind a legacy of producing some of the finest white wines in south west France.

*****

Jules remained Chief of Police and retired in 1950 to take care of his small vineyard in Noailles, south of Brive. Immediately after the surrender he struggled to live down painful accusations from several political factions, that the only reason he had kept his position was through collaboration with the Germans. Thanks to Henriette and several Maquis leaders who were able to demonstrate otherwise, he was not only cleared of the accusations, but served the town for another five years.

*****

Pierre-Michel eventually retired from the SNCF in Brive and

moved with his wife to live with his daughter in Nice. He died in 1977.

*****

Beatrice continued working at the museum until a new center was created in the 1970's, at the initiative of Marie Michelet, wife of Edmond, the man responsible for the very first act of Resistance in the area. The Michelet family home was ceded to an Historical Association in partnership with the city of Brive, to develop an establishment for the study of events that occurred during the Second World War, especially those concerning the Maquis and Jewish Deportations. Beatrice became the new director. She, Simone, and Jean Luc remained good friends.

*****

Jean Luc and Simone married in December 1944 and remained together raising a family of two girls and two boys in Brive. He grew his dental practice and opened a second office in Uzerche. She focused on raising her children. Every other month they would take the family to visit Henriette and enjoy her hospitality. They also visited the monastery to spend time with Père Louis.

Once the children were old enough, Simone went back to school and became a qualified teacher. She taught history classes at the local High school until she retired, and became a volunteer working with Beatrice at the new Historical Museum.

*****

Père Louis returned to his monastery and remained there as Abbot until his death in 1988. He was beloved and respected by his community and left them a journal he had kept since the first day he arrived at the Chateau.

******

Henriette continued her routine of daily Mass at the monastery and weekly confession with Père Yves. Only rarely did she see or speak with Père Louis, and when they met it always centered on business and finance.

Her sister Therese's oldest son, wishing to enter the wine business, came to live at the Chateau with his new wife, and Henriette was delighted to have somebody who would not only inherit but continue the family tradition. Her time was taken up with helping look after her grand nieces and nephews as they arrived, and Lucien's children whom she adored.

She decided to take up painting and attended classes in Brive, at first using watercolors, until finally settled on using oil. Her work was always sensitive, and she produced outstanding landscapes and portraits. She loved to entertain visitors at the Chateau and inevitably, it included a tour of what was fast becoming a private art gallery.

After the war, guided by her spiritual director Père Yves, she devoted most of her time, energy, and money, into helping develop and support a struggling orphanage for girls in the village of Aubergine, near Brive. Run by the Sisters of the Sacred Heart of Mary, it was overwhelmed by the number of war orphans. Henriette, even into her old age, had Basile drive her there two days each week, where she taught classes in English and painting.

When she died in 1991, with special permission from the Trappist Abbot General, as the major benefactor and donor, she was allowed to be buried in the monastery cemetery, and as it happened the monks unknowingly had prepared her grave next to that of Père Louis.

Michael Barrington was born in Manchester, England. He lived and studied in France and was member of a French Order of Missionary priests. His Memoir, "The Bishop Wears No Drawers" recounts 10 years spent ministering in West Africa. He is married to a beautiful French woman and they live near San Francisco, California. This is his first novel.

ABOOKS

ALIVE Book Publishing and ALIVE Publishing Group
are imprints of Advanced Publishing LLC,
3200 A Danville Blvd., Suite 204, Alamo, California 94507

Telephone: 925.837.7303
alivebookpublishing.com